The Ins

Mankind

CORDWAINER SMITH

The Instrumentality
of
Mankind

Introduction by Frederik Pohl

VGSF

VGSF is an imprint of Victor Gollancz Ltd
14 Henrietta Street, London WC2E 8QJ

First published in Great Britain 1988
by Victor Gollancz Ltd

First VGSF edition 1988

British Library Cataloguing in Publication Data
Smith, Cordwainer, 1913-1966
  The instrumentality of mankind.
  Rn: Paul Myron Anthony Linebarger   I. Title
813′.54[F]

ISBN 0-575-04167-6

Printed and bound in Great Britain
by Cox & Wyman Ltd, Reading

ACKNOWLEDGMENTS

Contents

Timeline from THE INSTRUMENTALITY OF MANKIND

A.D.	2,000 ▸▸▸▸▸ 3,000 ▸▸▸▸▸▸▸▸▸▸ 4,000 ▸▸▸▸▸ 5,000 ▸▸▸
STORIES	No, No, Not Rogov* / War No. 81-Q* / Mark* Elf / Queen of the* Afternoon
EVENTS	Forgotten First Age of Space / The Ancient Wars, culminating in the collapse of all nations save China. Retreat of the true men into isolated cities, with most of Earth left to Beasts, manshonyaggers and Unforgiven / Advent of the Vomacts and the return of vitality to mankind. Rule of the Jwindz succeeded by that of the Instrumentality

◂◂

A.D.	9,000 ▸▸▸▸▸▸▸▸▸▸▸▸▸ 10,000 ▸▸▸▸▸▸▸▸▸▸▸▸▸▸▸▸
STORIES	The Game of Rat and Dragon / The Burning of the Brain / From Gustible's Planet*
EVENTS	Age of Planoforming. Settlement of thousands of worlds, compared to 200 by sailship / Stabilization of Utopia. Life spans standardized at 400 years. Programming of embryos, growing use of robots, underpeople

◂◂

A.D.	14,000 ▸▸▸▸▸▸▸▸▸▸▸▸▸ 15,000 ▸▸▸▸▸▸▸▸▸▸▸▸▸▸
STORIES	The Dead Lady of Clown Town / Under Old Earth / Drunkboat*
EVENTS	Martyrdom of D'Joan, rebirth of old strong Religion. Founding of line of Jestocost / Appearance of Lady Alice More, partner to Lord Jestocost in the Rediscovery of Man. Holy Insurgency. Visions from space 3

*Stories in this collection.

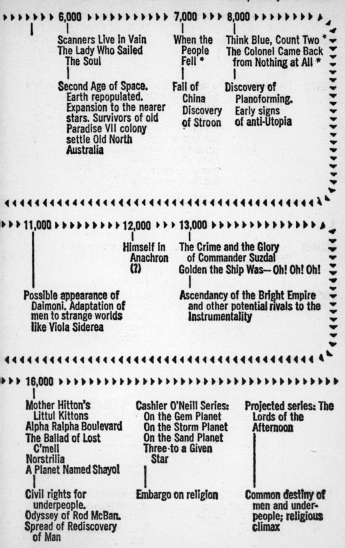

▶▶▶▶▶▶ 6,000 ▶▶▶▶▶▶▶▶▶ 7,000 ▶▶▶ 8,000 ▶▶▶▶▶▶▶ ▶

**Scanners Live in Vain
The Lady Who Sailed
  The Soul**

**When the
People
Fell ***

Think Blue, Count Two *
**The Colonel Came Back
from Nothing at All ***

**Second Age of Space.
Earth repopulated.
Expansion to the nearer
stars. Survivors of old
Paradise VII colony
settle Old North
Australia**

**Fall of
China
Discovery
of Stroon**

**Discovery of
Planoforming.
Early signs
of anti-Utopia**

▶▶▶ 11,000 ▶▶▶▶▶▶▶▶▶ 12,000 ▶▶▶ 13,000 ▶▶▶▶▶▶▶▶▶ ▶

**Himself in
Anachron
(?)**

**The Crime and the Glory
of Commander Suzdal
Golden the Ship Was— Oh! Oh! Oh!**

**Possible appearance of
Daimoni. Adaptation of
men to strange worlds
like Viola Siderea**

**Ascendancy of the Bright Empire
and other potential rivals to the
Instrumentality**

▶▶▶ 16,000 ▶▶▶▶▶▶▶▶▶▶▶▶▶▶▶▶▶▶▶▶▶▶▶▶▶▶▶

**Mother Hitton's
  Littul Kittons
Alpha Ralpha Boulevard
The Ballad of Lost
  C'mell
Norstrilia
A Planet Named Shayol**

**Cashier O'Neill Series:
  On the Gem Planet
  On the Storm Planet
  On the Sand Planet
  Three-to a Given
    Star**

**Projected series: The
Lords of the
Afternoon**

**Civil rights for
underpeople.
Odyssey of Rod McBan.
Spread of Rediscovery
of Man**

Embargo on religion

**Common destiny of
men and under-
people; religious
climax**

Note: With Smith's own notebooks lost, chronology is largely a matter of
    guesswork, based on internal evidence. But the order of stories
    and surrounding events can be fairly well established

Introduction

THIRTY YEARS AGO I had a story in a magazine called *Fantasy Book*. Actually it was only about half a story (it was a collaboration with Isaac Asimov called "Little Man on the Subway"), and for that matter *Fantasy Book* was only about half a magazine. It didn't last very long or reach a very big audience. It might not even have reached me if I hadn't been a contributor—half a contributor. But, by gosh, it had some good stories. And the best of them all was a piece called "Scanners Live in Vain" by an author called Cordwainer Smith.

"Cordwainer Smith," forsooth! The instant question that burned in my mind was who lay behind that disguise. Henry Kuttner had played hide-and-seek games with pennames in those days. So had Robert A. Heinlein, and "Scanners Live in Vain" seemed inventive enough, and *good* enough, to do credit to either of them. But it wasn't in the style, or any of the styles, that I had associated with them. Besides, they denied it. Theodore Sturgeon? A. E. van Vogt? No, neither of them. Then who?

It really did not seem probable that this was someone wholly new. Apart from the coyness of the by-line, there was too great a wealth of color and innovation and conceptually stimulating thought in "Scanners" for me to believe for one second that it was the creation of any but a top master in science fiction. It was not only good. It was expert. Even excellent writers are not usually that excellent the first time around.

Not long afterward I signed a contract to edit a science-fiction anthology for Doubleday's paperback subsidiary, to be entitled *Beyond the End of Time*. That pleased me a lot, not least because it meant I had a chance to display "Scanners Live in Vain" to an audience a hundred times larger than *Fantasy Book* had commanded. And there was a valuable fringe benefit. Somebody would have to sign the publishing agreement for the story. And then I would have him!

Only I didn't. The permission came back signed by Forrest J. Ackerman, as Cordwainer Smith's literary agent. For a brief, crazed period I suspected Forry of having written the story himself, but he assured me he hadn't. And there it rested. For the better part of a decade. Until the time came when I was doing some editorial work for *Galaxy* and my phone rang. The man on the other end said, "Mr. Pohl? I'm Paul Linebarger."

I said, "Yes?" in a tone that he easily translated to mean, *And who the hell is Paul Linebarger?* He quickly added: "I write under the name of Cordwainer Smith."

So who is Paul Linebarger, then?

Well, let me tell you a story. A couple of years ago I was traveling around Eastern Europe on behalf of the U.S. State Department, talking about science fiction to audiences of Poles and Macedonians and Soviet Georgians. Among others. American science fiction is kindly received in almost all parts of the world, that one included. I was received with cordial hospitality. By the Eastern Europeans, anyway; and often, but not always, by the American diplomats charged with keeping me busy and out of trouble. The least welcome I was ever made to feel was at an embassy dinner, at a post where the American ambassador was a stuffed shirt of the old school, had never read any science fiction, never intended to read any, and was visibly displeased with the malign turn of fate that compelled him to make dinner-table conversation with a person who made his living by writing the stuff. He didn't thaw until we got to the brandy, and Cordwainer Smith's name came up. I mentioned his real name. The ambassador almost dropped his snifter. "*Doctor* Paul Linebarger? The professor from Johns Hopkins?" The very one, I agreed. "But he was my *teacher*!" said the ambassador. And for what was left of the evening he could not have been more charming.

Professor Linebarger did not teach foreign affairs only to the ambassador; he taught any number of others. He didn't only teach events. He played a part in shaping them. Bilingual in Chinese (he grew up there) and fluent in half a dozen other languages, he was on call to the State Department to lecture, explain, discuss, or negotiate. Even in English. He once gave me his explanation of that. "It's because," he said, "I can speak a . . . lot . . . more . . . slowly . . . and . . . distinctly . . . than . . . most . . . people." And so he could. And I'm sure that was helpful with many persons who owned rusty or incomplete English. But I don't for one second believe that was the reason. What the State Department treasured was what we all treasure: not the habit of speech, but the mind that shaped it, wise, quick, and comprehending.

Traveler, teacher, writer, diplomat, scholar—Paul Linebarger led a fascinating life. If I don't say more about it here it is only because I don't want to repeat what has already been said very well in John Jeremy Pierce's excellent essay.* Most writers are dull as ditchwater in their personal lives. Paul Linebarger's life was as colorful as his novels.

If you have not happened to read a lot of science fiction, the next question that might come to your mind is: "So who is Cordwainer Smith, then?" So let me tell you something about what he wrote, and why to so many of us he was, and is, something special.

Start with this. All of science fiction is special. Not every person likes any of it. Hardly any one likes all of it. It comes in a wide variety of shapes and flavors. Some are bland and familiar, like vanilla. Some are strange and at first glance hardly assimilable, like a

*Published as the introduction to *The Best of Cordwainer Smith*, Ballantine-Del Rey, New York, 1975.

Tinguely sculpture happening. That is one of the things that attracts me to science fiction: its mind-stretching employment of incongruities. When this trait is pushed as far as it can go, it is a precarious tightrope-dance, daring balanced against disaster; the imagination of the writer and the tolerance of the reader stand stretched right up to the point of catastrophic collapse. One tiny millimeter more, and it would all fall apart. What was mind-bending and fresh would become simply absurd. A. E. van Vogt walked that narrow path marvelously, so did Jack Vance; Samuel R. Delany does it now; but no one, ever, has done it with more daredevil success than Cordwainer Smith. The outrageousness of his concepts, characters, and even words! Congohelium and stroon. Cat-people and laminated-mouse-brain robots. Mile-high abandoned freeways, and dead people who move and act and think and feel. Smith made wonderlands. And he made us believe they could be real.

Part of it was his finely tuned ear for the sound and sense of words. He had a prose style that changed and grew over the few years of his short career, and proved over and over that the right word was the unexpected word. The Smith word-selection is so privately his own that it can be detected even in the titles of his stories—though perhaps not as straightforwardly as one might imagine. Once James Blish looked up delightedly from the latest issue of *Galaxy* and said, "What I remember best about Cordwainer Smith is those marvelously individual titles." Which titles in particular? I asked, and Jim said, "Why, all of them. 'The Dead Lady of Clown Town,' 'The Ballad of Lost C'Mell,' and 'Think Blue, Count Two,' " for three. That was funny, and I told him so, because not one of those had been Smith's original title. I had put them on the stories when I published them. But Jim wasn't wrong, because I hadn't made any of them up. They had simply come out of Smith's own text.

Paul Linebarger was not at all a recluse. In fact, the opposite. He was gregarious and conversational, traveled immensely, spent a great deal of his time in classes and meetings. But he did not want to meet many science-fiction people. It was not that he did not like them. It was almost a superstition. Once before he had begun a career as a writer. He had published two novels—*Carola* and *Ria*, neither of them science fiction; what they remind me of most are Robert Briffault's novels of European politics, *Europa* and *Europa in Limbo*. He had had every intention of continuing, but he couldn't. The novels had been published under the pseudonym Felix C. Forrest. They had attracted enough attention to make a number of people wonder who "Felix C. Forrest" was, and a few of them had found out. Unfortunately. What was unfortunate was that when Paul found himself in face-to-face contact with "Forrest"'s audience, he could no longer write for them. Would the same thing happen with science fiction under the same circumstances? He didn't know. But he did not want to risk it.

So Paul Linebarger kept his pseudonym private. He stayed away from gatherings where science-fiction readers and writers were present. When the World Science Fiction Convention was in Washington in 1963, not more than a mile or two from his home, I urged him to drop in and test the water. I would not tell a soul who he was. If he chose, he could turn around and leave. If not . . . well, then not.

Paul weighed the thought and then, reluctantly, decided against the risk. But, he said, there were a couple of individuals whom he would like to meet if they wouldn't mind coming to his house. And so it happened. And of course it was a marvelous afternoon. It had to be. Paul was a fine host, and Genevieve—once his student, then his wife—a splendid hostess. Under the scarlet and gold birth scroll calligraphed by Paul's godfather, Sun Yat-sen, drinking "pukka pegs" (ginger ale and brandy highballs, which, Paul said, were what had kept the British army alive in India), in that discovering company the vibrations were optimal.

And it did not trouble his writing at all, then or

thereafter. He kept on writing, if anything better than ever. He enjoyed his guests—particularly, he said, Judith Merril and Algis Budrys—enough so that he felt easier about meeting others in the field. Little by little he did. Some in person, some only by mail, most by phone, and I think that the time was not far off when Paul Linebarger would have made an appearance at a science-fiction convention. Maybe a lot. But time ran out. He died of a stroke in 1966, at the bitterly unfair age of fifty-three.

Every important work of fiction is written partly in code. What we read in a sentence is not always what the author had in mind when he wrote it, and there are times—oh, *many* times—when the author's meaning may be unclear even to him. This is not always a flaw. It is sometimes a necessity. When a human mind, boxed inside its skull, perceiving the universe only through deceitful senses and communicating with it only in imprecise words, reaches for complex meanings and patterns of understanding, explicit statement is hard to achieve. The higher the reach, the harder the task. Cordwainer Smith's reach sometimes went clear out of sight.

Paul taught me how to decrypt some of his messages, but only the easy ones. Somewhere in the files of the manuscript collection at Syracuse University there is, or ought to be, an annotated copy of some of his manuscripts with decoding instructions. The particular stories were a parable of Middle-Eastern politics. He had taken the trouble to note in the margins for me which story characters from the remote future represented what current Egyptian and Lebanese political figures.

That is a game many writers play. It is sometimes fun, but I don't happen to consider it a whole *lot* of fun. What I wish I could decode in the work of Cordwainer Smith is far more complicated. His concerns went beyond current life and contemporary politics, and maybe beyond human experience entirely. Religion. Metaphysics. Ultimate meaning. The search for truth. When you set out to catch ultimate truth in a net of words, you need a lot of patience and a lot of skill. The quarry is elusive. Worse than that. You need a lot of faith, too, and a lot of stubbornness, because what you are seeking may not exist at all. *Does* religion refer to anything "real?" *Is* there such a thing in the universe as "meaning?"

The Cordwainer Smith stories are science fiction, all right. But they are, at least the best of them are, science fiction of the special kind that C. S. Lewis called "eschatological fiction." They aren't about the future of human beings like us. They are about what comes *after* human beings like us. They don't answer questions. They ask them, and command us to ask them too.

With the publication of this volume, nearly every science-fiction story "Cordwainer Smith" ever wrote is in print in a paperback edition. They fill just four volumes. His whole science-fiction writing career essentially took place in less than a decade, but how many writers in a full lifetime can match it?

—Frederik Pohl
Schaumberg, Illinois
July 1978

No, No, Not Rogov!

*That golden shape on the golden steps shook and flut-
tered like a bird gone mad—like a bird imbued with an
intellect and a soul, and, nevertheless, driven mad by
ecstasies and terrors beyond human understanding—
ecstasies drawn momentarily down into reality by the
consummation of superlative art. A thousand worlds
watched.*

*Had the ancient calendar continued this would have
been* A.D. *13,582. After defeat, after disappointment,
after ruin and reconstruction, mankind had leapt among
the stars.*

*Out of meeting inhuman art, out of confronting non-
human dances, mankind had made a superb esthetic effort and had leapt upon the stage of all the worlds.*

*The golden steps reeled before the eyes. Some eyes
had retinas. Some had crystalline cones. Yet all eyes
were fixed upon the golden shape which interpreted*
The Glory and Affirmation of Man *in the Inter-World
Dance Festival of what might have been* A.D. *13,582.*

*Once again mankind was winning the contest. Music
and dance were hypnotic beyond the limits of systems,
compelling, shocking to human and inhuman eyes. The
dance was a triumph of shock—the shock of dynamic
beauty.*

*The golden shape on the golden steps executed shim-
mering intricacies of meaning. The body was gold and
still human. The body was a woman, but more than a
woman. On the golden steps, in the golden light, she
trembled and fluttered like a bird gone mad.*

1

1

The Ministry of State Security had been positively shocked when they found that a Nazi agent, more heroic than prudent, had almost reached N. Rogov.

Rogov was worth more to the Soviet armed forces than any two air armies, more than three motorized divisions. His brain was a weapon, a weapon for the Soviet power.

Since the brain was a weapon, Rogov was a prisoner. He didn't mind.

Rogov was a pure Russian type, broad-faced, sandy-haired, blue-eyed, with whimsey in his smile and amusement in the wrinkles of the tops of his cheeks.

"Of course I'm a prisoner," Rogov used to say. "I am a prisoner of State service to the Soviet peoples. But the workers and peasants are good to me. I am an academician of the All Union Academy of Sciences, a major general in the Red Air Force, a professor in the University of Kharkov, a deputy works manager of the Red Flag Combat Aircraft Production Trust. From each of these I draw a salary."

Sometimes he would narrow his eyes at his Russian scientific colleagues and ask them in dead earnest, "Would I serve capitalists?"

The affrighted colleagues would try to stammer their way out of the embarrassment, protesting their common loyalty to Stalin or Beria, or Zhukov, or Molotov, or Bulganin, as the case may have been.

Rogov would look very Russian: calm, mocking, amused. He would let them stammer.

Then he'd laugh.

Solemnity transformed into hilarity, he would explode into bubbling, effervescent, good-humored laughter. "Of course I could not serve the capitalists. My little Anastasia would not let me."

The colleagues would smile uncomfortably and would wish that Rogov did not talk so wildly, or so comically, or so freely.

Even Rogov might wind up dead.

Rogov didn't think so.

They did.

Rogov was afraid of nothing.

Most of his colleagues were afraid of each other, of the Soviet system, of the world, of life, and of death.

Perhaps Rogov had once been ordinary and mortal like other people and full of fears.

But he had become the lover, the colleague, the husband of Anastasia Fyodorovna Cherpas.

Comrade Cherpas had been his rival, his antagonist, his competitor, in the struggle for scientific eminence in the daring Slav frontiers of Russian science. Russian science could never overtake the inhuman perfection of German method, the rigid intellectual and moral discipline of German teamwork, but the Russians could and did get ahead of the Germans by giving vent to their bold, fantastic imaginations. Rogov had pioneered the first rocket launchers of 1939. Cherpas had finished the job by making the best of the rockets radiodirected.

Rogov in 1942 had developed a whole new system of photomapping. Comrade Cherpas had applied it to color film. Rogov, sandy-haired, blue-eyed, and smiling, had recorded his criticisms of Comrade Cherpas's naïveté and unsoundness at the top-secret meetings of Russian scientists during the black winter nights of 1943. Comrade Cherpas, her butter-yellow hair flowing down like living water to her shoulders, her unpainted face gleaming with fanaticism, intelligence, and dedication, would snarl her own defiance at him, deriding his Communist theory, pinching at his pride, hitting his intellectual hypotheses where they were weakest.

By 1944 a Rogov-Cherpas quarrel had become something worth traveling to see.

In 1945 they were married.

Their courtship was secret, their wedding a surprise, their partnership a miracle in the upper ranks of Russian science.

The emigré press had reported that the great scientist, Peter Kapitza, once remarked, "Rogov and

Cherpas, there is a team. They're Communists, good Communists; but they're better than that! They're *Russian,* Russian enough to beat the world. Look at them. That's the future, our Russian future!" Perhaps the quotation was an exaggeration, but it did show the enormous respect in which both Rogov and Cherpas were held by their colleagues in Soviet science.

Shortly after their marriage strange things happened to them.

Rogov remained happy. Cherpas was radiant.

Nevertheless, the two of them began to have haunted expressions, as though they had seen things which words could not express, as though they had stumbled upon secrets too important to be whispered even to the most secure agents of the Soviet State Police.

In 1947 Rogov had an interview with Stalin. As he left Stalin's office in the Kremlin, the great leader himself came to the door, his forehead wrinkled in thought, nodding, "Da, da, da."

Even his own personal staff did not know why Stalin was saying "Yes, yes, yes," but they did see the orders that went forth marked ONLY BY SAFE HAND, and TO BE READ AND RETURNED, NOT RETAINED, and furthermore stamped FOR AUTHORIZED EYES ONLY AND UNDER NO CIRCUMSTANCES TO BE COPIED.

Into the true and secret Soviet budget that year by the direct personal order of a noncommittal Stalin an item was added for "Project Telescope." Stalin tolerated no inquiry, brooked no comment.

A village which had had a name became nameless.

A forest which had been opened to the workers and peasants became military territory.

Into the central post office in Kharkov there went a new box number for the *village of Ya. Ch.*

Rogov and Cherpas, comrades and lovers, scientists both and Russians both, disappeared from the everyday lives of their colleagues. Their faces were no longer seen at scientific meetings. Only rarely did they emerge.

On the few times they were seen, usually to and from Moscow at the time the All Union budget was made up each year, they seemed smiling and happy. But they did not make jokes.

What the outside world did not know was that Stalin in giving them their own project, granting them a paradise restricted to themselves, had seen to it that a snake went with them in the paradise. The snake this time was not one, but two personalities—Gausgofer and Gauck.

2

Stalin died.

Beria died too—less willingly.

The world went on.

Everything went into the forgotten village of Ya. Ch. and nothing came out.

It was rumored that Bulganin himself visited Rogov and Cherpas. It was even whispered that Bulganin said as he went to the Kharkov airport to fly back to Moscow, "It's big, big, big. There'll be no cold war if they do it. There won't be any war of any kind. We'll finish capitalism before the capitalists can ever begin to fight. If they do it. If they do it." Bulganin was reported to have shaken his head slowly in perplexity and to have said nothing more but to have put his initials on the unmodified budget of Project Telescope when a trusted messenger next brought him an envelope from Rogov.

Anastasia Cherpas became a mother. Their first boy looked like his father. He was followed by a little girl. Then another little boy. The children didn't stop Cherpas's work. They had a large dacha and trained nursemaids took over the household.

Every night the four of them dined together.

Rogov, Russian, humorous, courageous, amused.

Cherpas, older, more mature, more beautiful than ever but just as biting, just as cheerful, just as sharp as she had ever been.

But then the other two, the two who sat with them across the years of all their days, the two colleagues who had been visited upon them by the all-powerful word of Stalin himself.

Gausgofer was a female: bloodless, narrow-faced,

with a voice like a horse's whinny. She was a scientist and a policewoman, and competent at both jobs. In 1917 she had reported her own mother's whereabouts to the Bolshevic Terror Committee. In 1924 she had commanded her father's execution. He had been a Russian German of the old Baltic nobility and he had tried to adjust his mind to the new system, but he had failed. In 1930 she had let her lover trust her a little too much. He had been a Roumanian Communist, very high in the Party, but he had whispered into her ear in the privacy of their bedroom, whispered with the tears pouring down his face; she had listened affectionately and quietly and had delivered his words to the police the next morning.

With that she had come to Stalin's attention.

Stalin had been tough. He had addressed her brutally. "Comrade, you have some brains. I can see you know what Communism is all about. You understand loyalty. You're going to get ahead and serve the Party and the working class, but is that all you want?" He had spat the question at her.

She had been so astonished that she gaped.

The old man had changed his expression, favoring her with leering benevolence. He had put his forefinger on her chest. "Study science, Comrade. Study science. Communism plus science equals victory. You're too clever to stay in police work."

Gausgofer took a reluctant pride in the fiendish program of her German namesake, the wicked old geographer who made geography itself a terrible weapon in the Nazi anti-Soviet struggle.

Gausgofer would have liked nothing better than to intrude on the marriage of Cherpas and Rogov.

Gausgofer fell in love with Rogov the moment she saw him.

Gausgofer fell in hate—and hate can be as spontaneous and miraculous as love—with Cherpas the moment she saw *her*.

But Stalin had guessed that too.

With the bloodless, fanatic Gausgofer he had sent a man named B. Gauck.

Gauck was solid, impassive, blank-faced. In body he was about the same height as Rogov. Where Rogov was muscular, Gauck was flabby. Where Rogov's skin was fair and shot through with the pink and health of exercise, Gauck's skin was like stale lard, greasy, gray-green, sickly even on the best of days.

Gauck's eyes were black and small. His glance was as cold and sharp as death. Gauck had no friends, no enemies, no beliefs, no enthusiasm. Even Gausgofer was afraid of him.

Gauck never drank, never went out, never received mail, never sent mail, never spoke a spontaneous word. He was never rude, never kind, never friendly, never really withdrawn: he couldn't withdraw any more than the constant withdrawal of all his life.

Rogov had turned to his wife in the secrecy of their bedroom soon after Gausgofer and Gauck came and had said, "Anastasia, is that man sane?"

Cherpas intertwined the fingers of her beautiful, expressive hands. She who had been the wit of a thousand scientific meetings was now at a loss for words. She looked up at her husband with a troubled expression. "I don't know, Comrade . . . I just don't know . . ."

Rogov smiled his amused Slavic smile. "At the least then I don't think Gausgofer knows either."

Cherpas snorted with laughter and picked up her hairbrush. "That she doesn't. She really doesn't know, does she? I'll wager she doesn't even know to whom he reports."

That conversation had receded into the past. Gauck, Gausgofer, the bloodless eyes and the black eyes—they remained.

Every dinner the four sat down together.

Every morning the four met in the laboratory.

Rogov's great courage, high sanity, and keen humor kept the work going.

Cherpas's flashing genius fueled him whenever the routine overloaded his magnificent intellect.

Gausgofer spied and watched and smiled her bloodless smiles; sometimes, curiously enough, Gausgofer made genuinely constructive suggestions. She never understood the whole frame of reference of their work, but she knew enough of the mechanical and engineering details to be very useful on occasion.

Gauck came in, sat down quietly, said nothing, did nothing. He did not even smoke. He never fidgeted. He never went to sleep. He just watched.

The laboratory grew and with it there grew the immense configuration of the espionage machine.

3

In theory what Rogov had proposed and Cherpas seconded was imaginable. It consisted of an attempt to work out an integrated theory for all the electrical and radiation phenomena accompanying consciousness and to duplicate the electrical functions of mind without the use of animal material.

The range of potential products was immense.

The first product Stalin had asked for was a receiver, if possible, capable of tuning in the thoughts of a human mind and of translating those thoughts into either a punch-tape machine, an adapted German Hellschreiber machine, or phonetic speech. If the grids could be turned around and the brain-equivalent machine could serve not as a receiver but as a transmitter, it might be able to send out stunning forces which would paralyze or kill the process of thought.

At its best, Rogov's machine would be designed to confuse human thought over great distances, to select human targets to be confused, and to maintain an electronic jamming system which would jam straight into the human mind without the requirement of tubes or receivers.

He had succeeded—in part. He had given himself a violent headache in the first year of work.

In the third year he had killed mice at a distance of ten kilometers. In the seventh year he had brought on mass hallucinations and a wave of suicides in a neighboring village. It was this which impressed Bulganin.

Rogov was now working on the receiver end. No one had ever explored the infinitely narrow, infinitely subtle bands of radiation which distinguished one human mind from another, but Rogov was trying, as it were, to tune in on minds far away.

He had tried to develop a telepathic helmet of some kind, but it did not work. He had then turned away from the reception of pure thought to the reception of visual and auditory images. Where the nerve ends reached the brain itself he had managed over the years to distinguish whole pockets of microphenomena, and on some of these he had managed to get a fix.

With infinitely delicate tuning he had succeeded one day in picking up the eyesight of their second chauffeur and had managed, thanks to a needle thrust in just below his own right eyelid, to "see" through the other man's eyes as the other man, all unaware, washed their Zis limousine 1,600 meters away.

Cherpas had surpassed his feat later that winter and had managed to bring in an entire family having dinner over in a nearby city. She had invited B. Gauck to have a needle inserted into his cheekbone so that he could see with the eyes of an unsuspecting spied-on stranger. Gauck had refused any kind of needles, but Gausgofer had joined in the work.

The espionage machine was beginning to take form.

Two more steps remained. The first step consisted of tuning in on some remote target, such as the White House in Washington or the NATO Headquarters outside of Paris. The machine itself could obtain perfect intelligence by eavesdropping on the living minds of people far away.

The second problem consisted of finding a method of jamming those minds at a distance, stunning them so that the subject personnel fell into tears, confusion, or sheer insanity.

Rogov had tried, but he had never gotten more than thirty kilometers from the nameless village of Ya. Ch.

One November there had been seventy cases of hysteria, most of them ending in suicide, down in the city of Kharkov several hundred kilometers away, but Rogov was not sure that his own machine was doing it.

Comrade Gausgofer dared to stroke his sleeve. Her white lips smiled and her watery eyes grew happy as she said in her high, cruel voice, "*You* can do it, Comrade. You can do it."

Cherpas looked on with contempt. Gauck said nothing.

The female agent Gausgofer saw Cherpas's eyes upon her, and for a moment an arc of living hatred leapt between the two women.

The three of them went back to work on the machine.

Gauck sat on his stool and watched them.

The laboratory workers never talked very much and the room was quiet.

4

It was the year in which Eristratov died that the machine made a breakthrough. Eristratov died after the Soviet and People's democracies had tried to end the cold war with the Americans.

It was May. Outside the laboratory the squirrels ran among the trees. The leftovers from the night's rain dripped on the ground and kept the earth moist. It was comfortable to leave a few windows open and to let the smell of the forest into the workshop.

The smell of their oil-burning heaters and the stale smell of insulation, of ozone and the heated electronic gear was something with which all of them were much too familiar.

Rogov had found that his eyesight was beginning to suffer because he had to get the receiver needle somewhere near his optic nerve in order to obtain visual impressions from the machine. After months of experimentation with both animal and human subjects he had decided to copy one of their last experiments, successfully performed on a prisoner boy fifteen years of age, by having the needle slipped directly through the skull, up and behind the eye. Rogov had disliked using prisoners, because Gauck, speaking on behalf of security, always insisted that a prisoner used in experiments had to be destroyed in not less than five days from the beginning of the experiment. Rogov had satisfied himself that the skull-and-needle technique was safe, but he was very tired of trying to get frightened unscientific people to carry the load of intense, scientific attentiveness required by the machine.

Rogov recapitulated the situation to his wife and to their two strange colleagues.

Somewhat ill-humored, he shouted at Gauck, "Have you ever known what this is all about? You've been here years. Do you know what we're trying to do? Don't you ever want to take part in the experiments yourself? Do you realize how many years of mathematics have gone into the making of these grids and the calculation of these wave patterns? Are you good for anything?"

Gauck said, tonelessly and without anger, "Comrade Professor, I am obeying orders. You are obeying orders, too. I've never impeded you."

Rogov almost raved. "I know you never got in my way. We're all good servants of the Soviet State. It's not a question of loyalty. It's a question of enthusiasm. Don't you ever want to glimpse the science we're making? We are a hundred years or a thousand years ahead of the capitalist Americans. Doesn't that excite you? Aren't you a human being? Why don't you take part? Will you understand me when I explain it?"

Gauck said nothing: he looked at Rogov with his beady eyes. His dirty-gray face did not change expression. Gausgofer exhaled loudly in a grotesquely feminine sigh of relief, but she too said nothing. Cherpas, her winning smile and her friendly eyes looking at her husband and two colleagues, said, "Go ahead, Nikolai. The comrade can follow if he wants to."

Gausgofer looked enviously at Cherpas. She seemed inclined to keep quiet, but then had to speak. She said, "Do go ahead, Comrade Professor."

Said Rogov, "*Kharosho,* I'll do what I can. The machine is now ready to receive minds over immense distances." He wrinkled his lip in amused scorn. "We may even spy into the brain of the chief rascal himself and find out what Eisenhower is planning to do today against the Soviet people. Wouldn't it be wonderful if our machine could stun him and leave him sitting addled at his desk?"

Gauck commented, "Don't try it. Not without orders."

Rogov ignored the interruption and went on. "First I receive. I don't know what I will get, who I will get, or where they will be. All I know is that this machine will reach out across all the minds of men and beasts now living and it will bring the eyes and ears of a single mind directly into mine. With the new needle going directly into the brain it will be possible for me to get a very sharp fixation of position. The trouble with that boy last week was that even though we knew he was seeing something outside of this room, he appeared to be getting sounds in a foreign language and did not know enough English or German to realize where or what the machine had taken him to see."

Cherpas laughed. "I'm not worried. I saw then it was safe. You go first, my husband. If our comrades don't mind—?"

Gauck nodded.

Gausgofer lifted her bony hand breathlessly up to her skinny throat and said, "Of course, Comrade Rogov, of course. You did *all* the work. You *must* be the first."

Rogov sat down.

A white-smocked technician brought the machine over to him. It was mounted on three rubber-tired wheels and it resembled the small X-ray units used by dentists. In place of the cone at the head of the X-ray machine there was a long, incredibly tough needle. It had been made for them by the best surgical-steel craftsmen in Prague.

Another technician came up with a shaving bowl, a brush, and a straight razor. Under the gaze of Gauck's deadly eyes he shaved an area four centimeters square on the top of Rogov's head.

Cherpas herself then took over. She set her husband's head in the clamp and used a micrometer to get the skullfittings so tight and so clear that the needle would push through the dura mater at exactly the right point.

All this work she did deftly with kind, very strong fingers. She was gentle, but she was firm. She was his wife, but she was also his fellow scientist and his fellow colleague in the Soviet State.

She stepped back and looked at her work. She gave him one of their own very special smiles, the secret gay smiles which they usually exchanged with each other only when they were alone. "You won't want to do this every day. We're going to have to find some way of getting into the brain without using this needle. But it won't hurt you."

"Does it matter if it does hurt?" said Rogov. "This is the triumph of all our work. *Bring it down.*"

Gausgofer looked as though she would like to be invited to take part in the experiment, but she dared not interrupt Cherpas. Cherpas, her eyes gleaming with attention, reached over and pulled down the handle, which brought the tough needle to within a tenth of a millimeter of the right place.

Rogov spoke very carefully. "All I felt was a little sting. You can turn the power on now."

Gausgofer could not contain herself. Timidly she addressed Cherpas. "May *I* turn on the power?"

Cherpas nodded. Gauck watched. Rogov waited. Gausgofer pulled down the bayonet switch.

The power went on.

With an impatient twist of her hand, Anastasia Cherpas ordered the laboratory attendants to the other end of the room. Two or three of them had stopped working and were staring at Rogov, staring like dull sheep. They looked embarrassed and then they huddled in a white-smocked herd at the other end of the laboratory.

The wet May wind blew in on all of them. The scent of forest and leaves was about them.

The three watched Rogov.

Rogov's complexion began to change. His face became flushed. His breathing was so loud and heavy they could hear it several meters away. Cherpas fell on her knees in front of him, eyebrows lifted in mute inquiry.

Rogov did not dare nod, not with a needle in his brain. He said through flushed lips, speaking thickly and heavily, "Do—not—stop—now."

Rogov himself did not know what was happening. He thought he might see an American room, or a Russian room, or a tropical colony. He might see palm trees, or forests, or desks. He might see guns or buildings, washrooms or beds, hospitals, homes, churches. He might see with the eyes of a child, a woman, a man, a soldier, a philosopher, a slave, a worker, a savage, a religious one, a Communist, a reactionary, a governor, a policeman. He might hear voices; he might hear English, or French, or Russian, Swahili, Hindu, Malay, Chinese, Ukrainian, Armenian, Turkish, Greek. He did not know.

Something strange was happening.

It *seemed* to him that he had left the world, that he had left time. The hours and the centuries shrank up as the meters and the machine, unchecked, reached out for the most powerful signal which any humankind had transmitted. Rogov did not know it, but the machine had conquered time.

The machine reached the dance, the human challenger, and the dance festival of the year that was not A.D. 13,582, but which might have been.

Before Rogov's eyes the golden shape and the golden steps shook and fluttered in a ritual a thousand times more compelling than hypnotism. The rhythms meant nothing and everything to him. This was Russia, this was Communism. This was his life—indeed it was his soul acted out before his very eyes.

For a second, the last second of his ordinary life, he looked through flesh-and-blood eyes and saw the shabby woman whom he had once thought beautiful. He saw Anastasia Cherpas, and he did not care.

His vision concentrated once again on the dancing image, this woman, those postures, that dance!

Then the sound came in—music which would have made a Tschaikovsky weep, orchestras which would have silenced Shostakovich or Khachaturian forever, so much did it surpass the music of the twentieth century.

The people-who-were-not-people between the stars had taught mankind many arts. Rogov's mind was the best of its time, but his time was far, far behind the time of the great dance. With that one vision Rogov went firmly and completely mad. He became blind to the sight of Cherpas, Gausgofer, and Gauck. He forgot the village of Ya. Ch. He forgot himself. He was like a fish, bred in stale fresh water, which is thrown for the first time into a living stream. He was like an insect emerging from the chrysalis. His twentieth-century mind could not hold the imagery and the impact of the music and the dance.

But the needle was there and the needle transmitted into his mind more than his mind could stand.

The synapses of his brain flicked like switches. The future flooded into him.

He fainted. Cherpas leapt forward and lifted the needle. Rogov fell out of the chair.

5

It was Gauck who got the doctors. By nightfall they had Rogov resting comfortably and under heavy sedation. There were two doctors, both from the military headquarters. Gauck had obtained authorization for their services by dint of a direct telephone call to Moscow.

Both the doctors were annoyed. The senior one never stopped grumbling at Cherpas.

"You should not have done it, Comrade Cherpas. Comrade Rogov should not have done it either. You can't go around sticking things into brains. That's a medical problem. None of you people are doctors of medicine. It's all right for you to contrive devices with the prisoners, but you can't inflict things like this on

Soviet scientific personnel. I'm going to get blamed because I can't bring Rogov back. You heard what he was saying. All he did was mutter, 'That golden shape on the golden steps, that music, that me is a true me, that golden shape, that golden shape, I want to be with that golden shape,' and rubbish like that. Maybe you've ruined a first-class brain forever—" He stopped himself short as though he had said too much. After all, the problem was a security problem and apparently both Gauck and Gausgofer represented the security agencies.

Gausgofer turned her watery eyes on the doctor and said in a low, even, unbelievably poisonous voice, "Could *she* have done it, Comrade Doctor?"

The doctor looked at Cherpas, answering Gausgofer. "How? You were there. I wasn't. *How* could she have done it? *Why* should she do it? You were there."

Cherpas said nothing. Her lips were compressed tight with grief. Her yellow hair gleamed, but her hair was all that remained, at that moment, of her beauty. She was frightened and she was getting ready to be sad. She had no time to hate foolish women or to worry about security; she was concerned with her colleague, her lover, her husband, Rogov.

There was nothing much for them to do except to wait. They went into a large room and tried to eat.

The servants had laid out immense dishes of cold sliced meat, pots of caviar, and an assortment of sliced breads, pure butter, genuine coffee, and liquors.

None of them ate much.

They were all waiting.

At 9:15 the sound of rotors beat against the house. The big helicopter had arrived from Moscow.

Higher authorities took over.

6

The higher authority was a deputy minister, a man by the name of V. Karper.

Karper was accompanied by two or three uniformed colonels, by an engineer civilian, by a man from the headquarters of the Communist Party of the Soviet Union, and by two doctors.

They dispensed with the courtesies. Karper merely said, "You are Cherpas. I have met you. You are Gausgofer. I have seen your reports. You are Gauck."

The delegation went into Rogov's bedroom. Karper snapped, "Wake him."

The military doctor who had given him sedatives said, "Comrade, you mustn't—"

Karper cut him off. "Shut up." He turned to his own physician, pointed at Rogov. "Wake him up."

The doctor from Moscow talked briefly with the senior military doctor. He too began shaking his head. He gave Karper a disturbed look. Karper guessed what he might hear. He said, "Go ahead. I know there is some danger to the patient, but I've got to get back to Moscow with a report."

The two doctors worked over Rogov. One of them asked for his bag and gave Rogov an injection. Then all of them stood back from the bed.

Rogov writhed in his bed. He squirmed. His eyes opened, but he did not see them. With childishly clear and simple words Rogov began to talk: ". . . that golden shape, the golden stairs, the music, take me back to the music, I want to be with the music, I really am the music . . ." and so on in an endless monotone.

Cherpas leaned over him so that her face was directly in his line of vision. "My darling! My darling, wake up. This is serious."

It was evident to all of them that Rogov did not hear her, because he went on muttering about golden shapes.

For the first time in many years Gauck took the initiative. He spoke directly to the man from Moscow, Karper. "Comrade, may I make a suggestion?"

Karper looked at him. Gauck nodded at Gausgofer. "We were both sent here by orders of Comrade Stalin. She is senior. She bears the responsibility. All I do is double-check."

The deputy minister turned to Gausgofer. Gausgofer had been staring at Rogov on the bed; her blue, watery eyes were tearless and her face was drawn into an expression of extreme tension.

Karper ignored that and said to her firmly, clearly, commandingly, "What do you recommend?"

Gausgofer looked at him very directly and said in a measured voice, "I do not think that the case is one of brain damage. I believe that he has obtained a communication which he must share with another human being and that unless one of us follows him there may be no answer."

Karper barked, "Very well. But what do we do?"

"Let *me* follow—into the machine."

Anastasia Cherpas began to laugh slyly and frantically. She seized Karper's arm and pointed her finger at Gausgofer. Karper stared at her.

Cherpas slowed down her laughter and shouted at Karper, "The woman's mad. She has loved my husband for many years. She has hated my presence, and now she thinks that she can save him. She thinks that she can follow. She thinks that he wants to communicate with her. That's ridiculous. I will go myself!"

Karper looked about. He selected two of his staff and stepped over into a corner of the room. They could hear him talking, but they could not distinguish the words. After a conference of six or seven minutes he returned.

"You people have been making serious security charges against each other. I find that one of our finest weapons, the mind of Rogov, is damaged. Rogov's not just a man. He is a Soviet project." Scorn entered his voice. "I find that the senior security officer, a policewoman with a notable record, is charged by another Soviet scientist with a silly infatuation. I disregard such charges. The development of the Soviet State and the work of Soviet science cannot be impeded by personalities. Comrade Gausgofer will follow. I am acting tonight because my own staff physician says that Rogov may not live and it is very important for us to find out just what has happened to him and why."

He turned his baneful gaze on Cherpas. "You will not protest, Comrade. Your mind is the property of the

Russian State. Your life and your education have been paid for by the workers. You cannot throw these things away because of personal sentiment. If there is anything to be found Comrade Gausgofer will find it for both of us."

The whole group of them went back into the laboratory. The frightened technicians were brought over from the barracks. The lights were turned on and the windows were closed. The May wind had become chilly.

The needle was sterilized.

The electronic grids were warmed up.

Gausgofer's face was an impassive mask of triumph as she sat in the receiving chair. She smiled at Gauck as an attendant brought the soap and the razor to shave a clean patch on her scalp.

Gauck did not smile back. His black eyes stared at her. He said nothing. He did nothing. He watched.

Karper walked to and fro, glancing from time to time at the hasty but orderly preparation of the experiment.

Anastasia Cherpas sat down at a laboratory table about five meters away from the group. She watched the back of Gausgofer's head as the needle was lowered. She buried her face in her hands. Some of the others thought they heard her weeping, but no one heeded Cherpas very much. They were too intent on watching Gausgofer.

Gausgofer's face became red. Perspiration poured down the flabby cheeks. Her fingers tightened on the arm of her chair.

Suddenly she shouted at them, *"That golden shape on the golden steps."*

She leapt to her feet, dragging the apparatus with her.

No one had expected this. The chair fell to the floor. The needle holder, lifted from the floor, swung its weight sidewise. The needle twisted like a scythe in Gausgofer's brain. Neither Rogov nor Cherpas had ever expected a struggle within the chair. *They did not know that they were going to tune in on* A.D. *13,582.*

The body of Gausgofer lay on the floor, surrounded by excited officials.

Karper was acute enough to look around at Cherpas.

She stood up from the laboratory table and walked toward him. A thin line of blood flowed down from her cheekbone. Another line of blood dripped down from a position on her cheek, one and a half centimeters forward of the opening of her left ear.

With tremendous composure, her face as white as fresh snow, she smiled at him. "I eavesdropped."

Karper said, "What?"

"I eavesdropped, eavesdropped," repeated Anastasia Cherpas. "I found out where my husband has gone. It is not somewhere in this world. It is something hypnotic beyond all the limitations of our science. We have made a great gun, but the gun has fired upon us before we could fire it. You may think you will change my mind, Comrade Deputy Minister, but you will not.

"I know what has happened. My husband is never coming back. And I am not going any further forward without him.

"Project Telescope is finished. You may try to get someone else to finish it, but you will not."

Karper stared at her and then turned aside.

Gauck stood in his way.

"What do you want?" snapped Karper.

"To tell you," said Gauck very softly, "to tell you, Comrade Deputy Minister, that Rogov is gone as she says he is gone, that she is finished if she says she is finished, that all this is true. I know."

Karper glared at him. "How do you know?"

Gauck remained utterly impassive. With superhuman assurance and perfect calm he said to Karper, "Comrade, I do not dispute the matter. I know these people, though I do not know their science. Rogov is done for."

At last Karper believed him. Karper sat down in a chair beside a table. He looked up at his staff. "Is it possible?"

No one answered.

"I ask you, is it possible?"

They all looked at Anastasia Cherpas, at her beautiful hair, her determined blue eyes, and the two thin lines of blood where she had eavesdropped with small needles.

Karper turned to her. "What do we do now?"

For an answer she dropped to her knees and began sobbing, "No, no, not Rogov! No, no, not Rogov!"

And that was all that they could get out of her. Gauck looked on.

On the golden steps in the golden light, a golden shape danced a dream beyond the limits of all imagination, danced and drew the music to herself until a sigh of yearning, yearning which became a hope and a torment, went through the hearts of living things on a thousand worlds.

Edges of the golden scene faded raggedly and unevenly into black. The gold dimmed down to a pale gold-silver sheen and then to silver, last of all to white. The dancer who had been golden was now a forlorn white-pink figure standing, quiet and fatigued, on the immense white steps. The applause of a thousand worlds roared in upon her.

She looked blindly at them. The dance had overwhelmed her too. Their applause could mean nothing. The dance was an end in itself. She would have to live, somehow, until she danced again.

War No. 81-Q*

It came to war.

Tibet and America, each claiming the Radiant Heat Monopoly, applied for a War Permit for 2127, A.D.

*"War No. 81-Q" originally appeared under the pseudonym Karloman Jungahr in *The Adjutant*, a publication of the Washington, D.C., public school system, Vol. IX, No. 1, June 1928. Long feared lost, this is its first appearance since.

The Universal War Board granted it, stating, of course, the conditions. It was, after a few compromises and amendments had been effected, accepted by the belligerent nations.

The conditions were:

a.   Five 22,000-ton aero-ships, combinations of aero and dirigible, were to be the only combatants.

b.   They were to be armed with machine-guns firing nonexplosive bullets only.

c.   The War Territory of Kerguelen was to be rented by the two nations, the United American Nations and the Mongolian Alliance, for the two hours of the war, which was to begin on January 5, 2127, at noon.

d.   The nation vanquished was to pay all the expenses of the war, excepting the War Territory Rent.

e.   No human beings should be on the battlefield. The Mongolian controllers must be in Lhasa; the American ones, in the City of Franklin.

The belligerent nations had no difficulty in renting the War Territory of Kerguelen. The rent charged by the Austral League was, as usual, forty million dollars an hour.

Spectators from all over the world rushed to the borders of the Territory, eager to obtain good places. Q-ray telescopes came into tremendous demand.

Mechanics carefully worked over the giant war-machines.

The radio-controls, delicate as watches, were brought to perfection, both at the control stations in Lhasa and in the City of Franklin, and on the war-flyers.

The planes arrived on the minute decided.

Controlled by their pilots thousands of miles away, the great planes swooped and curved, neither fleet daring to make the first move.

There were five American ships, the *Prospero, Ariel, Oberon, Caliban*, and *Titania*, and five Chinese ships, rented by the Mongolians, the *Han, Yuen, Tsing, Tsin*, and *Sung*.

The Mongolian fleet incurred the displeasure of the spectators by casting a smoke screen, which greatly interfered with the seeing. The *Prospero*, every gun throbbing, hurled itself into the smoke screen and came out on the other side, out of control, quivering with incoordinating machinery. As it neared the boundary, it was blown up by its pilot, safe and sound, thousands of miles away. But the sacrifice was not in vain. The *Han* and *Sung*, both severely crippled, swung slowly out of the mist. The *Han*, with a list that clearly showed it was doomed, was struck by a lucky shot from the *Caliban* and fell several hundred feet, its left wing ablaze. But for a second or two, the pilot regained control, and, with a single shot, disabled the *Caliban*, and then the *Han* fell to its doom on the rocky islands below.

The *Caliban* and *Sung* continued to drift, firing at each other. As soon as it was seen that neither would be of any further use in the battle, they were, by common consent, taken from the field.

There now remained three ships on each side, darting in and out of the smoke screen, occasionally ascending to cool the engines.

Among the spectators, excitement prevailed, for it was announced from the City of Franklin that a new and virtually unknown pilot, Jack Bearden, was going to take command of three ships at once! And never before had one pilot commanded, by radio, more than two ships! Besides, two of the most famous Mongolian aces, Baartek and Soong, were on the field, while an even more famous person, the Chinese mercenary T'ang, commanded the *Yuen*.

The Americans among the spectators protested that a pilot so young and inexperienced should not be allowed to endanger the ships.

The Government replied that it had a thorough confidence in Bearden's abilities.

But when the young pilot stepped before the television screen, on which was pictured the battle, and the maze of controls, he realized that his ability had been overestimated, by himself and by everyone else.

He climbed up on the high stool and reached for the speed control levers, which were directly behind him.

He leaned back, and fell! His head struck against two buttons: and he saw the *Oberon* and *Titania* blow themselves up.

The three enemy ships cooperated in an attack on the *Ariel*. Bearden swung his ship around and rushed it into the smoke screen.

He saw the huge bulk of the *Tsing* bear down upon him. He fired instinctively—and hit the control center.

Dodging aside as the *Tsing* fell past him, he missed the *Tsin* by inches. The pilot of the *Tsin* shot at the reinforcements of the *Ariel*'s right wing, loosening it.

For a few moments, he was alone, or, rather, the *Ariel* was alone. For he was at the control board in the War Building in the City of Franklin.

The *Yuen*, controlled by the master-pilot T'ang, rose up from beneath him, shot off the end of his left wing, and vanished into the mists of the smoke screen before the astonished Bearden was able to register a single hit.

He had better luck with the *Tsin*. When this swooped down on the *Ariel,* he disabled its firing control. Then, when this plane rose from beneath, intending to ram itself into the *Ariel*, Bearden dropped half his machineguns overboard. They struck the *Tsin*, which exploded immediately.

Now only the *Ariel* and the *Yuen* remained! Masterpilot faced master-pilot.

Bearden placed a lucky shot in the *Yuen*'s rudder, but only partially disabled it.

Yuen threw more smoke-screen bombs overboard.

Bearden rose upward; no, he was still safe and sound in America, but the *Ariel* rose upward.

The spectators in their helicopters blew whistles, shot off pistols, went mad in applause.

T'ang lowered the *Yuen* to within several hundred feet of the water.

He was applauded, too.

Bearden inspected his ship with the autotelevision. It would collapse at the slightest strain.

He wheeled his ship to the right, preparatory to descending.

His left wing broke under the strain: and the *Ariel* began hurtling downward. He turned his autotelevisation on the *Yuen*, not daring to see the ship, which carried his reputation, his future, crash.

The *Yuen* was struck by his left wing, which was falling like a stone. The *Yuen* exploded, and the *Ariel* crashed forty-six seconds later.

And, by international law, Bearden had won the war for America, with it the honors of war and the possession of the enormous Radiant Heat revenue.

All the world hailed this Lindbergh of the twenty second century.

Mark Elf

THE YEARS ROLLED by; the Earth lived on, even when a stricken and haunted mankind crept through the glorious ruins of an immense past.

1. Descent of a Lady

Stars wheeled silently over an early summer sky, even though men had long ago forgotten to call such nights by the name of June.

Laird tried to watch the stars with his eyes closed. It was a ticklish and terrifying game for a telepath: at any moment he might feel the heavens opening up and might, as his mind touched the image of the nearer stars, plunge himself into a nightmare of perpetual falling. Whenever he had this sickening shocking ghastly suffocating feeling of limitless fall, he had to close his mind against telepathy long enough to let his powers heal.

He was reaching with his mind for objects just above the Earth, burnt-out space stations which flitted in their

*multiplex orbits, spinning forever, left over from the
wreckage of ancient atomic wars.*

He found one.

*Found one so ancient it had no surviving cryotronic
controls. Its design was archaic beyond belief; chemical
tubes had apparently once lifted it out of Earth's atmosphere.*

He opened his eyes and promptly lost it.

*Closing his eyes he groped again with his seeking
mind until he found the ancient derelict. As his mind
reached for it again the muscles of his jaw tightened. He
sensed life within it, life as old as the archaic machine
itself.*

*In an instant he made contact with his friend Tong
Computer.*

*He poured his knowledge into Tong's mind. Keenly
interested, Tong shot back at him an orbit which would
cut the mildly parabolic pattern of the old device and
bring it back down into Earth's atmosphere.*

Laird made a supreme effort.

*Calling on his unseen friends to aid him, he searched
once more through the rubbish that raced and twinkled
unseen just above the sky. Finding the ancient machine
he managed to give it a push.*

*In this fashion, about sixteen thousand years after she
left Hitler's Reich, Carlotta vom Acht began her return
to the Earth of men.*

In all those years she had not changed.

Earth had.

The ancient rocket tipped. Four hours later it had begun to graze the stratosphere, and its ancient controls,
preserved by cold and time against all change, went
back into effect. As they thawed they became activated.

The course flattened out.

Fifteen hours later the rocket was seeking a destination.

Electronic controls which had really been dead for
thousands of years, out in the changeless time of space
itself, began to look for German territory, seeking the

territory by feedbacks which selected characteristic Nazi patterns of electronic communications scramblers.

There were none.

How could the machine know this? The machine had left the town of Pardubice on April 2, 1945, just as the last German hideouts were being mopped up by the Red Army. How could the machine know that there was no Hitler, no Reich, no Europe, no America, no nations? The machine was keyed to German codes. Only German codes.

This did not affect the feedback mechanisms.

They looked for German codes anyway. There were none. The electronic computer in the rocket began to go mildly neurotic. It chattered to itself like an angry monkey, rested, chattered again, and then headed the rocket for something which seemed to be vaguely electrical. The rocket descended and the girl awoke.

She knew she was in the box in which her daddy had placed her. She knew that she was not a cowardly swine like the Nazis whom her father despised. She was a good Prussian girl of noble military family. She had been ordered to stay in the box by her father. What daddy told her to do she had always done. That was the first kind of rule for her kind of girl, a sixteen-year-old of the Junker class. The noise increased.

The electronic chattering flared up into a wild medley of clicks.

She could smell something perfectly dreadful burning, something awful and rotten like flesh. She was afraid that it was herself, but she felt no pain.

"*Vadi, Vadi,* what is happening to me?" she cried to her father.

(Her father had been dead sixteen thousand and more years. Obviously enough he did not answer.)

The rocket began to spin. The ancient leather harness holding her broke loose. Even though her section of the rocket was no bigger than a coffin she was cruelly bruised.

She began to cry.

She vomited, even though very little came up. Then

she slid in her own vomit and felt nasty and ashamed because of something which was a terribly simple human reaction.

The noises all met in a screaming shrieking climax. The last thing she remembered was the firing of the forward decelerators. The metal had become fatigued so that the tubes not only fired forward; they blew themselves to pieces sidewise as well.

She was unconscious when the rocket crashed. Perhaps that saved her life, since the least muscular tension would have led to the ripping of muscle and the crack of bone.

2. A Moron Found Her

His metals and plumes beamed in the moonlight as he scampered about the dark forest in his gorgeous uniform. The government of the world had long since been left to the Morons by the true men, who had no interest in such things as politics or administration.

Carlotta's weight, not her conscious will, had tripped the escape handle.

Her body lay half in, half out of the rocket.

She had gotten a bad burn on her left arm where her skin touched the hot outer surface of the rocket.

The Moron parted the bushes and approached.

"I am the Lord High Administrator of Area Seventy-three," he said, identifying himself according to the rules.

The unconscious girl did not answer. He rose up close to the rocket, crouching low lest the dangers of the night devour him, and listened intently to the radiation counter built in under the skin of his skull behind his left ear. He lifted the girl dextrously, flung her gently over his shoulder, turned about, ran back into the bushes, made a right-angle turn, ran a few paces, looked about him undecidedly, and then ran (still uncertain, still rabbitlike) down to the brook.

He reached into his pocket and found a burn-balm. He applied a thick coating to the burn on her arm. It

would stay, killing the pain and protecting the skin until
the burn was healed.

He splashed cool water on her face. She awakened.
"Wo bin ich?" said she in German.

On the other side of the world Laird, the telepath,
had forgotten for the moment about the rocket. He
might have understood her, but he was not there. The
forest was around her and the forest was full of life,
fear, hate, and pitiless destruction.

The Moron babbled in his own language.

She looked at him and thought that he was a Russian.

Said she in German, "Are you a Russian? Are you a
German? Are you part of General Vlasov's army? How
far are we from Prague? You must treat me cour-
teously. I am an important girl . . ."

The Moron stared at her.

His face began to grin with innocent and consummate
lust. (The true men had never felt it necessary to inhibit
the breeding habits of Morons between the Beasts, the
Unforgiven, and the Menschenjägers. It was hard for
any kind of human being to stay alive. The true men
wanted the Morons to go on breeding, to carry reports,
to gather up a few necessaries, and to distract the other
inhabitants of the world enough to let the true men have
the quiet and contemplation which their exalted but
weary temperaments demanded.)

This Moron was typical of his kind. To him food
meant eat, water meant drink, woman meant lust.

He did not discriminate.

Weary, confused, and bruised though she was, Carlotta still recognized his expression.

Sixteen thousand years ago she had expected to be
raped or murdered by the Russians. This soldier was a
fantastic little man, plump and grinning, with enough
medals for a Soviet colonel general. From what she
could see in the moonlight, he was clean-shaven and
pleasant, but he looked innocent and stupid to be so

high-ranking an officer. Perhaps the Russians were all
like that, she thought.

He reached for her.

Tired as she was, she slapped him.

The Moron was mixed up in his thoughts. He knew
that he had the right to capture any Moron woman
whom he might find. Yet he also knew that it was worse
than death to touch any woman of the true men. Which
was this—this thing—this power—this entity who had
descended from the stars?

Pity is as old and emotional as lust. As his lust receded, his elemental human pity took over. He reached
in his jerkin pocket for a few scraps of food.

He held them out to her.

She ate, looking at him trustfully, very much the
child.

Suddenly there was a crashing in the woods.

Carlotta wondered what had happened.

When she first saw him his face had been full of concern. Then he had grinned and had talked. Later he had
become lustful. Finally he had acted very much the
gentleman. Now he looked blank, brain and bone and
skin all concentrated into the act of listening—listening
for something else, beyond the crashing, which she
could not hear. He turned back to her.

"You must run. You must run. Get up and run. I tell
you, run!"

She listened to his babble without comprehension.

Once again he crouched to listen.

He looked at her with blank horror on his face. Carlotta tried to understand what was the matter, but she
could not riddle his meaning.

Three more strange little men dressed exactly like
him came crashing out of the woods.

They ran like elk or deer before a forest fire. Their
faces were blank with the exertion of running. Their
eyes looked straight ahead so that they seemed almost
blind. It was a wonder that they evaded the trees. They
came crashing down the slope scattering leaves as
they ran. They splashed the waters of the brook as they

stomped recklessly through it. With a half-animal cry Carlotta's Moron joined them.

The last she saw of him, he was running away into the woods, his plumes grinning ridiculously as his head nodded with the exertion of running.

From the direction from which the Morons had come an unearthly creepy sound whistled through the woods. It was whistling, stealthy and low, accompanied by the very quiet sound of machinery.

The noise sounded like all the tanks in the world compressed into the living ghost of a tank, into the heart of a machine which survived its own destruction and, spiritlike, haunted the scenes of old battles.

As the sound approached Carlotta turned toward it. She tried to stand up and could not. She faced the danger. (All Prussian girls, destined to be the mothers of officers, were taught to face danger and never to turn their backs on it.) As the noise came close to her she could hear the high crazy inquiry of soft electronic chatter. It resembled the sonar she had once heard in her father's laboratory at the Reichs' secret offices project of Nordnacht.

The machine came out of the woods.

And it did look like a ghost.

3. The Death of All Men

Carlotta stared at the machine. It had legs like a grasshopper, a body like a ten-foot turtle, and three heads which moved restlessly in the moonlight.

From the forward edge of the top shell a hidden arm leapt forth, seeming to strike at her, deadlier than a cobra, quicker than a jaguar, more silent than a bat flitting across the face of the moon.

"Don't!" Carlotta screamed in German. The arm stopped suddenly in the moonlight.

The stop was so sudden that the metal twanged like the string of a bow.

The heads of the machine all turned toward her.

Something like surprise seemed to overtake the machine. The whistling dropped down to a soothing purr. The electronic chatter burst up to a crescendo and then stopped. The machine dropped to its knees.

Carlotta crawled over to it.

Said she in German, "What are you?"

"I am the death of all men who oppose the Sixth German Reich," said the machine in fluted singsong German. "If the Reichsangehöriger wishes to identify me, my model and number are written on my cara- pace."

The machine knelt at a height so low that Carlotta could seize one of the heads and look in the moonlight at the edge of the top shell. The head and neck, though made of metal, felt much more weak and brittle than she expected. There was about the machine an air of immense age.

"I can't see," wailed Carlotta, "I need a light."

There was the ache and grind of long-unused machi- nery. Another mechanical arm appeared, dropping flakes of near-crystalized dirt as it moved. The tip of the arm exuded light, blue, penetrating and strange.

Brook, forest, small valley, machine, even herself, were all lit up by the soft penetrating blue light which did not hurt her eyes. The light even gave her a sense of well-being. With the light she could read. Traced on the carapace just above the three heads was this inscription:

WAFFENAMT DES SECHSTEN DEUTSCHEN
REICHES
BURG EISENHOWER, A.D. 2495
And then below it in much larger Latin letters:
MENSCHENJAGER MARK ELF

"What does 'Man-hunter, Model Eleven' mean?"

"That's me," whistled the machine. "How is it you don't know me if you are a German?"

"Of course, I'm a German, you fool!" said Carlotta. "Do I look like a Russian?"

"What is a Russian?" said the machine.

Carlotta stood in the blue light wondering, dreaming,

dreading—dreading the unknown which had materialized around her.

When her father, Heinz Horst Ritter vom Acht, professor and doctor of mathematical physics at project
Nordnacht, had fired her into the sky before he himself
awaited a gruesome death at the hands of the Soviet sol-
diery, he had told her nothing about the Sixth Reich,
nothing about what she might meet, nothing about the
future. It came to her mind that perhaps the world was
dead, that the strange little men were not near Prague,
that she was in Heaven or Hell, herself being dead, or if
herself alive, was in some other world, or her own world
in the future, or things beyond all human ken, or problems which no mind could solve . . .

She fainted again.

The Menschenjäger could not know that she was unconscious and addressed her in serious high-pitched
singsong German. "German citizen, have confidence
that I will protect you. I am built to identify German
thoughts and to kill all men who do not have true German thoughts."

The machine hesitated. A loud chatter of electronic
clicks echoed across the silent woods while the machine
tried to compute its own mind. It was not easy to select
from the long-unused store of words for so ancient and
so new a situation. The machine stood in its own blue
light. The only sound was the sound of the brook moving irresistibly about its gentle and unliving business.
Even the birds in the trees and the insects round about
were hushed into silence by the presence of the dreaded
whistling machine.

To the sound-receptors of the Menschenjäger the
running of the Morons, by now some two miles distant,
came as a very faint pitter-patter.

The machine was torn between two duties, the long-
current and familiar duty of killing all men who were
not German, and the ancient and forgotten duty of suc-
coring all Germans, whoever they might be. After another period of electronic chatter the machine began to
speak again. Beneath the grind of its singsong German

there was a curious warning, a reminder of the whistle which it made as it moved, a sound of immense mechanical and electronic effort.

Said the machine, "You are German. It has been long since there has been any German anywhere. I have gone around the world two thousand three and twenty-eight times. I have killed seventeen thousand four hundred and sixty-nine enemies of the Sixth German Reich for sure, and I have probably killed forty-two thousand and seven additional ones. I have been back to the automatic restoration center eleven times. The enemies who call themselves the True Men always elude me. One of them I have not killed for more than three thousand years. The ordinary men whom some call the Unforgiven are the ones I kill most of all, but frequently I catch Morons and kill them, too. I am fighting for Germany, but I cannot find Germany anywhere. There are no Germans in Germany. There are no Germans anywhere. I accept orders from no one but a German. Yet there have been no Germans anywhere, no Germans anywhere, no Germans anywhere . . ."

The machine seemed to get a catch in its electronic brain because it went on repeating *no Germans anywhere* three or four hundred times.

Carlotta came to as the machine was dreamily talking to itself, repeating with sad and lunatic intensity *no Germans anywhere.*

Said she, "I'm a German."

". . . no Germans anywhere, no Germans anywhere, except you, except you, except you."

The mechanical voice ended in a thin screech.

Carlotta tried to come to her feet.

At last the machine found words again. "What—do—I—do—now?"

"Help me," said Carlotta firmly.

This command seemed to tap an operable feedback in the ancient cybernetic assembly. "I cannot help you, member of the Sixth German Reich. For that you need a rescue machine. I am not a rescue machine. I am a hunter of men, designed to kill all the enemies of the German Reich."

"Get me a rescue machine then," said Carlotta.

The blue light went off, leaving Carlotta standing blinded in the dark. She was shaky on her legs. The voice of the Menschenjäger came to her.

"I am not a rescue machine. There are no rescue machines. There are no rescue machines anywhere. There is no Germany anywhere. There are no Germans anywhere, no Germans anywhere, no Germans anywhere, except you. You must ask a rescue machine. Now I go. I must kill men. Men who are enemies of the Sixth German Reich. That is all I can do. I can fight forever. I shall find a man and kill him. Then I shall find another man and kill him. I depart on the work of the Sixth German Reich."

The whistling and clicking resumed.

With incredible daintiness the machine stepped as lightly as a cat across the brook. Carlotta listened intently in the darkness. Even the dry leaves of last year did not stir as the Menschenjäger moved through the shadow of the fresh leafy trees.

Abruptly there was silence.

Carlotta could hear the agonized clickety-clack of the computers in the Menschenjäger. The forest became a weird silhouette as the blue light went back on.

The machine returned.

Standing on the far side of the brook it spoke to her in the dry, high-fluted singing German voice.

"Now that I have found a German I will report to you once every hundred years. That is correct. Perhaps that is correct. I do not know. I was built to report to officers. You are not an officer. Nevertheless you are a German. So I will report every hundred years. Meanwhile watch out for the Kaskaskia Effect."

Carlotta, sitting again, was chewing some of the dry cubic food scraps which the Moron had left behind. They tasted like a mockery of chocolate. With her mouth full she tried to shout to the Menschenjäger, *Was ist das?*

Apparently the machine understood, because it answered, "The Kaskaskia Effect is an American weapon. The Americans are all gone. There are no Americans anywhere, no Americans anywhere, no Americans anywhere—"

"Stop repeating yourself," said Carlotta. "What is that effect you are talking about?"

"The Kaskaskia Effect stops the Menschenjägers, stops the true men, stops the Beasts. It can be sensed, but it cannot be seen or measured. It moves like a cloud. Only simple men with clean thoughts and happy lives can live inside it. Birds and ordinary beasts can live inside it, too. The Kaskaskia Effect moves about like clouds. There are more than twenty-one and less than thirty-four Kaskaskia Effects moving slowly about this planet Earth. I have carried other Menschenjägers back for restoration and rebuilding, but the restoration center can find no fault. The Kaskaskia Effect ruins us. Therefore, we run away even though the officers told us to run from nothing. If we did not run away we would cease to exist. You are a German. I think the Kaskaskia Effect would kill you. Now I go to hunt a man. When I find him I will kill him."

The blue light went off.

The machine whistled and clicked its way into the dark silence of the wooded night.

4. Conversation with the Middle-Sized Bear

Carlotta was completely adult.

She had left the screaming uproar of Hitler Germany as it fell to ruins in its Bohemian outposts. She had obeyed her father, the Ritter vom Acht, as he passed her and her sisters into missiles which had been designed as personnel and supply carriers for the First German National Socialist Moon Base.

He and his medical brother, Professor Doctor Joachim vom Acht, had harnessed the girls securely in their missiles.

Their uncle the Doctor had given them shots.

Karla had gone first, then Juli, and then Carlotta.

Then the barbed-wire fortress of Pardubice and the monotonous grind of Wehrmacht trucks trying to escape the air strikes of the Red Air Force and the American fighter-bombers died in the one night and this mysterious "forest in the middle of nothing-at-all" was born in the next night.

Carlotta was completely dazed.

She found a smooth-looking place at the edge of the brook. The old leaves were heaped high here. Without regard for further danger, she slept.

She had not been asleep more than a few minutes before the bushes parted again.

This time it was a bear. The bear stood at the edge of the darkness and looked into the moonlit valley with the brook running through it. He could hear no sound of Morons, no whistle of manshonyagger, as he and his kind called the hunting machines. When he was sure all was safe, he twitched his claws and reached delicately into a leather bag which was hanging from his neck by a thong. Gently he took out a pair of spectacles and fitted them slowly and carefully in front of his tired old eyes.

He then sat down next to the girl and waited for her to wake up.

She did not wake until dawn.

Sunlight and birdsong awakened her.

(Could it have been the probing of Laird's mind, whose far-reaching senses told him that a woman had magically and mysteriously emerged from the archaic rocket and that there was a human being unlike all the other kinds of mankind waking at a brookside in a place which had once been called Maryland?)

Carlotta awoke, but she was sick.

She had a fever.

Her back ached.

Her eyelids were almost stuck together with foam. The world had had time to develop all sorts of new allergenic substances since she had last walked on the surface of the Earth. Four civilizations had come and vanished. They and their weapons were sure to leave membrane-inflaming residua behind.

Her skin itched.

Her stomach felt upset.

Her arm was numb and covered with some kind of sticky black. She did not know it was a burn covered by the salve which the Moron had given her the previous night.

Her clothes were dry and seemed to be falling off her in shreds.

She felt so bad that when she noticed the bear she did not even have strength to run.

She just closed her eyes again.

Lying there with her eyes closed she wondered all over again where she was.

Said the bear in perfect German, "You are at the edge of the Unselfing Zone. You have been rescued by a Moron. You have stopped a Menschenjäger very mysteriously. For the first time in my own life I can see into a German mind and see that the word manshon-yagger should really be Menschenjäger, a hunter of men. Allow me to introduce myself. I am the Middle-Sized Bear who lives in these woods."

The voice not only spoke German, but it spoke exactly the right kind of German. The voice sounded like the German which Carlotta had heard throughout her life from her father. It was a masculine voice, confident, serious, reassuring. With her eyes still closed she realized that it was a bear who was doing the talking. With a start, she recalled that the bear had been wearing spectacles.

Said she, sitting up, "What do *you* want?"

"Nothing," said the bear mildly.

They looked at each other for a while.

Then said Carlotta, "Who are you? Where did you learn German? What's going to happen to me?"

"Does the Fräulein," asked the bear, "wish me to answer the questions in order?"

"Don't be silly," said Carlotta. "I don't care what order. Anyhow, I'm hungry. Do you have anything I could eat?"

The bear responded gently, "You wouldn't like hunting for insect grubs. I have learned German by reading your mind. Bears like me are friends of the True Men and we are good telepaths. The Morons are afraid of us, but we are afraid of the manshonyaggers. Anyhow, you don't have to worry very much because your husband is coming soon."

Carlotta had been walking down toward the brook to get a drink. His last words stopped her in her tracks.

"My husband?" she gasped.

"So probably that it is certain. There is a True Man named Laird who has brought you down. He already knows what you are thinking, and I can see his pleasure in finding a human being who is wild and strange, but not really wild and not really strange. At this moment he is thinking that you may have left the centuries to bring the gift of vitality back among mankind. He is thinking that you and he will have wonderful children. Now he is telling me not to tell you what I think he thinks, for fear that you will run away." The bear chuckled.

Carlotta stood, her mouth agape.

"You may sit in my chair," said the Middle-Sized Bear, "or you can wait here until Laird comes to get you. Either way you will be taken care of. Your sickness will heal. Your ailments will go away. You will be happy again. I know this because I am one of the wisest of all known bears."

Carlotta was angry, confused, frightened, and sick again. She started to run.

Something as solid as a blow hit her.

She knew without being told that it was the bear's mind reaching out and encompassing hers.

It hit—boom!—and that was all.

She had never before stopped to think of how comfortable a bear's mind was. It was like lying in a great big bed and having mother take care of one when one was a very little girl, glad to be petted and sure of getting well.

The anger poured out of her. The fear left her. The sickness began to lighten. The morning seemed beautiful.

She herself felt beautiful as she turned—

Out of the blue sky, dropping swiftly but gracefully, came the figure of a bronze young man. A happy thought pulsed against her mind. *That is Laird, my beloved. He is coming. He is coming. I shall be happy forever after.*

It *was* Laird.

And so she was.

The Queen of the Afternoon

Above all, as she began to awaken, she wished for her family. She called to them, "Mutti, Vati, Carlotta, Karla! Where are you?" But of course she cried it in German since she was a good Prussian girl. Then she remembered.

How long had it been since her father had put her and her two sisters into the space capsules? She had no idea. Even her father, the Ritter vom Acht, and her uncle, Professor Doctor Joachim vom Acht—who had administered the shots in Parbudice, Germany, on April 2, 1945—could not have imagined that the girls would remain in suspended animation for thousands of years. But so it was.

AFTERNOON SUNLIGHT GLEAMED orange and gold on the rich purple shades of the Fighting Trees. Charls looked at the trees, knowing that as the sunset moved from orange to red and as darkness crept over the eastern horizon, they would once again glow with quiet fire.

How long was it since the trees were planted— Fighting Trees, the True Men called them—for the express purpose of sending their immense roots down into the earth, seeking out the radioactives in the soil and the waters beneath, concentrating the poisonous wastes into their hard pods, then dropping the waxy pods until, at some later time, the waters which came from above the earth, and those yet in the earth, would once more be clean? Charls did not know.

One thing he did know. To touch one of the trees, to touch it directly, was certain death.

He wanted very much to break a twig but he did not dare. Not only was it *tambu,* but he feared the sickness. His people had made much progress in the last few generations, enough so that at times they did not fear to face True Men and to argue with them. But the sickness was not something with which one could argue.

At the thought of a True Man, an unaccountable thickness gripped him in the throat. He felt sentimental, tender, fearful; the yearning that gripped him was a kind of love, and yet he knew that it could not be love since he had never seen a True Man except at a distance.

Why, Charls wondered, was he thinking so much about True Men? Was there, perhaps, one nearby?

He looked at the setting sun, which was by now red enough to be looked at safely. Something in the atmosphere was making him uneasy. He called to his sister.

"Oda, Oda!"

She did not answer.

Again he called. "Oda, Oda!"

This time he heard her coming, plowing recklessly through the underbrush. He hoped she would remember to avoid the Fighting Trees. Oda was sometimes too impatient.

Suddenly there she was before him.

"You called me, Charls? You called me? You've found something? Shall we go somewhere together? What do you want? Where are mother and father?"

Charls could not help laughing. Oda was always like that.

"One question at a time, little sister. Weren't you afraid you would die the burning death, going through the trees like that? I know you don't want to believe in the *tambu,* but the sickness is real."

"It isn't," she said. She shook her head. "Maybe it was once . . . I guess it really was once"—granting him a concession—"but do you, yourself, know of anybody who has died from the trees for a thousand years?"

"Of course not, silly. I haven't been alive a thousand years."

Oda's impatience returned. "*You* know what I mean. And anyway, I decided the whole thing is silly. We all accidentally brush against the trees. So one day I *ate* a pod. And nothing happened."

He was appalled. "You *ate* a pod?"

"That's what I said. And nothing happened."

"Oda, one of these days you're going to go too far."

She smiled at him. "And now I suppose you are going to say that the oceans' beds were not always filled with grass."

He was indignant. "No, of course I know better than that. I know that the grass was put into the oceans for the same reason that the Fighting Trees were planted— to eat up all the poisons that the Old Ones left in the days of the Ancient Wars."

How long they would have bickered he did not know, but just then his ears caught an unfamiliar noise. He knew the sound the True Men made as they sped on their mysterious errands in the upper air. He knew the ominous buzz that the Cities gave off should he approach them too closely. He knew also the clicking noises that the few remaining manshonyaggers made as they crept through the Wild, alert for any non-German to kill. Poor blind machines, they were so easy to outsmart.

But this noise, this noise was different. It was nothing he had ever heard before.

The whistling sound rose and throbbed against the upper reaches of his hearing. It had a curiously spiral quality about it as though it approached and receded, all the while veering toward him. Charls was filled with terror, feeling threatened beyond all understanding.

Now Oda heard it too. Their quarrel forgotten, she seized his arm. "What is it, Charls? What could it be?"

His voice was hesitant and full of wonder. "I don't know."

"Are the True Men doing something, something new that we never heard before? Do they want to hurt us, or enslave us? Do they want to catch us? Do we want to be caught? Charls, tell me, do we want to be caught? Could it be the True Men coming? I seem to smell True Man. They *did* come once before and caught some of us and took them away and did strange things to them, so that they looked like True Men, didn't they, Charls? Could it be the True Men again?"

In spite of his fear, Charls had a certain amount of impatience with Oda. She talked so much.

The noise persisted and intensified. Charls sensed that it was directly over his head, but he could see nothing.

Oda said, "Charls, I think I see it. Do you see it, Charls?"

Suddenly he too saw the circle—a dim whiteness, a vapor train that increased in size and volume. Concomitantly the sound increased, until he felt his eardrums would burst. It was nothing ever before seen in his world. . . .

A thought struck him. It was as hard as a physical blow; it sapped his courage and manhood as nothing before had ever done; he did not feel young and strong any more. He could hardly frame his words.

"Oda, could that be—"

"Be what?"

"Could it be one of the old, old weapons from the Ancient Past? Could it be coming back to destroy us all, as the legends have always foretold? People have always said they would come back. . . ." His voice trailed off.

Whatever the danger, he knew that he was completely helpless, helpless to protect himself, helpless to protect Oda.

Against the ancient weapons there was no defense. This place was no safer than that place, that place no better than this. People still had to live their lives under the threat of weapons from long, long ago. This was the first time that he personally had met the threat, but he had heard of it. He reached for Oda's hand.

Oda, singularly courageous now that there was real danger, drew him over onto the bank, away from the *cenote*. With half his mind he wondered why she seemed to want to move away from the water. She tugged at his arm, and he sat down beside her.

Already, he knew, it was too late to go looking for their parents or others of their pack. Sometimes it took a whole day to round up the entire family—the *thing* was coming down relentlessly, and Charls felt so drained of energy that he stopped talking. He thought at her: *Let's just wait it out here,* and she squeezed his hand as she thought back: *Yes, my brother.*

The long box in the circle of light continued to descend, inexorable.

It was odd. Charls could feel a human presence, but the mind was strangely closed to him. He felt a quality of mind that he had never felt before. He had read the minds of True Men as they flew far overhead; he knew the minds of his own people; he could distinguish the thoughts of most of the birds and beasts; it was no trouble to detect the crude electronic hunger of the mechanical mind of a manshonyagger.

But this—this being had a mind that was raw, elemental, hot. And closed.

Now the box was very near. Would it crash in this valley or the next? The screams from within it were extremely shrill. Charls's ears hurt and his eyes smarted from the intensity of heat and noise. Oda held his hand tightly.

The object crashed into the ground.

It ripped the hillside just across the *cenote*. Had Oda

not instinctively moved away from the *cenote*, the box would have hit *them*, Charls realized.

Charls and Oda stood up cautiously.

Somehow the box must have decelerated: It was hot, but not hot enough to make the broken trees around it burst into flame. Steam rose from the crushed leaves.

The noise was gone.

Charls and Oda moved to within ten man-lengths of the object. Charls framed his clearest thought and flung it at the box: *Who are you?*

The being within obviously did not perceive him as he was. There came forth a wild thought, directed at living beings in general.

Fools, fools, help me! Get me out of here!

Oda caught the thought, as did Charls. She stepped in mentally and Charls was astonished at the clarity and force of her inquiry. It was simple but beautifully strong and hard. She thought the one idea:

How?

From the box there came again the frantic babble of demand: *The handles, you fools. The handles on the outside. Take the handles and let me out!*

Charls and Oda looked at each other. Charls was not sure that he really wanted to let this creature "out." Then he thought further. Maybe the unpleasantness that radiated from the box was simply the result of imprisonment. He knew that he himself would hate to be encased like that.

Together Charls and Oda risked the broken leaves, walking gingerly up to the box itself. It was black and old; it looked like something the elders called "iron"—and never touched. They saw the handles, pitted and scarred.

With the ghost of a smile, Charls nodded to his sister. Each took a handle and lifted.

The sides of the box crackled. The iron was hot but not unbearably so. With a rusty shriek, the ancient door flew open.

They looked into the box.

There lay a young woman.

She had no fur, only long hair on her head.

Instead of fur, she had strange, soft objects on her body but as she sat up, these objects began to disintegrate.

At first the girl looked frightened; then, as she glanced at Oda and Charls, she began to laugh. Her thought came through, clearly and rather cruelly: *I guess I don't have to worry about modesty in front of puppy dogs.*

Oda did not seem to mind the thought but Charls's feelings were hurt. The girl said words with her mouth but they could not understand them. Each of them took an elbow and led her to the ground.

They reached the edge of the *cenote* and Oda gestured to the strange girl to sit down. She did, and made more words.

Oda was as puzzled as Charls, but then she began to smile. Spieking had worked before, when the girl was in the box. Why not now? The only thing was, this odd girl did not seem to know how to control her thoughts. Everything she thought was directed at the world at large—at the valley, at the sunset sky, at the *cenote*. She did not seem to realize that she was shouting every thought aloud.

Oda put her question to the young woman: *Who are you?*

The hot, strange mind flung back quickly: *Juli, of course.*

At this point Charls intervened. *There's no "of course" about it,* he spieked.

What am I doing? the girl's thoughts ran. *I'm in mental telepathy with puppy-dog people.*

Embarrassed, Charls and Oda watched her as her thoughts splashed out.

"Doesn't she know how to close off her thoughts?" Charls wondered. And why had her mind seemed so closed when she was in the box?

Puppy-dog people. Where can I be if I'm mixed up with puppy-dog people? Can this be Earth? Where have I been? How long have I been gone? Where is Ger-

many? *Where are Carlotta and Karla? Where are Daddy and Mother and Uncle Joachim? Puppy-dog people!*

Charls and Oda felt the sharp edge of the mind that was so recklessly flinging all these thoughts. There was a kind of laughter that was cruel each time she thought *puppy-dog people*. They could feel that this mind was as bright as the brightest minds of the True Men—but this mind was different. It did not have the singleness of devotion or the wary wisdom that saturated the minds of the True Men.

Then Charls remembered something. His parents had once told him of a mind that was something like this one.

Juli continued to pour out her thoughts like sparks from a fire, like raindrops from a big splash. Charls was frightened and did not know what to do; and Oda began to turn away from the strange girl.

Then Charls perceived it. Juli was frightened. She was calling them *puppy-dog people* to cover her fear. She really did not know where she was.

He mused, not directing his thought at Juli: *Just because she's frightened, it doesn't mean she has the right to think sharp, bright things at us.*

Perhaps it was his posture that betrayed his attitude; Juli seemed to catch the thought.

Suddenly she burst into words again, words that they could not understand. It sounded as though she were begging, asking, pleading, expostulating. She seemed to be calling for specific persons or things. Words poured forth, and there were names that the True Men used. Was it her parents? Her lover? Her siblings? It had to be someone she had known before entering that screaming box, where she had been captive in the blue of the sky for . . . for how long?

Suddenly she was quiet. Her attention had shifted.

She pointed to the Fighting Trees.

The sunset had so darkened that the trees were beginning to light up. The soft fire was coming to life as it had during all the years of Charls's life and those of his forefathers.

As she pointed, Juli made words again. She kept repeating them. It sounded like *v-a-s-i-s-d-a-s*.

Charls could not help being a little irritated. *Why doesn't she just think?* It was odd that they could not read her mind when she was using the words.

Again, although Charls had not aimed the question at her, Juli seemed to catch it. From her there came a flame of thought, a single idea, that leapt like a fountain of fire from that tired little female head:

What is this world?

Then the thought shifted focus slightly. *Vati, Vati, where am I? Where are you? What has become of me?* There was something forlorn and desolate to it.

Oda put out a soft hand toward the girl. Juli looked at her and some of the harsh, fearful thoughts returned. Then the sheer compassion of Oda's posture seemed to catch Juli's attention, and with relaxation came complete collapse. The great and terrifying thought disappeared. Juli burst into tears. She put her long arms about Oda. Oda patted her back and Juli sobbed even harder.

Out of the sobbing came a funny, friendly thought, loving and no longer contemptuous: *Dear little puppy dogs, dear little puppy dogs, please help me. You are supposed to be our best friends . . . do help me now. . . .*

Charls perked up his ears. Something—or someone—was coming over the top of the hill.

Certainly a thought as big and as sharp as Juli's could attract all living forms within kilometers. It might even catch the attention of the aloof but ominous True Men.

A moment later Charls relaxed. He recognized the stride of his parents. He turned to Oda.

"Hear that?"

She smiled. "It's father and mother. They must have heard that big thought the girl had."

Charls watched with pride as his parents approached. It was a well-justified pride. Bil and Kae both appeared, as they were, sensitive and intelligent. In addition, their fur was well-matched. Bil's beautiful caramel coat had spots of white and black only along his cheekbones and nose and at the tip of his tail; Kae was a uniform fawn-beige with which her beautiful green eyes made a striking contrast.

"Are you both all right?" Bil asked as they approached. "Who is that? She looks like a True Man. Is she friendly? Has she hurt you? Was she the one who was doing all that violent thinking? We could feel it clear across the hillside."

Oda burst into a giggle. "You ask as many questions as I do, Daddy."

Charls said, "All we know is that a box came from the sky and that she was in it. You heard that shrieking noise as it came down first, didn't you?"

Kae laughed. "Who didn't hear it?"

"The box hit right over there. You can see where it hurt the hillside."

The area where the box had landed was black and forbidding. Around it the fallen Fighting Trees gleamed in tangled confusion on the ground.

Bil looked at Juli and shook his head. "I don't see why she wasn't killed if it hit that hard."

Juli began to speak in words again, but at last she seemed to understand. Shouting her language would not help any. Instead, she thought: *Please, dear little puppy dogs. Please help me. Please understand me.*

Bil kept his dignity but he noticed with dismay that his tail was wagging of its own accord. He realized that the urge was uncontrollable. He felt both resentful and happy as he thought back at her: *Of course we understand you and we'll try to help you; but please don't think your thoughts so hard or so recklessly. They hurt our minds when they are so bright and sharp.*

Juli tried to turn down the intensity of her thought. She pleaded: *Take me to Germany.*

The four Unauthorized Men—mother, father, daughter and son—looked at each other. They had no idea of what a Germany might be.

It was Oda who turned to Juli, girl to girl, and spieked: *Think some Germany at us so we can know what it is.*

There came forth from the strange girl images of unbelievable beauty. Picture after clear picture emerged until the little family was almost blinded by the magnificence of the display. They saw the whole ancient world come to life. Cities stood bright in a green-encircled world. There were no aloof and languid True Men; instead, all the people they saw in Juli's mind resembled Juli herself. They were vital, sometimes fierce, forceful; they were tall, erect, long-fingered; and of course they did not have the tails of the Unauthorized Men. The children were pretty beyond belief.

The most amazing thing about this world was the tremendous number of people in it. The people were thicker than the birds of passage, more crowded than the salmon at running time.

Charls had thought himself a well-traveled young man. He had met at least four dozen other persons besides his own family, and he had seen True Men in the skies above him hundreds of times. He had often witnessed the intolerable brightness of Cities and had walked around them more than once until, each time, he had been firmly assured that there was no way for him to enter. He thought his valley a good one. In a few more years he would be old enough to visit the nearby valleys and to look for a wife for himself.

But this vision that came from Juli's mind . . . he could not imagine how so many people could live together. How could they all greet each other in the mornings? How could they all agree on anything? How could they all ever become still enough to be aware of each other's presence, each other's needs?

There came a particularly strong, bright image. Small-wheeled boxes were hurtling people at insensate speed up and down smooth, smooth roads.

"So that's what *roads* were for," he gasped to himself.

Among the people he saw many dogs. They were nothing like the creatures of Charls's world. They were

not the long, otterlike animals whom the Unauthorized
Men despised as lowly kindred; nor were they like the
Unauthorized Men themselves, and they were certainly
not like those modified animals who in appearance were
almost indistinguishable from True Men. No, these dogs
of Juli's world were bounding, happy creatures with few
responsibilities. There seemed to be an affectionate relationship between them and the people there. They
shared laughter and sorrow.

Juli had closed her eyes as she tried to bring Germany to them. Concentrating hard, now she brought
into the picture of beauty and happiness something
else—fearful flying things that dropped fire; thunder
and noise; a most unpleasant face, a screaming face
with a dab of black fur above the mouth; a licking of
flame in the night; a thunder of death machines. Across
this thunder there was the image of Juli and two other
girls who resembled her; they were moving with a man,
obviously their father, toward three iron boxes that
looked like the one Juli had landed in. Then there was
darkness.

That was Germany.

Juli slumped to the ground.

Gently the four of them probed at her mind. To them
it was like a diamond, as clear and transparent as a sun-
lit pool in the forest, but the light it shot back to them
was not a reflection. It was rich and bright and daz-
zling. Now that it was at rest, they could see deeply into
it. They saw hunger, hurt and loneliness. They saw a
loneliness so great that each of them in turn tried to
think of a way to assuage it. *Love,* they thought, *what
she needs is love, and her own kind.* But where would
they find an Ancient One? Would a True Man answer?

Bil said, "There's only one thing to do. We've got to
take her to the house of the Wise Old Bear. He has
communications with the True Men."

Oda cried out, "But she hasn't done anything
wrong!"

Her father looked at her. "Darling, we don't know

what this is. She's an Ancient One come back to this world after a sleep in space itself. It's been thousands of years since her world lived; I think she's beginning to realize that, and that's what put her into shock. We need help. Our people may once have been dogs, and that's what she thinks we are. We can't let that bother us. But she needs a house, and the only unauthorized house that I know of belongs to the Wise Old Bear."

Charls looked at his parents. His eyes were troubled. "What is this business about dogs? Is that why we feel so mixed up when we think about True Men? I'm confused about her too. Do you suppose I really want to belong to her?"

"Not really," his father said. "That's just a feeling left over from long, long ago. We lead our own lives now. But this girl, she's too big a problem for us. We will take her to the Bear. At least he has a house."

Juli was still unconscious, and to them she was so big. Each took a limb and with difficulty they managed to carry her. Within less than a tenth of a night they had reached the house of the Wise Old Bear. Fortunately they had not met any manshonyaggers or other dangers of the forest.

At the door of the house of the Wise Old Bear they gently laid the girl on the ground.

Bil shouted, "Bear, Bear, come out, come out!"

"Who is there?" a voice boomed from within.

"Bil and his family. We have an Ancient with us. Come out. We need your help."

The light that had been streaming from the doorway with a yellow glare was suddenly reduced to endurable proportions as the immense bulk of the Bear loomed in the doorway before them.

He pulled his spectacles from a case attached to his belt, put them on his nose and squinted at Juli.

"Bless my soul," he said. "Another one. Where on earth did you get an ancient girl?"

Pompous but happy, Charls spoke up. "She came out of the sky in a screaming box."

The Bear nodded wisely.

Then Bil spoke up. "You said 'another one.' What did you mean?"

The Bear winced slightly. "Forget I said that," he told them. "I forgot for a moment that you are not True Men. Please forget it."

Bil said, "You mean it's something Unauthorized Men are not supposed to know about?"

The Bear nodded unhappily.

Understanding, Bil said, "Well, if you *can* ever tell us about it, will you, please?"

"Of course," the Bear replied. "And now I think I'd better call my housekeeper to take care of her. Herkie, Herkie, come here."

A blonde woman appeared, peering anxiously. Obviously there was something the matter with her blue eyes but she seemed to be functioning adequately.

Bil backed away from the door. "That's an Experimental person," he said. "That's a cat!"

The Bear was completely uninterested. "So it is, but you can see that her eyes are imperfect. That's why she is allowed to be my housekeeper and why her name isn't prefaced by a C'."

Bil understood. The errors True Men made in trying to breed Underpersons were often destroyed but occasionally one was allowed to live if it seemed able to function at some necessary task. The Bear had connections with True Men. If he needed a housekeeper, an imperfect modified animal provided an ideal solution.

Herkie bent over Juli's still form. She peered in puzzlement at Juli's face. Then she looked up at the Bear. "I don't understand," she said. "I don't see how it could be."

"Later," the Bear said. "When we are alone."

Herkie strained to see into the darkness and perceived the dog family. "Oh, I see," she said.

Bil and Charls were embarrassed. Oda and Kae did not seem to notice the slight.

Bil waved his hand. "Well, good-bye. I hope you can take care of her all right."

"Thank you for bringing her," the Bear said. "The True Men will probably give you a reward."

In spite of himself, Bil felt his tail beginning to wag again.

"Will we ever see her again?" Oda asked. "Do you think we'll ever see her again? I love her, I love her . . ."

"Perhaps," her father answered. "She will know who saved her, and I think she will seek us out."

Juli awoke slowly. *Where am I? What is this place?* She had a partial return of memory. *The puppy-dog people. Where are they?* She felt conscious of someone at her bedside. She looked up into clouded blue eyes staring anxiously into hers.

"I'm Herkie," the woman said. "I'm the Bear's housekeeper."

Juli felt as though she had awakened in a mental hospital. It was all so impossible. Puppy-dog people and now a *bear*? And surely the blonde woman with the bad eyes was not a human?

Herkie patted her hand. "Of course you're confused," she said.

Juli was taken aback. "You're *talking!* You're talking and I understand you. You're talking German. We're not just communicating telepathically."

"Of course," Herkie said. "I speak true Doych. It's one of the Bear's favorite languages."

"One of . . ." Juli broke off. "It's all so confusing."

Again Herkie patted her hand. "Of course it is."

Juli lay back and looked at the ceiling. *I must be in some other world.*

No, Herkie thought at her, *but you've been gone a long time.*

The Bear came into the room. "Feeling better?" he asked.

Juli merely nodded.

"In the morning we will decide what to do," he said. "I have some connections with the True Men, and I think that we had best take you to the Vomact."

Juli sat up as if hit by a bolt of lightning. "What do you mean, 'the Vomacht'? That is my name, vom Acht!"

"I thought it might be," the Bear said. Herkie, peering at her from the bedside, nodded wisely.

"I was sure of it," she said. Then, "I think you need some good hot soup and a rest. In the morning it will all straighten itself out."

The tiredness of years seemed to settle in Juli's bones. *I do need to rest,* she thought. *I need to get things sorted out in my mind.* So suddenly that she did not even have a chance to be startled by it, she was asleep.

Herkie and the Bear studied her face. "There's a remarkable resemblance," the Bear said. Herkie nodded in agreement. "It's the time differential I'm worried about. Do you think that will be important?"

"I don't know," Herkie replied. "Since I'm not human, I don't know what bothers people." She straightened and stretched to her full length. "I know!" she said. "I *do* know! She must have been sent here to help us with the rebellion!"

"No," the Bear said. "She has been too long in Time for her arrival to have been intentional. It is true that she may help us, she may very well help us, but I think that her arrival at this particular time and place is fortuitous rather than planned."

"Sometimes I think I understand a particular human mind," Herkie said, "but I'm sure you're correct. I can hardly wait for them to meet each other!"

"Yes," he said, "although I'm afraid that it's going to be rather traumatic. In more than one way."

When Juli awoke after her deep sleep, she found a thoughtful Herkie awaiting her.

Juli stretched and her mind, still uncontrolled, asked: *Are you really a cat?*

Yes, Herkie thought back at her. *But you are going to have to discipline that thought process of yours. Everyone can read your thoughts.*

I'm sorry, Juli spieked, *but I'm just not used to all this telepathy.*

"I know." Herkie had switched to German.

"I still don't understand how you know German," Juli said.

"It's rather a long story. I learned it from the Bear. I think, perhaps, you had better ask him how he learned it."

"Wait a minute. I'm beginning to remember what happened before I fell asleep. The Bear mentioned my name, my family name, vom Acht."

Herkie switched the subject. "We've made you some clothes. We tried to copy the style of those you had on, but they were coming to pieces so badly that we are not sure we got the new ones right."

She looked so anxious to please that Juli reassured her immediately. *If they fit, I'm sure they'll be just fine.*

Oh, they fit, Herkie spieked. *We measured you. Now, after your bath and meal, you will dress and the Bear and I will take you to the City. Underpersons like me are not ordinarily allowed in the City, but this time I think that an exception will be made.*

There was something sweet and wise in the face with the clouded blue eyes. Juli felt that Herkie was her friend. *I am,* Herkie spieked, and Juli was once more made aware that she must learn to control her thoughts, or at least the broadcasting of them.

You'll learn, Herkie spieked. *It just takes some practice.*

They approached the City on foot, the Bear leading the way, Juli behind him and Herkie bringing up the rear. They encountered two manshonyaggers along the road but the Bear spoke true Doych to them from some distance and they turned silently and slunk away.

Juli was fascinated. "What *are* they?" she asked.

"Their real name is 'Menschenjäger' and they were invented to kill people whose ideas did not accord with those of the Sixth German Reich. But there are very few of them still functional, and so many of us have learned Doych since . . . since . . ."

"Yes?"

"Since an event you'll find out about in the City. Now let's get on with it."

They neared the City wall and Juli became conscious of a buzzing sound, and of a powerful force that excluded them. Her hair stood on end and she felt a tingling sensation of mild electrical shock. Obviously there was a force field around the City.

"What is it?" she cried out.

"Just a static charge to keep back the Wild," the Bear said soothingly. "Don't worry, I have a damper for it."

He held up a small device in his right paw, pushed a button on it and immediately a corridor opened before them.

When they reached the City wall, the Bear felt carefully along the upper ridge. At a certain point he paused, then reached for a strange-looking key that hung from a cord around his neck.

Juli could see no difference between this section of the wall and any other but the Bear inserted his key into a notch he had located and a section of the barrier swung up. The three passed through and silently the wall fell back into position.

The Bear hurried them along dusty streets. Juli saw a number of people but most of them seemed to her aloof, austere, uncaring. They bore little resemblance to the lusty Prussians she remembered.

Eventually they arrived at the door of a large building that looked old and imposing. Beside the door there was an inscription. The Bear was hurrying them through the entryway.

Oh, please, Mr. Bear, may I stop to read it?

Just plain Bear is all right. And yes, of course you may. It may even help you to understand some of the things that you are going to learn today.

The inscription was in German, and it was in the form of a poem. It looked as though it had been carved

hundreds of years earlier (as indeed it had. Juli could
not know that at this time).

Herkie looked up. "Oh, the first . . ."

"Hush," said the Bear.

Juli read the poem to herself silently.

> Youth
> Fading, fading, going
> Flowing
> Like life blood from your veins. . . .
> Little remains.
> The glorious face
> Erased,
> Replaced
> By one which mirrors tears,
> The years
> Gone by.
> Oh, Youth,
> Linger yet a while!
> Smile
> Still upon us
> The wretched few
> Who worship
> You. . . .

"I don't understand it," said Juli.

"You will," the Bear said. "Unfortunately, you will."

An official in a bright green robe trimmed with gold
approached.

"We have not had the honor of your presence for
some time," he said respectfully to the Bear.

"I've been rather busy," the Bear replied. "But how
is she?"

Juli realized with a start that the conversation was
not telepathic but was in German. *How do all these
people know German?* She unthinkingly flung her
thought abroad.

Hush came back the simultaneous warnings from
Herkie and the Bear.

Juli felt thoroughly admonished. "I'm sorry," she almost whispered. "I don't know how I'll ever learn the trick."

Herkie was immediately sympathetic. "It *is* a trick," she said, "but you're already better at it than you were when you arrived. You just have to be careful. You can't fling your thoughts everywhere."

"Never mind that now," the Bear said and he turned to the green-uniformed official. "Is it possible to have an audience? I think it's important."

"You may have to wait a little while," the official said, "but I'm sure she will always grant audience to *you*."

The Bear looked a little smug at that, Juli noticed.

They sat down to wait and from time to time Herkie patted Juli's arm reassuringly.

It was actually not long before the official reappeared. "She will see you now," he said.

He led them through a long corridor to a large room at the end of which was a dais with a chair. "Not quite a throne," Juli thought to herself. Behind the chair stood a young and handsome male, a True Man. In the chair sat a woman, old, old beyond imagining; her wrinkled hands were claws, but in the haggard, wrinkled face one could still detect some trace of beauty.

Juli's sense of bewilderment grew. She *knew* this person, but she did not. Her sense of orientation, already splintered by the events of the past "day," almost disintegrated. She grabbed Herkie's hand as if it were the only familiar element in a world she could not understand.

The woman spoke. Her voice was old and weak, but she spoke in German.

"So, Juli, you have come. Laird told me he was bringing you in. I am so happy to see you, and to know that you are all right."

Juli's senses reeled. She *knew*, she *knew*, but she could not believe. Too much had changed, too much had happened, in the short time that she had returned to life.

Gasping, tentatively she whispered, "Carlotta?"

Her sister nodded. "Yes, Juli, it is I. And this is my husband, Laird." She nodded her head toward the handsome young man behind her. "He brought me in about two hundred years ago, but unfortunately as an Ancient I cannot undergo the rejuvenation process that has been developed since we left the Earth."

Juli began to sob. "Oh, Carlotta, it's all so hard to believe. And you're so old! You were only two years older than I."

"Darling, I've had two hundred years of bliss. They couldn't rejuvenate me but they could at least prolong my life. Now, it is not from purely altruistic purposes that I have had Laird bring you in. Karla is still out there, but since she was only sixteen when she was suspended, we thought that you would be better suited to the task.

"In fact, we really didn't do you any favor in bringing you in because now you too will begin to age. But to be forever in suspended animation is not any life either."

"Of course not," Juli said. "And anyway, if I had lived a normal life, I would have aged."

Carlotta leaned over to kiss her.

"At least we're together at last," Juli sighed.

"Darling," Carlotta said, "it is wonderful to have even this little time together. You see, I'm dying. There comes a point when, with all technology, the scientists cannot keep a body alive. And we need help, help with the rebellion."

"The rebellion?"

"Yes. Against the Jwindz. They were Chinesians, philosophers. Now they are the true rulers of the Earth, and we—so they believe—are merely their Instrumentality, their police force. Their power is not over the body of man but over the *soul*. That is almost a forgotten word here now. Say 'mind' instead. They call themselves the Perfect Ones and have sought to remake man in their own image. But they are remote, removed, bloodless.

"They have recruited persons of all races, but man has not responded well. Only a handful aspire to the kind of esthetic perfection the Jwindz have as their goal. So the Jwindz have resorted to their knowledge of drugs and opiates to turn True Man into a tranquilized, indifferent people—to make it easy to govern them, to control everything that they do. Unfortunately some of our"—she nodded toward Laird—"descendants have joined them.

"We need you, Juli. Since I came back from the ancient world, Laird and I have done what we could to free True Men from this form of slavery, because it *is* slavery. It is a lack of vitality, a lack of meaning to life. We used to have a word for it in the old days. Remember? 'Zombie.' "

"What do you want me to do?"

During the entire conversation between the sisters, Herkie, the Bear and Laird had remained silent.

Now Laird spoke. "Until Carlotta came to us, we were drifting along, uncaring, in the power of the Jwindz. We did not know what it was, really, to be a human being. We felt that our only purpose in life was to serve the Jwindz: If they were perfect, what other function could we perform? It was our duty to serve their needs—to maintain and guard the cities, to keep out the Wild, to administer the drugs. Some of the Instrumentality even preyed upon the Unauthorized Men, the Unforgiven and, as a last resort, the True Men, to supply their laboratories.

"But now many of us no longer believe in the perfection of the Jwindz—or perhaps we have come to believe in something more than human perfection. We have been serving men. We should have been serving *mankind*.

"Now we feel that the time has come to put an end to this tyranny. Carlotta and I have allies among some of our descendants and among some of the Unforgiven and, as you have seen, even among the Unauthorized

Men and other animal-derived persons. I think there must still be a connection from the time that human beings had 'pets' in the old days."

Juli looked about her and realized that Herkie was quietly purring. "Yes," she said, "I see what you mean."

Laird continued, "What we want to do is to set up a *real* Instrumentality—not a force for the service of the Jwindz, but one for the service of man. We are determined that never again shall man betray his own image. We will establish the Instrumentality of Mankind, one benevolent but not manipulative."

Carlotta nodded slowly. Her aged face showed concern. "I will die in a few days and you will marry Laird. You will be the new Vomact. With any luck by the time you are as old as I am, your descendants and some of mine should have freed the Earth from the power of the Jwindz."

Juli again felt completely disoriented. "I'm to marry your husband?"

Again Laird spoke. "I have loved your sister well for more than two hundred years. I shall love you too, because you are so much like her. Do not think that I am being disloyal. She and I have discussed this for some time before I brought you in. If she were not dying, I should continue to be faithful to her. But now we need you."

Carlotta concurred. "It is true. He has made me very happy, and he will make you happy too, through all the years of your life. Juli, I could not have had you brought in had I not had some plan for your future. You could never be happy with one of those drugged, tranquilized True Men. Trust me in this, please. It is the only thing to do."

Tears formed in Juli's eyes. "To have found you at last and then to lose you after such a short time. . . ."

Herkie patted her hand and Juli looked up to see sympathetic tears in her clouded blue eyes.

It was three days later that Carlotta died. She died with a smile on her face and Laird and Juli each holding one of her hands. She spoke at the last and pressed their hands. "I'll see you later. Out among the stars."

Juli wept uncontrollably.

They postponed the wedding ceremony for seven days of mourning. For once the City gates were opened and the static fields of electricity cut off because even the Jwindz could not control the feelings of the animal-derived persons, the Unauthorized Men, even some of the True Men, toward this woman who had come to them from an ancient world.

The Bear was particularly mournful. "I was the one who found her, you know, after you brought her in," he said to Laird.

"I remember."

So that's what the Bear meant when he said 'another one,' Bil said.

Charls and Oda, Bil and Kae were among the mourners, Juli saw them and thought, *My dear little puppy-dog people,* but this time the thought was loving and not contemptuous.

Oda's tail wagged. *I've thought of something,* she spieked at Juli. *Can you meet me down by the cenote in two days' time?*

Yes, thought Juli, proud of herself at being sure, for the first time, that her thought had gone only to the person for whom it was meant. She knew that she had been successful when she glanced at Laird's face and saw that he had not read her thought.

When she met Oda at the *cenote,* Juli did not know what was expected of her—nor what she herself expected.

You must be very careful in directing your thoughts, Oda spieked. *We never know when some of the Jwindz are overhead.*

I think I'm learning, Juli spieked. Oda nodded.

What my idea was, it was to make use of the Fighting Trees. The True Men are still afraid of the sickness.

*But, you see, I know that the sickness is gone. I got so
tired of brushing past the trees and always worrying
about it that I decided to test it out, and I ate a pod
from one of the Fighting Trees—and nothing happened.
I've never been afraid of them since. So if we met there,
we rebels, in a grove of the Fighting Trees, the officials
of the Jwindz would never find us. They'd be afraid to
hunt for us there.*

Juli's face lightened. *That's a very good idea. May I
consult with Laird?*

*Certainly. He has always been one of us. And your
sister was too.*

Juli was sad again. *I feel so alone.*

*No. You have Laird, and you have us, and the Bear
and his housekeeper. And in time there will be others.
Now we must part.*

Juli returned from her meeting with Oda at the *cenote* to find Laird deep in conference with the Bear and
a young man who bore a singular resemblance to
Laird—and to the youthful Carlotta that Juli remembered.

Laird smiled at her. "This is your great-nephew," he
said, "my grandson."

Juli's perspective of time and age received another
jolt. Laird appeared to be no older than his grandson.
How do I fit in to this? she wondered, and accidentally
broadcast the thought.

"I know that all of this must be difficult for you to
comprehend," Laird said, taking her hand. "Carlotta
had some difficulty in adjusting too. But try, please try,
my dear, because we need you so desperately and I, I
particularly, have already become dependent on you. I
could not face Carlotta's loss without you."

Juli felt a vague sense of embarrassment. "What is
my"—she could not say it—"what is his name?"

"I beg your pardon. He is named Joachim for your
uncle."

Joachim smiled and then gave her a brief hug. "You
see," he said, "the reason we need your help with the
rebellion is the cult that was built up around your sister,

my grandmother. When she returned to earth as an Ancient One, there was a kind of cult set up about her. That is why she was 'The Vomact' and why you must also be. It is a rallying point for those of us who oppose the power of the Jwindz. Grandmother Carlotta had a minikingdom here, and even the Jwindz could not keep people from coming to pay her court. You must have realized that at the mourning session for her."

"Yes, I could see that she had a great deal of respect from many kinds of people. If she was in favor of a rebellion, I am sure she must have been correct. Carlotta was always a most upright person. And now I must tell you about the plan that Oda proposes." She proceeded to do so.

"It might work," the Bear said. "True Men have been very careful about observing the *tambu* of the Fighting Trees. In fact, I may even have an improvement on Oda's idea." He began to get excited and dropped his spectacles. Joachim picked them up.

"Bear," he said, "you always do that when you're excited."

"I think it means I have a good idea," the Bear said. "Look, why don't we use the manshonyaggers?"

The others looked at him in bewilderment and Laird said slowly, "I think I may see what you're getting at. The manshonyaggers, although there are not many of them left, respond only to German and—"

"And the leaders of the Jwindz are Chinesian, too proud to have learned another language," the Bear broke in, smiling.

"Yes. So if we establish headquarters in the Fighting Trees and let it be known that the new Vomact is there—"

"And surround the grove with manshonyaggers—"

They were breaking in upon each other as the idea began to take shape. The excitement grew.

"I think it will work," Laird said.

"I think so too," Joachim reassured him. "I will get together the Band of Cousins and after you're established in the Fighting Trees, we'll make a raid on the drug center and bring the tranquilizers to the grove, where we can destroy them."

"The Band of Cousins?" Juli asked.

"Carlotta's and my descendants who have not joined the Instrumentality of the Jwindz," Laird told her.

"Why would *any* of them have joined?"

Laird shrugged. "Greed, power, all kinds of very human motives. Even an illusion of physical immortality. We tried to give our children ideals but the corruption of power is very great. You must know that."

Remembering a howling, hateful face with a black mustache above the mouth, a face from her own time and place, Juli nodded.

Herkie and the Bear, Charls and Oda, Bil and Kae accompanied Juli into the grove of Fighting Trees. At first Bil and Kae were reluctant. It was only after Oda's confession of having eaten a pod that they agreed to go, and then Bil's reaction was that of a typical father.

"How *could* you take such a chance?" he asked Oda.

Her eyes were bright and her tail wagged furiously. "I just had to," she said.

He glanced at Herkie. "Now if *she* had done it. . . ."

Herkie drew herself up to her full height. "I think that the relationship of curiosity and cats has, perhaps, been a little exaggerated," she said. "Actually, we're generally rather careful."

"I didn't mean to be disrespectful," Bil said hastily, and Herkie saw his tail droop.

"It's a common misconception," she said kindly, and Bil's tail straightened.

When they reached the center of the grove, they spread a picnic and gathered around. Juli was hungry. In the City she had been offered synthetic food, no doubt healthful and full of vitamins but not satisfying to the appetite of an Ancient Prussian girl. The animal-derived persons had brought real *food* and Juli ate happily.

The Bear, in particular, noticed her enjoyment. "You see," he said, "that's how they did it."

"Did what?" asked Juli, her mouth full of bread.

"How they drugged the majority of True Men. True Men were so accustomed to living on synthetic food-stuffs that when the Jwindz introduced tranquilizers into the synthetics, True Men never knew the difference. I hope that if the Band of Cousins succeeds in capturing the drug supply, the withdrawal symptoms for the True Men will not be too severe."

Bil looked up. "That's something we should consider," he said. "If there *are* severe withdrawal symptoms, a number of the True Men may be tempted to join the Jwindz in an attempt to recover the drugs."

The Bear nodded. "That's what I was thinking," he said.

It was several days before Laird, Joachim and the Band of Cousins joined them. By this time Juli had become almost accustomed to the daylight darkness under the thick leaves and branches of the Fighting Trees, and the soft-glowing illumination at night.

Laird greeted her affectionately. "I have missed you," he said simply. "Already I have grown very attached to you."

Juli blushed and changed the subject. "Did you—or, rather, the Band of Cousins—succeed?"

"Oh, yes. There was very little difficulty. The officials of the Jwindz had grown quite careless since they have had the minds of most True Men under their control for generations. It was only a matter of Joachim's pretending to be tranquilized, and he had free access to the drug room. Over a period of days he managed to transfer the entire supply to the Cousins and to substitute placebos. I wonder when *that* will be discovered."

"As soon as the first withdrawal symptoms occur, I should think," Joachim ventured.

Something that had been nagging at the back of Juli's mind surfaced. "You have your *grand*son here, and the Band of Cousins. But where are your and Carlotta's own children? Obviously you had some."

His face saddened. "Of course. But since they were

half-Ancient, they could not only not be rejuvenated, but the combination of the chemistry made it such that their lives could not even be prolonged. They all died in their seventies and eighties. It was a great sadness to Carlotta and me. You too, my dear, if we have children, must be prepared for that. By the time of the next generation, however, the Ancient blood is sufficiently diluted that rejuvenation may take place. Joachim is a hundred and fifty years old."

"And you? And you?" she said.

He looked at her. "This is very hard on you, isn't it? I'm over three hundred years old."

Juli could not disbelieve but neither could she quite comprehend. Laird was so handsome and youthful; Carlotta had been so old.

She tried to shake the cobwebs from her mind. "What do we do with the tranquilizers now that we have them?"

Oda had approached at the latter part of the conversation. Her eyes sparkled and her tail wagged madly. "I have an idea," she announced.

"I hope it's as good as your last one," Laird said.

"I hope so too. Look, why don't we just feed the tranquilizers back to the officials? The Jwindz probably will never notice. Then we won't have to worry about fighting them. They could just gradually die off; or maybe . . . do you think . . . we could send them out into space? To another planet?"

Laird nodded slowly. "You do have good ideas. Yes, to feed the tranquilizers back to them . . . but how?"

"We work well together," the Bear said, indicating Oda. "She has an idea and it triggers another one in my mind." Carefully he put on his spectacles. "I have here a map of the terrain in this vicinity. Except for the *cenote* there is no water for many kilometers in any direction. If we dropped the tranquilizers—all of them—into the *cenote*, and then if one of the Cousins could prepare the synthetic food of the Jwindz's officials so it was very spicy—I think that the problem would be solved."

Laird said, "We do have one of the Cousins who has

infiltrated the Jwindz. But what would induce them to drink the water?"

Charls had joined the group. "I have heard," he said, "of an ancient spice people used to like which eventually produced thirst. It used to be found in the oceans, before they were filled with grass. But some of it remains on the banks of the sea. I believe that it was called 'salt.' "

"Now that you mention it, I've heard of that too." The Bear nodded wisely. "So that is what we need to do. 'Salt.' We introduce it into their food, then we entice them to the grove with the knowledge that the new Vomact is here together with the heart of a rebellion. It's risky but I think it's the best idea, or combination of ideas, yet."

Laird agreed. "It's as you say, risky, but it may work, and they're not likely to execute any of us if it doesn't. They'll just tranquilize us. I think that we have a better than even chance of winning. And if True Man is not revitalized, not freed from this bondage of tranquility and apathy, I believe that the entire breed will be extinguished within a few hundred years. They have come to the point that they care about nothing."

All worlds know how the plan was carried out. It was exactly as the Bear had foretold. The thirsty officials of the Jwindz, their food highly salted, drank eagerly from the water of the *cenote* and were quickly tranquilized. They put up no opposition to the members of the rebellion who soon thereafter emerged from the shelter of the Fighting Trees.

Joachim was sad. "One of my brothers had joined them," he said.

Laird laid a comforting arm across his shoulder. "Well, he's only tranquilized. We may be able to help him as he comes out of it."

"Perhaps, but it violates all my principles."

"Don't be too high-minded, Joachim. Principles are fine, but there is such a thing as rehabilitation."

And this was the way that the Instrumentality of

Mankind was established. In time it would govern many worlds. Juli, by virtue of being the Vomact, became one of the first Ladies of the Instrumentality. Laird, as her husband, was one of the first Lords.

Juli lived to see some of her descendants among the first great scanners in space. She was very proud of them, and she was very old. Laird, of course, was as young as ever. All of her animal-descended friends had long since died. She missed them, although Laird was ever faithful.

At last, so old that she had difficulty in moving, Juli called Laird to her. She looked up into his handsome face. "My darling, you have made me very happy, just as you did Carlotta. But now I am old and, I think, dying. You are still so young and vital. I wish it were possible for me to undergo the rejuvenation, but since it isn't possible, I think we should call in Karla."

He responded so rapidly that her feelings were somewhat hurt. "Yes, I think that we should call in Karla."

He turned away from her momentarily.

She said, with a hint of tears in her voice, "I know that you will make her happy and love her very much."

His silence continued for a moment before he turned back to her.

She saw suddenly that there were lines in his face, lines she had never seen before.

"What is happening to you?" she asked.

"My darling and last love," he said, "I will be losing you twice. I cannot bear it. I have asked the physician for medicine to counteract the rejuvenation. In an hour I shall be as old as you. We are going together. And somewhere out there we will meet Carlotta and we will hold hands, the three of us, among the stars. Karla will find her own man and her own fate."

Together they sat and watched the descent of Karla's spacecraft.

When the People Fell

"CAN YOU IMAGINE a rain of people through an acid fog? Can you imagine thousands and thousands of human bodies, without weapons, overwhelming the unconquerable monsters? Can you—"

"Look, sir," interrupted the reporter.

"Don't interrupt me! You ask me silly questions. I tell you I saw the Goonhogo itself. I saw it take Venus. Now ask me about that!"

The reporter had called to get an old man's reminiscences about bygone ages. He did not expect Dobyns Bennett to flare up at him.

Dobyns Bennett thrust home the psychological advantage he had gotten by taking the initiative. "Can you imagine showhices in their parachutes, a lot of them dead, floating out of a green sky? Can you imagine mothers crying as they fell? Can you imagine people pouring down on the poor helpless monsters?"

Mildly, the reporter asked what showhices were.

"That's old Chinesian for children," said Dobyns Bennett. "I saw the last of the nations burst and die, and you want to ask me about fashionable clothes and things. Real history never gets into the books. It's too shocking. I suppose you were going to ask me what I thought of the new striped pantaloons for women!"

"No," said the reporter, but he blushed. The question was in his notebook and he hated blushing.

"Do you know what the Goonhogo did?"

"What?" asked the reporter, struggling to remember just what a Goonhogo might be.

"It took Venus," said the old man, somewhat more calmly.

Very mildly, the reporter murmured, "It *did*?"

"You bet it did!" said Dobyns Bennett belligerently.

"Were you there?" asked the reporter.

"You bet I was there when the Goonhogo took Venus," said the old man. "I was there and it's the damnedest thing I've ever seen. You know who I am. I've seen more worlds than you can count, boy, and yet when the nondies and the needies and the showhices came pouring out of the sky, that was the worst thing that any man could ever see. Down on the ground, there were the loudies the way they'd always been—"

The reporter interrupted, very gently. Bennett might as well have been speaking a foreign language. All of this had happened three hundred years before. The reporter's job was to get a feature from him and to put it into a language which people of the present time could understand.

Respectfully he said, "Can't you start at the beginning of the story?"

"You bet. That's when I married Terza. Terza was the prettiest girl you ever saw. She was one of the Vomacts, a great family of scanners, and her father was a very important man. You see, I was thirty-two, and when a man is thirty-two, he thinks he is pretty old, but I wasn't really old, I just thought so, and he wanted Terza to marry me because she was such a complicated girl that she needed a man's help. The Court back home had found her unstable and the Instrumentality had ordered her left in her father's care until she married a man who then could take on proper custodial authority. I suppose those are old customs to you, boy—"

The reporter interrupted again. "I am sorry, old man," said he. "I know you are over four hundred years old and you're the only person who remembers the time the Goonhogo took Venus. Now the Goonhogo was a government, wasn't it?"

"Anyone knows that," snapped the old man. "The

Goonhogo was a sort of separate Chinesian government.
Seventeen billion of them all crowded in one small part
of Earth. Most of them spoke English the way you and
I do, but they spoke their own language, too, with all
those funny words that have come on down to us. They
hadn't mixed in with anybody else yet. Then, you see,
the Waywanjong himself gave the order and that is
when the people started raining. They just fell right out
of the sky. You never saw anything like it—"

The reporter had to interrupt him again and again to
get the story bit by bit. The old man kept using terms
that he couldn't seem to realize were lost in history and
that had to be explained to be intelligible to anyone of
this era. But his memory was excellent and his descrip-
tive powers as sharp and alert as ever. . . .

Young Dobyns Bennett had not been at Experimental Area A very long, before he realized that the most
beautiful female he had ever seen was Terza Vomact.
At the age of fourteen, she was fully mature. Some of
the Vomacts did mature that way. It may have had
something to do with their being descended from unreg-
istered, illegal people centuries back in the past. They
were even said to have mysterious connections with the
lost world back in the age of nations when people could
still put numbers on the years.

He fell in love with her and felt like a fool for doing
it.

She was so beautiful, it was hard to realize that she
was the daughter of Scanner Vomact himself. The scanner was a powerful man.

Sometimes romance moves too fast and it did with
Dobyns Bennett because Scanner Vomact himself called
in the young man and said, "I'd like to have you marry
my daughter Terza, but I'm not sure she'll approve of
you. If you can get her, boy, you have my blessing."

Dobyns was suspicious. He wanted to know why a
senior scanner was willing to take a junior technician.

All that the scanner did was to smile. He said, "I'm a
lot older than you, and with this new santaclara drug

coming in that may give people hundreds of years, you
may think that I died in my prime if I die at a hundred
and twenty. You may live to four or five hundred. But I
know my time's coming up. My wife has been dead for
a long time and we have no other children and I know
that Terza needs a father in a very special kind of way.
The psychologist found her to be unstable. Why don't
you take her outside the area? You can get a pass
through the dome anytime. You can go out and play
with the loudies."

Dobyns Bennett was almost as insulted as if someone
had given him a pail and told him to go play in the
sandpile. And yet he realized that the elements of play
in courtship were fitted together and that the old man
meant well.

The day that it all happened, he and Terza were outside the dome. They had been pushing loudies around.

Loudies were not dangerous unless you killed them.
You could knock them down, push them out of the
way, or tie them up; after a while, they slipped away
and went about their business. It took a very special
kind of ecologist to figure out what their business was.
They floated two meters high, ninety centimeters in diameter, gently just above the land of Venus, eating mi-
croscopically. For a long time, people thought there was
radiation on which they subsisted. They simply multi-
plied in tremendous numbers. In a silly sort of way, it
was fun to push them around, but that was about all
there was to do.

They never responded with intelligence.

Once, long before, a loudie taken into the laboratory
for experimental purposes had typed a perfectly clear
message on the typewriter. The message had read,
"Why don't you Earth people go back to Earth and
leave us alone? We are getting along all—"

And that was all the message that anybody had
ever got out of them in three hundred years. The best
laboratory conclusion was that they had very high intelligence if they ever chose to use it, but that their voli-
tional mechanism was so profoundly different from the

psychology of human beings that it was impossible to force a loudie to respond to stress as people did on Earth.

The name *loudie* was some kind of word in the old Chinesian language. It meant the "ancient ones." Since it was the Chinesians who had set up the first outposts on Venus, under the orders of their supreme boss the Waywonjong, their term lingered on.

Dobyns and Terza pushed loudies, climbed over the hills and looked down into the valleys where it was impossible to tell a river from a swamp. They got thoroughly wet, their air converters stuck, and perspiration itched and tickled along their cheeks. Since they could not eat or drink while outside—at least not with any reasonable degree of safety—the excursion could not be called a picnic. There was something mildly refreshing about playing child with a very pretty girl-child—but Dobyns wearied of the whole thing.

Terza sensed his rejection of her. Quick as a sensitive animal, she became angry and petulant. "You didn't have to come out with me!"

"I wanted to," he said, "but now I'm tired and want to go home."

"You treat me like a child. All right, play with me. Or you treat me like a woman. All right, be a gentleman. But don't seesaw all the time yourself. I just got to be a little bit happy and you have to get middle-aged and condescending. I won't take it."

"Your father—" he said, realizing the moment he said it that it was a mistake.

"My father this, my father that. If you're thinking about marrying me, do it yourself." She glared at him, stuck her tongue out, ran over a dune, and disappeared.

Dobyns Bennett was baffled. He did not know what to do. She was safe enough. The loudies never hurt anyone. He decided to teach her a lesson and to go on back himself, letting her find her way home when she pleased. The Area Search Team could find her easily if she really got lost.

He walked back to the gate.

When he saw the gates locked and the emergency lights on, he realized that he had made the worst mistake of his life.

His heart sinking within him, he ran the last few meters of the way, and beat the ceramic gate with his bare hands until it opened only just enough to let him in.

"What's wrong?" he asked the doortender.

The doortender muttered something which Dobyns could not understand.

"Speak up, man!" shouted Dobyns. "What's wrong?"

"The Goonhogo is coming back and they're taking over."

"That's impossible," said Dobyns. "They couldn't—" He checked himself. *Could* they?

"The Goonhogo's taken over," the gatekeeper insisted. "They've been given the whole thing. The Earth Authority has voted it to them. The Waywonjong has decided to send people right away. They're sending them."

"What do the Chinesians want with Venus? You can't kill a loudie without contaminating a thousand acres of land. You can't push them away without them drifting back. You can't scoop them up. Nobody can live here until we solve the problem of these things. We're a long way from having solved it," said Dobyns in angry bewilderment.

The gatekeeper shook his head. "Don't ask me. That's all I hear on the radio. Everybody else is excited too."

Within an hour, the rain of people began.

Dobyns went up to the radar room, saw the skies above. The radar man himself was drumming his fingers against the desk. He said, "Nothing like this has been seen for a thousand years or more. You know what there is up there? Those are warships, the warships left over from the last of the old dirty wars. I knew the Chinesians were inside them. Everybody knew about it. It was sort of like a museum. Now they don't have any weapons in them. But do you know—there are millions

of people hanging up there over Venus and I don't
know what they are going to do!"

He stopped and pointed at one of the screens. "Look,
you can see them running in patches. They're behind
each other, so they cluster up solid. We're never had a
screen look like that."

Dobyns looked at the screen. It was, as the operator
said, full of blips.

As they watched, one of the men exclaimed, "What's
that milky stuff down there in the lower left? See, it's—
it's pouring," he said. "It's pouring somehow out of
those dots. How can you pour things into a radar? It
doesn't really show, does it?"

The radar man looked at his screen. He said, "Search
me. I don't know what it is, either. You'll have to find
out. Let's just see what happens."

Scanner Vomact came into the room. He said, once
he had taken a quick, experienced glance at the screens,
"This may be the strangest thing we'll ever see, but I
have a feeling they're dropping people. Lots of them.
Dropping them by the thousands, or by the hundreds of
thousands, or even by the millions. But people are coming down there. Come along with me, you two. We'll go
out and see it. There may be somebody that we can
help."

By this time, Dobyns's conscience was hurting him
badly. He wanted to tell Vomact that he had left Terza
out there, but he had hesitated—not only because he
was ashamed of leaving her, but because he did not
want to tattle on the child to her father. Now he spoke.

"Your daughter's still outside."

Vomact turned on him solemnly. The immense eyes
looked very tranquil and very threatening, but the silky
voice was controlled.

"You may find her." The scanner added, in a tone
which sent the thrill of menace up Dobyns's back, "And
everything will be well if you bring her back."

Dobyns nodded as though receiving an order.

"I shall," said Vomact, "go out myself, to see what I
can do, but I leave the finding of my daughter to you."

They went down, put on the extra-long-period converters, carried their miniaturized survey equipment so
that they could find their way back through the fog, and
went out. Just as they were at the gate, the gatekeeper
said, "Wait a moment, sir and excellency. I have a message for you here on the phone. Please call Control."

Scanner Vomact was not to be called lightly and he
knew it. He picked up the connection unit and spoke
harshly.

The radar man came on the phone screen in the gatekeeper's wall. "They're overhead now, sir."

"Who's overhead?"

"The Chinesians are. They're coming down. I don't
know how many there are. There must be two thousand
warships over our heads right here and there are more
thousands over the rest of Venus. They're down now. If
you want to see them hit ground, you'd better get outside quick."

Vomact and Dobyns went out.

Down came the Chinesians. People's bodies were
raining right out of the milk-cloudy sky. Thousands
upon thousands of them with plastic parachutes that
looked like bubbles. Down they came.

Dobyns and Vomact saw a headless man drift down.
The parachute cords had decapitated him.

A woman fell near them. The drop had torn her
breathing tube loose from her crudely bandaged throat
and she was choking in her own blood. She staggered
toward them, tried to babble but only drooled blood
with mute choking sounds, and then fell face forward
into the mud.

Two babies dropped. The adult accompanying them
had been blown off course. Vomact ran, picked them up
and handed them to a Chinesian man who had just
landed. The man looked at the babies in his arms, sent
Vomact a look of contemptuous inquiry, put the weeping children down in the cold slush of Venus, gave them
a last impersonal glance and ran off on some mysterious
errand of his own.

Vomact kept Bennett from picking up the children.

"Come on, let's keep looking. We can't take care of all of them."

The world had known that the Chinesians had a lot of unpredictable public habits, but they never suspected that the nondies and the needies and the showhices could pour down out of a poisoned sky. Only the Goonhogo itself would make such a reckless use of human life. *Nondies* were men and *needies* were women and *showhices* were the little children. And the *Goonhogo* was a name left over from the old days of nations. It meant something like republic or state or government. Whatever it was, it was the organization that ran the Chinesians in the Chinesian manner, under the Earth Authority.

And the ruler of the Goonhogo was the Waywonjong.

The Waywonjong didn't come to Venus. He just sent his people. He sent them floating down into Venus, to tackle the Venusian ecology with the only weapons which could make a settlement of that planet possible— people themselves. Human arms could tackle the loudies, the loudies who had been called "old ones" by the first Chinesian scouts to cover Venus.

The loudies had to be gathered together so gently that they would not die and, in dying, each contaminate a thousand acres. They had to be kept together by human bodies and arms in a gigantic living corral.

Scanner Vomact rushed forward.

A wounded Chinesian man hit the ground and his parachute collapsed behind him. He was clad in a pair of shorts, had a knife at his belt, canteen at his waist. He had an air converter attached next to his ear, with a tube running into his throat. He shouted something unintelligible at them and limped rapidly away.

People kept on hitting the ground all around Vomact and Dobyns.

The self-disposing parachutes were bursting like bubbles in the misty air, a moment or two after they touched the ground. Someone had done a tricky, efficient job with the chemical consequences of static electricity.

And as the two watched, the air was heavy with people. One time, Vomact was knocked down by a person. He found that it was two Chinesian children tied together.

Dobyns asked, "What are you doing? Where are you going? Do you have any leaders?"

He got cries and shouts in an unintelligible language. Here and there someone shouted in English "This way!" or "Leave us alone!" or "Keep going . . ." but that was all.

The experiment worked.

Eighty-two million people were dropped in that one day.

After four hours which seemed barely short of endless, Dobyns found Terza in a corner of the cold hell. Though Venus was warm, the suffering of the almost-naked Chinesians had chilled his blood.

Terza ran toward him.

She could not speak.

She put her head on his chest and sobbed. Finally she managed to say, "I've—I've—I've tried to help, but they're too many, too many, too many!" And the sentence ended as shrill as a scream.

Dobyns led her back to the experimental area.

They did not have to talk. Her whole body told him that she wanted his love and the comfort of his presence, and that she had chosen that course of life which would keep them together.

As they left the drop area, which seemed to cover all of Venus so far as they could tell, a pattern was beginning to form. The Chinesians were beginning to round up the loudies.

Terza kissed him mutely after the gatekeeper had let them through. She did not need to speak. Then she fled to her room.

The next day, the people from Experimental Area A tried to see if they could go out and lend a hand to the settlers. It wasn't possible to lend a hand; there were too many settlers. People by the millions were scattered all over the hills and valleys of Venus, sludging through the mud and water with their human toes, crushing the alien mud, crushing the strange plants. They didn't know what to eat. They didn't know where to go. They had no leaders.

All they had were orders to gather the loudies together in large herds and hold them there with human arms.

The loudies didn't resist.

After a time-lapse of several Earth days the Goonhogo sent small scout cars. They brought a very different kind of Chinesian—these late arrivals were uniformed, educated, cruel, smug men. They knew what they were doing. And they were willing to pay any sacrifice of their own people to get it done.

They brought instructions. They put the people together in gangs. It did not matter where the nondies and needies had come from on Earth; it didn't matter whether they found their own showhices or somebody else's. They were shown the jobs to do and they got to work. Human bodies accomplished what machines could not have done—they kept the loudies firmly but gently encircled until every last one of the creatures was starved into nothingness.

Rice fields began to appear miraculously.

Scanner Vomact couldn't believe it. The Goonhogo biochemists had managed to adapt rice to the soil of Venus. And yet the seedlings came out of boxes in the scout cars and weeping people walked over the bodies of their own dead to keep the crop moving toward the planting.

Venusian bacteria could not kill human beings, nor could they dispose of human bodies after death. A problem arose and was solved. Immense sleds carried dead men, women and children—those who had fallen wrong, or drowned as they fell, or had been trampled by others—to an undisclosed destination. Dobyns suspected the material was to be used to add Earth-type organic waste to the soil of Venus, but he did not tell Terza.

The work went on.

The nondies and needies kept working in shifts. When they could not see in the darkness, they proceeded without seeing—keeping in line by touch or by shout. Foremen, newly trained, screeched commands. Workers lined up, touching fingertips. The job of building the fields kept on.

"That's a big story," said the old man. "Eighty-two million people dropped in a single day. And later I heard that the Waywonjong said it wouldn't have mattered if seventy million of them had died. Twelve million survivors would have been enough to make a spacehead for the Goonhogo. The Chinesians got Venus, all of it.

"But I'll never forget the nondies and the needies and the showhices falling out of the sky, men and women and children with their poor scared Chinesian faces. That funny Venusian air made them look green instead of tan. There they were, falling all around.

"You know something, young man?" said Dobyns Bennett, approaching his fifth century of age.

"What?" said the reporter.

"There won't be things like that happening on any world again. Because now, after all, there isn't any separate Goonhogo left. There's only one Instrumentality and they don't care what a man's race may have been in the ancient years. Those were the rough old days, the ones I lived in. Those were the days *men* still tried to do things."

Dobyns almost seemed to doze off, but he roused himself sharply and said, "I tell you, the sky was full of people. They fell like water. They fell like rain. I've seen the awful ants in Africa, and there's not a thing among the stars to beat them for prowling horror. Mind you, they're worse than anything the stars contain. I've seen the crazy worlds near Alpha Centauri, but I never saw anything like the time the people fell on Venus.

More than eighty-two million in one day and my own little Terza lost among them.

"But the rice did sprout. And the loudies died as the walls of people held them in with human arms. Walls of people, I tell you, with volunteers jumping in to take the places of the falling ones.

"They were people still, even when they shouted in the darkness. They tried to help each other even while they fought a fight that had to be fought without violence. They were people still. And they did so win. It was crazy and impossible, but they won. Mere human beings did what machines and science would have taken another thousand years to do . . .

"The funniest thing of all was the first house that I saw a nondie put up, there in the rain of Venus. I was out there with Vomact and with a pale sad Terza. It wasn't much of a house, shaped out of twisted Venusian wood. There it was. *He* built it, the smiling half-naked Chinesian nondie. We went to the door and said to him in English, 'What are you building here, a shelter or a hospital?'

"The Chinesian grinned at us. 'No,' he said, 'gambling.'

"Vomact wouldn't believe it: 'Gambling?'

" 'Sure,' said the nondie. 'Gambling is the first thing a man needs in a strange place. It can take the worry out of his soul.' "

"Is that all?" said the reporter.

Dobyns Bennett muttered that the personal part did not count. He added, "Some of my great-great-great-great-great-grandsons may come along. You count those greats. Their faces will show you easily enough that I married into the Vomact line. Terza saw what happened. She saw how people build worlds. This was the hard way to build them. She never forgot the night with the dead Chinese babies lying in the half-illuminated mud, or the parachute ropes dissolving slowly. She heard the needies weeping and the helpless nondies comforting them and leading them off to nowhere. She remembered the cruel, neat officers coming out of the scout cars. She got home and saw the rice come up, and saw how the Goonhogo made Venus a Chinesian place."

"What happened to you personally?" asked the reporter.

"Nothing much. There wasn't any more work for us, so we closed down Experimental Area A. I married Terza.

"Any time later, when I said to her, 'You're not such a bad girl!' she was able to admit the truth and tell me she was not. That night in the rain of people would test anybody's soul and it tested hers. She had met a big test and passed it. She used to say to me, 'I saw it once. I saw the people fall, and I never want to see another person suffer again. Keep me with you, Dobyns, keep me with you forever.'

"And," said Dobyns Bennett, "it wasn't forever, but it was a happy and sweet three hundred years. She died after our fourth diamond anniversary. Wasn't that a wonderful thing, young man?"

The reporter said it was. And yet, when he took the story back to his editor, he was told to put it into the archives. It wasn't the right kind of story for entertainment and the public would not appreciate it any more.

Think Blue, Count Two

1

BEFORE THE GREAT ships whispered between the stars
by means of planoforming, people had to fly from star
to star with immense sails—huge films assorted in space
on long, rigid, coldproof rigging. A small spaceboat
provided room for a sailor to handle the sails, check the
course and watch the passengers who were sealed, like
knots in immense threads, in their little adiabatic pods
which trailed behind the ship. The passengers knew
nothing, except for going to sleep on earth and waking
up on a strange new world forty, fifty or two hundred
years later.

This was a primitive way to do it. But it worked.

On such a ship Helen America had followed Mr.
Gray-no-more. On such ships, the Scanners retained
their ancient authority over space. Two hundred planets
and more were settled in this fashion, including Old
North Australia, destined to be the treasure house of
them all.

The Emigration Port was a series of low, square
buildings—nothing like Earthport, which towers above
the clouds like a frozen nuclear explosion.

Emigration Port is dour, drab, dreary and efficient.
The walls are black-red like old blood merely because
they are cheaper to heat that way. The rockets are ugly
and simple; the rocket pits, as inglorious as machine
shops. Earth has a few showplaces to tell visitors about.
Emigration Port is not one of them. The people who
work there get the privilege of real work and secure

professional honors. The people who *go* there become unconscious very soon. What they remember about Earth is a little room like a hospital room, a little bed, some music, some talk, the sleep and (perhaps) the cold.

From Emigration Port they go to their pods, sealed in. The pods go to the rockets and these to the sailing ship. That's the old way of doing it.

The new way is better. All a person does now is visit a pleasant lounge, or play a game of cards, or eat a meal or two. All he needs is half the wealth of a planet, or a couple hundred years' seniority marked "excellent" without a single break.

The photonic sails were different. Everyone took chances.

A young man, bright of skin and hair, merry at heart, set out for a new world. An older man, his hair touched with gray, went with him. So, too, did thirty thousand others. And also, the most beautiful girl on earth.

Earth could have kept her, but the new worlds needed her.

She had to go.

She went by light-sail ship. And she had to cross space—space, where the danger always waits.

Space sometimes commands strange tools to its uses—the screams of a beautiful child, the laminated brain of a long-dead mouse, the heartbroken weeping of a computer. Most space offers no respite, no relay, no rescue, no repair. All dangers must be anticipated; otherwise they become mortal. And the greatest of all hazards is the risk of man himself.

"She's beautiful," said the first technician.

"She's just a child," said the second.

"She won't look like much of a child when they're two hundred years out," said the first.

"But she *is* a child," said the second, smiling, "a beautiful doll with blue eyes, just going tiptoe into the beginnings of grown-up life." He sighed.

"She'll be frozen," said the first.

"Not all the time," said the second. "Sometimes they wake up. They have to wake up. The machines defreeze them. You remember the crimes on the *Old Twenty-two*. Nice people, but the wrong combinations. And everything went wrong, dirtily, brutally wrong."

They both remembered *Old Twenty-two*. The hell-ship had drifted between the stars for a long time before its beacon brought rescue. Rescue was much too late.

The ship was in immaculate condition. The sails were set at a correct angle. The thousands of frozen sleepers, strung out behind the ship in their one-body adiabatic pods, would have been in excellent condition, but they had merely been left in open space too long and most of them had spoiled. The inside of the ship—there was the trouble. The sailor had failed or died. The reserve passengers had been awakened. They did not get on well with one another. Or else they got on too horribly well, in the wrong way. Out between the stars, encased only by a frail limited cabin, they had invented new crimes and committed them upon each other—crimes which a million years of Earth's old wickedness had never brought to the surface of man before.

The investigators of *Old Twenty-two* had become very sick, reconstructing the events that followed the awakening of the reserve crew. Two of them had asked for blanking and had obviously retired from service.

The two technicians knew all about *Old Twenty-two* as they watched the fifteen-year-old woman sleeping on the table. Was she a woman? Was she a girl? What would happen to her if she did wake up on the flight?

She breathed delicately.

The two technicians looked across her figure at one another and then the first one said:

"We'd better call the psychological guard. It's a job for him."

"He can try," said the second.

The psychological guard, a man whose number-name ended in the digits Tiga-belas, came cheerfully into the room a half-hour later. He was a dreamy-looking old man, sharp and alert, probably in his fourth rejuvenation. He looked at the beautiful girl on the table and inhaled sharply,

"What's this for—a ship?"

"No," said the first technician, "it's a beauty contest."

"Don't be a fool," said the psychological guard. "You mean they are really sending that beautiful child into the Up-and-Out?"

"It's stock," said the second technician. "The people out on Wereld Schemering are running dreadfully ugly, and they flashed a sign to the Big Blink that they had to have better-looking people. The Instrumentality is doing right by them. All the people on this ship are handsome or beautiful."

"If she's that precious, why don't they freeze her and put her in a pod? That way she would either get there or she would not. A face as pretty as that," said Tigabelas, "could start trouble anywhere. Let alone a ship. What's her name-number?"

"On the board there," said the first technician. "It's all on the board there. You'll want the others too. They're listed, too, and ready to go on the board."

"Veesey-koosey," read the psychological guard, saying the words aloud, "or five-six. That's a silly name, but it's rather cute." With one last look back at the sleeping girl, he bent to his work of reading the case histories of the people added to the reserve crew. Within ten lines, he saw why the girl was being kept ready for emergencies, instead of sleeping the whole trip through. She had a Daughter Potential of 999.999, meaning that any normal adult of either sex could *and would* accept her as a daughter after a few minutes of relationship. She had no skill in herself, no learning, no trained capacities. But she could remotivate almost anyone older than herself, and she showed a probability of making that remotivated person put up a gigantic fight for life. For her sake. And secondarily the adopter's.

That was all, but it was special enough to put her in the cabin. She had tested out into the literal truth of the ancient poetic scrap, "the fairest of the daughters of old, old earth."

When Tiga-belas finished taking his notes from the records, the working time was almost over. The technicians had not interrupted him. He turned around to look one last time at the lovely girl. She was gone. The second technician had left and the first was cleaning his hands.

"You haven't frozen her?" cried Tiga-belas. "I'll have to fix her too, if the safeguard is to work."

"Of course you do," said the first technician. "We've left you two minutes for it."

"You give me two minutes," said Tiga-belas, "to protect a trip of four hundred and fifty years!"

"Do you need more," said the technician, and it was not even a question, except in form.

"Do I?" said Tiga-belas. He broke into a smile. "No, I don't. That girl will be safe long after I am dead."

"When do you die?" said the technician, socially.

"Seventy-three years, two months, four days," said Tiga-belas agreeably. "I'm a fourth-and-last."

"I thought so," said the technician. "You're smart. Nobody starts off that way. We all learn. I'm sure you'll take care of that girl."

They left the laboratory together and ascended to the surface and the cool restful night of Earth.

2

Late the next day, Tiga-belas came in, very cheerful indeed. In his left hand he held a drama spool, full commercial size. In his right hand there was a black plastic cube with shimmering silver contact-points gleaming on its sides. The two technicians greeted him politely.

The psychological guard could not hide his excitement and his pleasure.

"I've got that beautiful child taken care of. The way she is going to be fixed, she'll keep her Daughter Potential, but it's going to be a lot closer to one thousand point double zero than it was with all those nines. I've used a mouse-brain."

"If it's frozen," said the first technician, "we won't be able to put it in the computer. It will have to go forward with the emergency stores."

"This brain isn't frozen," said Tiga-belas indignantly. "It's been laminated. We stiffened it with celluprime and then we veneered it down, about seven thousand layers. Each one has plastic of at least two molecular thicknesses. This mouse can't spoil. As a matter of fact, this mouse is going to go on thinking forever. He won't think much, unless we put the voltage on him, but he'll think. And he can't spoil. This is ceramic plastic, and it would take a major weapon to break it."

"The contacts? . . ." said the second technician.

"They don't go through," said Tigas-belas. "This mouse is tuned into that girl's personality, up to a thousand meters. You can put him anywhere in the ship. The case has been hardened. The contacts are just attached on the outside. They feed to nickel-steel counterpart contacts on the inside. I told you, this mouse is going to be thinking when the last human being on the last known planet is dead. And it's going to be thinking about that girl. Forever."

"Forever is an awfully long time," said the first technician, with a shiver. "We only need a safety period of two thousand years. The girl herself would spoil in less than a thousand years, if anything did go wrong."

"Never you mind," said Tiga-belas, "that girl is going to be guarded whether she is spoiled or not." He spoke to the cube. "You're going along with Veesey, fellow, and if she is an *Old Twenty-two* you'll turn the whole thing into a toddle-garden frolic complete with ice cream and hymns to the West Wind." Tiga-belas looked up at the other men and said, quite unnecessarily, "He can't hear me."

"Of course not," said the first technician, very dryly.

They all looked at the cube. It was a beautiful piece of engineering. The psychological guard had reason to be proud of it.

"Do you need the mouse any more?" said the first technician.

"Yes," said Tiga-belas. "One-third of a millisecond at forty megadynes. I want him to get her whole life printed on his left cortical lobe. Particularly her screams. She screamed badly at ten months. Something she got in her mouth. She screamed at ten when she thought the air had stopped in her drop-shaft. It hadn't, or she wouldn't be here. They're in her record. I want the mouse to have those screams. And she had a pair of red shoes for her fourth birthday. Give me the full two minutes with her. I've printed the key on the complete series of *Marcia and the Moon Men*—that was the best box drama for teen-age girls that they ran last year. Veesey saw it. This time she'll see it again, but the mouse will be tied in. She won't have the chance of a snowball in hell of forgetting it."

Said the first technician, "What was that?"

"Huh?" said Tiga-belas.

"What was that you just said, that, at the end?"

"Are you deaf?"

"No," said the technician huffily. "I just didn't understand what you meant."

"I said that she would not have the chance of a snowball in hell of forgetting it."

"That's what I thought you said," replied the technician. "What is a snowball? What is hell? What sort of chances do they make?"

The second technician interrupted eagerly. "I know," he explained. "Snowballs are ice formations on Neptune. Hell is a planet out near Khufu VII. I don't know how anybody would get them together."

Tiga-belas looked at them with the weary amazement of the very old. He did not feel like explaining, so he said gently:

"Let's leave the literature till another time. All I meant was, Veesey will be safe when she's cued into this mouse. The mouse will outlast her and everybody else, and no teen-age girl is going to forget *Marcia and the*

Moon Men. Not when she saw every single episode twice over. This girl did."

"She's not going to render the other passengers ineffectual? That wouldn't help," said the first technician.

"Not a bit," said Tiga-belas.

"Give me those strengths again," said the first technician.

"Mouse—one-third millisecond at forty megadynes."

"They'll hear that way beyond the moon," said the technician. "You can't put that sort of stuff into people's heads without a permit. Do you want us to get a special permit from the Instrumentality?"

"For one-third of a millisecond?"

The two men faced each other for a moment; then the technician began creasing his forehead, his mouth began to smile and they both laughed. The second technician did not understand it and Tiga-belas said to him:

"I'm putting the girl's whole lifetime into one-third of a millisecond at top power. It will drain over into the mouse-brain inside this cube. What is the normal human reaction within one-third millisecond?"

"Fifteen milliseconds—" The second technician started to speak and stopped himself.

"That's right," said Tiga-belas. "People don't get anything at all in less than fifteen milliseconds. This mouse isn't only veneered and laminated; *he's fast*. The lamination is faster than his own synapses ever were. Bring on the girl."

The first technician had already gone to get her.

The second technician turned back for one more question. "Is the mouse dead?"

"No. Yes. Of course not. What do you mean? Who knows?" said Tiga-belas all in one breath.

The younger man stared but the couch with the beautiful girl had already rolled into the room. Her skin had chilled down from pink to ivory and her respiration was no longer visible to the naked eye, but she was still beautiful. The deep freezing had not yet begun.

The first technician began to whistle. "Mouse—forty

megadynes, one-third of a millisecond. Girl, output maximum, same time. Girl input, two minutes, what volume?"

"Anything," said Tiga-belas. "Anything. Whatever you use for deep personality engraving."

"Set," said the technician.

"Take the cube," said Tiga-belas.

The technician took it and fitted it into the coffinlike box near the girl's head.

"Good-bye, immortal mouse," said Tiga-belas. "Think about the beautiful girl when I am dead and don't get too tired of *Marcia and the Moon Men* when you've seen it for a million years . . ."

"Record," said the second technician. He took it from Tiga-belas and put it into a standard drama-shower, but one with output cables heavier than any home had ever installed.

"Do you have a code word?" said the first technician.

"It's a little poem," said Tiga-belas. He reached in his pocket. "Don't read it aloud. If any of us misspoke a word, there is a chance she might hear it and it would heterodyne the relationship between her and the laminated mouse."

The two looked at a scrap of paper. In clear, archaic writing there appeared the lines:

Lady if a man
Tries to bother you, you can
   Think blue,
   Count two,
And look for a red shoe.

The technicians laughed warmly. "That'll do it," said the first technician.

Tiga-belas gave them an embarrassed smile of thanks.

"Turn them both on," he said. "Good-bye, girl," he murmured to himself. "Good-bye, mouse. Maybe I'll see you in seventy-four years."

The room flashed with a kind of invisible light inside their heads.

In moon orbit a navigator wondered about his mother's red shoes.

Two million people on Earth started to count "one-two" and then wondered why they had done so.

A bright young parakeet, in an orbital ship, began reciting the whole verse and baffled the crew as to what the meaning might be.

Apart from this, there were no side-effects.

The girl in the coffin arched her body with terrible strain. The electrodes had scorched the skin at her temples. The scars stood bright red against the chilled fresh skin of the girl.

The cube showed no sign from the dead-live live-dead mouse.

While the second technician put ointment on Veesey's scars, Tiga-belas put on a headset and touched the terminals of the cube very gently without moving it from the snap-in position it held in the coffin-shaped box.

He nodded, satisfied. He stepped back.

"You're sure the girl got it?"

"We'll read it back before she goes to deep-freeze."

"*Marcia and the Moon Men,* what?"

"Can't miss it," said the first technician. "I'll let you know if there's anything missing. There won't be."

Tiga-belas took one last look at the lovely, lovely girl. Seventy-three years, two months, three days, he thought to himself. And she, beyond Earth rules, may be awarded a thousand years. And the mouse-brain has got a million years.

Veesey never knew any of them—neither the first technician, nor the second technician, nor Tiga-belas, the psychological guard.

To the day of her death, she knew that *Marcia and the Moon Men* had included the most wonderful blue lights, the hypnotic count of "one-two, one-two" and the prettiest red shoes that any girl had seen on or off Earth.

3

Three hundred and twenty-six years later she had to wake up.

Her box had opened.

Her body ached in every muscle and nerve.

The ship was screaming emergency and she had to get up.

She wanted to sleep, to sleep, or to die.

The ship kept screaming.

She had to get up.

She lifted an arm to the edge of her coffin-bed. She had practiced getting in and out of the bed in the long training period before they sent her underground to be hypnotized and frozen. She knew just what to reach for, just what to expect. She pulled herself over on her side. She opened her eyes.

The lights were yellow and strong. She closed her eyes again.

This time a voice sounded from somewhere near her. It seemed to be saying, "Take the straw in your mouth."

Veesey groaned.

The voice kept on saying things.

Something scratchy pressed against her mouth.

She opened her eyes.

The outline of a human head had come between her and the light.

She squinted, trying to see if it might be one more of the doctors. No, this was the ship.

The face came into focus.

It was the face of a very handsome and very young man. His eyes looked into hers. She had never seen anyone who was both handsome and sympathetic, quite the way that he was. She tried to see him clearly, and found herself beginning to smile.

The drinking-tube thrust past her lips and teeth. Automatically she sucked at it. The fluid was something like soup, but it had a medicinal taste too.

The face had a voice. "Wake up," he said, "wake up. It doesn't do any good to hold back now. You need some exercise as soon as you can manage it."

She let the tube slip from her mouth and gasped, "Who are you?"

"Trece," he said, "and that's Talatashar over there. We've been up for two months, recueing the robots. We need your help."

"Help," she murmured, "my help?"

Trece's face wrinkled and crinkled in a delightful grin. "Well, we sort of needed you. We really do need a third mind to watch the robots when we think we've fixed them. And besides, we're lonely. Talatashar and I aren't much company to each other. We looked over the list of reserve crew and we decided to wake you." He reached out a friendly hand to her.

When she sat up she saw the other man, Talatashar. She immediately recoiled: she had never seen anyone so ugly. His hair was gray and cropped. Piggy little eyes peered out of eye-sockets which looked flooded with fat. His cheeks hung down in monstrous jowls on either side. On top of all that, his face was lopsided. One side seemed wide awake but the other was twisted in an end-less spasm which looked like agony. She could not help putting her hand to her mouth. And it was with the back of her hand against her lips that she spoke.

"I thought—I thought everybody on this ship was supposed to be handsome."

One side of Talatashar's face smiled at her while the other half stayed with its expression of frozen hurt.

"We were," his voice rumbled, and it was not of itself an unpleasant voice, "we all were. Some of us always get spoiled in the freezing. It will take you a while to get used to me." He laughed grimly. "It took *me* a while to get used to me. In two months, I've managed. Pleased to meet you. Maybe you'll be pleased to meet me, after a while. What do you think of that, eh, Trece?"

"What?" said Trece, who had watched them both with friendly worry.

"The girl. So tactful. The direct diplomacy of the

very young. Was I handsome, she said. No, say I. What is she, anyhow?"

Trece turned to her. "Let me help you sit," he said. She sat up on the edge of her box.

Wordlessly he passed the skin of fluid to her with its drinking tube, and she went back to sucking her broth. Her eyes peered up at the two men like the eyes of a small child. They were as innocent and troubled as the eyes of a kitten which has met worry for the first time.

"What are you?" said Trece.

She took her lips away from the tube for a moment. "A girl," she said.

Half of Talatashar's face smiled a sophisticated smile. The other half moved a little with muscular drag, but expressed nothing. "We see that," said he, grimly.

"He means," said Trece conciliatorily, "what have you been trained for?"

She took her mouth away again. "Nothing," said she.

The men laughed—both of them. First, Trece laughed with all the evil in the world in his voice. Then Talatashar laughed, and he was too young to laugh his own way. His laughter, too, was cruel. There was something masculine, mysterious, threatening and secret in it, as though he knew all about things which girls could find out only at the cost of pain and humiliation. He was as alien, for the moment, as men have always been from women: filled with secret motives and concealed desires, driven by bright sharp thoughts which women neither had nor wished to have. Perhaps more than his body had spoiled.

There was nothing in Veesey's own life to make her fear that laugh, but the instinctive reaction of a million years of womanhood behind her was to disregard the evil, go on the alert for more trouble and hope for the best at the moment. She knew, from books and tapes, all about sex. This laugh had nothing to do with babies or with love. There was contempt and power and cruelty in it—the cruelty of men who are cruel merely because they are men. For an instant she hated both of them, but she was not alarmed enough to set off the trigger of the protective devices which the psychological guard had built into her mind itself. Instead, she looked down the cabin, ten meters long and four meters wide.

This was home now, perhaps forever. There were sleepers somewhere, but she did not see their boxes. All she had was this small space and the two men—Trece with his warm smile, his nice voice, his interesting gray-blue eyes; and Talatashar, with his ruined face. And their laughter. That wretchedly mysterious masculine laughter, hostile and laughing-at in its undertones.

Life's life, she thought, and I must live it. Here.

Talatashar, who had finished laughing, now spoke in a very different voice.

"There will be time for the fun and games later. First, we have to get the work done. The photonic sails aren't picking up enough starlight to get us anywhere. The mainsail is ripped by a meteor. We can't repair it, not when it's twenty miles across. So we have to jury-rig the ship—that's the right old word."

"How does it work?" asked Veesey sadly, not much interested in her own question. The aches and pains of the long freeze were beginning to bedevil her.

Talatashar said, "It's simple. The sails are coated. We were put into orbit by rockets. The pressure of light is bigger on one side than on the other. With some pressure on one side and virtually no pressure on the other, the ship has to go somewhere. Interstellar matter is very fine and does not give us enough drag to slow us down. The sails pull away from the brightest source of light at any time. For the first eighty years it was the sun. Then we began trying to get both the sun and some bright patches of light behind it. Now we have more light coming at us than we want, and we will be pulled away from our destination if we do not point the blind side of the sails at the goal and the pushing sides at the next best source. The sailor died, for some reason we can't figure out. The ship's automatic mechanism woke us up and the navigation board explained the situation to us. Here we are. We have to fix the robots."

"But what's the matter with them? Why don't they do

it themselves? Why did they have to wake up people? They're supposed to be so smart." She particularly wondered, Why did they have to wake up *me*? But she suspected the answer—that the men had done it, not the robots—and she did not want to make them say it. She still remembered how their masculine laughter had turned ugly.

"The robots weren't programmed to tear up sails—only to fix them. We've got to condition them to accept the damage that we want to leave, and to go ahead with the new work which we are adding."

"Could I have something to eat?" asked Veesey.

"Let me get it!" cried Trece.

"Why not?" said Talatashar.

While she ate, they went over the proposed work in detail, the three of them talking it out calmly. Veesey felt more relaxed. She had the sensation that they were taking her in as a partner.

By the time they completed their work schedules, they were sure it would take between thirty-five and forty-two normal days to get the sails stiffened and rehung. The robots did the outside work, but the sails were seventy thousand miles long by twenty thousand miles wide.

Forty-two days!

The work was not forty-two days at all.

It was one year and three days before they finished.

The relationships in the cabin had not changed much. Talatashar left her alone except to make ugly remarks. Nothing he had found in the medicine cabinet had made him look any better, but some of the things drugged him so that he slept long and well.

Trece had long since become her sweetheart, but it was such an innocent romance that it might have been conducted on grass, under elms, at the edge of an Earthside silky river.

Once she had found them fighting and had exclaimed:

"Stop it! Stop it! You can't!"

When they did stop hitting each other, she said wonderingly:

"I thought you *couldn't*. Those boxes. Those safeguards. Those things they put in with us."

And Talatashar said, in a voice of infinite ugliness and finality, "That's what *they* thought. I threw those things out of the ship months ago. Don't want them around."

The effect on Trece was dramatic, as bad as if he had walked into one of the Ancient Unselfing Grounds unaware. He stood utterly still, his eyes wide and his voice filled with fear when, at last, he did speak.

"So—that's—why—we—fought!"

"You mean the boxes? They're gone, all right."

"But," gasped Trece, "each was protected by each one's box. We were all protected—from ourselves. God help us all!"

"What is God?" said Talatashar.

"Never mind. It's an old word. I heard it from a robot. But what are we going to do? What are *you* going to do?" said he accusingly to Talatashar.

"Me," said Talatashar, "I'm doing nothing. Nothing has happened." The working side of his face twisted in a hideous smile.

Veesey watched both of them.

She did not understand it, but she feared it, that unspecific danger.

Talatashar gave them his ugly, masculine laugh, but this time Trece did not join him. He stared openmouthed at the other man.

Talatashar put on a show of courage and indifference. "Shift's up," he said, "and I'm turning in."

Veesey nodded and tried to say good night but no words came. She was frightened and inquisitive. Of the two, feeling inquisitive was worse. There were thirty-odd thousand people all around her, but only these two were alive and present. They knew something which she did not know.

Talatashar made a brave show of it by bidding her,

"Mix up something special for the big eating tomorrow. Mind you do it, girl."

He climbed into the wall.

When Veesey turned toward Trece, it was he who fell into her arms.

"I'm frightened," he said. "We can face anything in space, but we can't face us. I'm beginning to think that the sailor killed himself. *His* psychological guard broke down too. And now we're all alone with just us."

Veesey looked instinctively around the cabin. "It's all the same as before. Just the three of us, and this little room, and the Up-and-Out outside."

"Don't you see it, darling?" He grabbed her by the shoulders. "The little boxes protected us from ourselves. And now there aren't any. We are helpless. There isn't anything here to protect us from us. What hurts man like man? What kills people like people? What danger to us could be more terrible than ourselves?"

She tried to pull away. "It's not that bad."

Without answering he pulled her to him. He began tearing at her clothes. The jacket and shorts, like his own, were omni-textile and fitted tight. She fought him off but she was not the least bit frightened. She was sorry for him, and at this moment the only thing that worried her was that Talatashar might wake up and try to help her. That would be too much.

Trece was not hard to stop.

She got him to sit down and they drifted into the big chair together.

His face was as tear-stained as her own.

That night, they did not make love.

In whispers, in gasps, he told her the story of *Old Twenty-two*. He told her that people poured out among the stars and that the ancient things inside people woke up, so that the deeps of their minds were more terrible than the blackest depth of space. Space never committed crimes. It just killed. Nature could transmit death, but only man could carry crime from world to world. Without the boxes, they looked into the bottomless depths of their own unknown selves.

She did not really understand, but she tried as well as she possibly could.

He went to sleep—it was long after his shift should have ended—murmuring over and over again:

"Veesey, Veesey, protect me from me! What can I do now, now, now, so that I won't do something terrible later on? What *can* I do? *Now* I'm afraid of me, Veesey, and afraid of *Old Twenty-two*. Veesey, Veesey, you've got to save me from me. What can I do now, now, now . . . ?"

She had no answer and after he slept, she slept. The yellow lights burned brightly on them both. The robot-board, reading that no human being was in the "on" position, assumed complete control of the ship and sails.

Talatashar woke them in the morning.

No one that day, nor any of the succeeding days, said anything about the boxes. There was nothing to say.

But the two men watched each other like unrelated beasts and Veesey herself began watching them in turn. Something wrong and vital had come into the room, some exuberance of life which she had never known existed. It did not smell; she could not see it; she could not reach it with her fingers. It was something real, nevertheless. Perhaps it was what people once called *danger*.

She tried to be particularly friendly to both the men. It made the feeling diminish within her. But Trece became surly and jealous and Talatashár smiled his untruthful lopsided smile.

4

Danger came to them by surprise.

Talatashar's hands were on her, pulling her out of her own sleeping-box.

She tried to fight but he was as remorseless as an engine.

He pulled her free, turned her around and let her float in the air. She would not touch the floor for a minute or two, and he obviously counted on getting control of her again. As she twisted in the air, wondering what had happened, she saw Trece's eyes rolling as they followed her movement. Only a fraction of a second later did she realize that she saw Trece too. He was tied up with emergency wire, and the wire which bound him was tied to one of the stanchions in the wall. He was more helpless than she.

A cold deep fear came upon her.

"Is this a crime?" she whispered to the empty air. "Is this what crime is, what you are doing to me?"

Talatashar did not answer her, but his hands took a firm terrible grip on her shoulders. He turned her around. She slapped at him. He slapped her back, hitting so hard that her jaw felt like a wound.

She had hurt herself accidentally a few times; the doctor-robots had always hurried to her aid. But no other human being had ever hurt her. Hurting people—why, that wasn't done, except for the games of men! It wasn't done. It couldn't happen. It did.

All in a rush she remembered what Trece had told her about *Old Twenty-two,* and about what happened to people when they lost their own outsides in space and began making up evil from the people-insides which, after a million and more years of becoming human, still followed them everywhere—even into space itself.

This was crime come back to man.

She managed to say it to Talatashar. "You are going to commit crimes? On this ship? With me?"

His expression was hard to read, with half of his face frozen in a perpetual rictus of unfulfilled laughter. They were facing each other now. Her face was feverish from the pain of his slap, but the good side of his face showed no corresponding imprint of pain from having been struck by her. It showed nothing but strength, alertness and a kind of attunement which was utterly and unimaginably wrong.

At last he answered her, and it was as if he wandered among the wonders of his own soul.

"I'm going to do what I please. What *I* please. Do you understand?"

"Why don't you just ask us?" she managed to say. "Trece and I will do anything you want. We're all alone in this little ship, millions of miles from nowhere. Why shouldn't we do what you want? Let him go. And talk to me. We'll do what you want. Anything. You have rights too "

His laugh was close to a crazy scream.

He put his face close to her and hissed at her so sharply that droplets of his spittle sprayed against her cheek and ear.

"I don't want rights!" he shouted at her. "I don't want what's mine. I don't want to do right. Do you think I haven't heard the two of you, night after night, making soft loving sounds when the cabin has gone dark? Why do you think I threw the cubes out of the ship? Why do you think I needed power?"

"I don't know," she said, sadly and meekly. She had not given up hope. As long as he was talking he might talk himself out and become reasonable again. She had heard of robots blowing their circuits, so that they had to be hunted down by other robots. But she had never thought that it might happen to people too.

Talatashar groaned. The history of man was in his groan—the anger at life, which promises so much and gives so little, and despair about time, which tricks man while it shapes him. He sat back on the air and let himself drift toward the floor of the cabin, where the magnetic carpeting drew the silky iron filaments in their clothing.

"You're thinking he'll get over this, aren't you?" said he, speaking of himself.

She nodded.

"You're thinking he'll get reasonable and let both of us alone, aren't you?"

She nodded again.

"You're thinking—Talatashar, he'll get well when we arrive at Wereld Schemering, and the doctors will fix his face, and then we'll all be happy again. That's what you're thinking, isn't it?"

She still nodded. Behind her she heard Trece give a

loud groan against his gag, but she did not dare take her eyes off Talatashar and his spoiled, horrible face.

"Well, it won't be that way, Veesey," he said. The finality in his voice was almost calm.

"Veesey, you're not going to get there. I'm going to do what I have to do. I'm going to do things to you that no one ever did in space before, and then I'm going to throw your body out the disposal door. But I'll let Trece watch it all before I kill him too. And then, do you know what I'll do?"

Some strange emotion—it was probably fear—began tightening the muscles in her throat. Her mouth had become dry. She barely managed to croak, "No, I don't know what you'll do then . . ."

Talatashar looked as though he were staring inward.

"I don't either," said he, "except that it's not something I want to do. I don't want to do it at all. It's cruel and messy and when I get through I won't have you and him to talk to. But this is something I have to do. It's justice, in a strange way. You've got to die because you're bad. And I'm bad too; but if you die, I won't be so bad."

He looked up at her brightly, almost as though he were normal. "Do you know what I'm talking about? Do you understand any of it?"

"No. No. No," Veesey stammered, but she could not help it.

Talatashar stared not at her but at the invisible face of his crime-to-come and said, almost cheerfully:

"You might as well understand. It's you who will die for it, and then him. Long ago you did me a wrong, a dirty, intolerable wrong. It wasn't the you who's sitting here. You're not big enough or smart enough to do anything as awful as the things that were done to me. It wasn't this you who did it, it was the real, true you instead. And now you are going to be cut and burned and choked and brought back with medicines and cut and choked and hurt again, as long as your body can stand it. And when your body stops, I'm going to put on an emergency suit and shove your dead body out into space with him. He can go out alive, for all I care. Without a suit, he'll last two gasps. And then part of my justice will be done. That's what people have called crime. It's just justice, private justice that comes out of the deep insides of man. Do you understand, Veesey?"

She nodded. She shook her head. She nodded again. She didn't know how to respond.

"And then there are more things which I'll have to do," he went on, with a sort of purr. "Do you know what there is outside this ship, waiting for my crime?"

She shook her head, and so he answered himself.

"There are thirty thousand people following in their pods behind this ship. I'll pull them in by two and two and I will get young girls. The others I'll throw loose in space. And with the girls I'll find out what it is—what it is I've always had to do, and never knew. Never knew, Veesey, till I found myself out in space with you."

His voice almost went dreamy as he lost himself in his own thoughts. The twisted side of his face showed its endless laugh, but the mobile side looked thoughtful and melancholy, so that she felt there was something inside him which might be understood, if only she had the quickness and the imagination to think of it.

Her throat still dry, she managed to half-whisper at him:

"Do you hate me? Why do you want to hurt me? Do you hate girls?"

"I don't hate girls," he blazed, "I hate *me*. Out here in space I found it out. You're not a person. Girls aren't people. They are soft and pretty and cute and cuddly and warm, but they have no feelings. I was handsome before my face spoiled, but that didn't matter. I always knew that girls weren't people. They're something like robots. They have all the power in the world and none of the worry. Men have to obey, men have to beg, men have to suffer, because they are built to suffer and to be sorry and to obey. All a girl has to do is to smile her pretty smile or to cross her pretty legs, and the man gives up everything he has ever wanted and fought for, just to be her slave. And then the girl"—and at this point he got to screaming again, in a high shrill shout—"and then the girl gets to be a woman and she has children, more girls to pester men, more men to be the victims of girls, more cruelty and more slaves. You're so cruel to me, Veesey! You're so cruel that you don't even know you're cruel. If you'd known how I wanted you, you'd have suffered like a person. But you didn't suffer. You're a girl. Well, you're going to find out now. You will suffer and then you will die. But you won't die until you know how men feel about women."

"Tala," she said, using the nickname they had so rarely used to him, "Tala, that's not so. I never meant you to suffer."

"Of course you didn't," he snapped. "Girls don't know what they do. That's what makes them girls. They're worse than snakes, worse than machines." He was mad, crazy-mad, in the outer deep of space. He stood up so suddenly that he shot through the air and had to catch himself on the ceiling.

A noise in the side of the cabin made them both turn for a moment. Trece was trying to break loose from his bonds. It did no good. Veesey flung herself toward Trece, but Talatashar caught her by the shoulder. He twisted her around. His eyes blazed at her out of his poor, misshapen face.

Veesey had sometime wondered what death would be like. She thought:

This is it.

Her body still fought Talatashar, there in the spaceboat cabin. Trece groaned behind his shackles and his gag. She tried to scratch at Talatashar's eyes, but the thought of death made her seem far away. Far away, inside herself.

Inside herself, where other people could not reach, ever—no matter what happened.

Out of that deep nearby remoteness, words came into her head:

Lady if a man
Tries to bother you, you can
      Think blue,
      Count two,
And look for a red shoe . . .

Thinking blue was not hard. She just imagined the
yellow cabin lights turning blue. Counting "one-two"
was the simplest thing in the world. And even with Talatashar straining to catch her free hand, she managed to
remember the beautiful, beautiful red shoes which she
had seen in *Marcia and the Moon Men*.

The lights dimmed momentarily and a huge voice
roared at them from the control board.

"Emergency, top emergency! People! People out of
repair!"

Talatashar was so astonished that he let her go.

The board whined at them like a siren. It sounded as
though the computer had become flooded with weeping.

In an utterly different voice from his impassioned
talkative rage, Talatashar looked directly at her and
asked, very soberly, "Your cube. Didn't I get your cube
too?"

There was a knocking on the wall. A knocking from
the millions of miles of emptiness outside. A knocking
out of nowhere.

A person they had never seen before stepped into the
ship, walking through the double wall as though it had
been nothing more than a streamer of mist.

It was a man. A middle-aged man, sharp of face,
strong in torso and limbs, clad in very old-style clothes.
In his belt he had a whole collection of weapons, and in
his hand a whip.

"You there," said the stranger to Talatashar, "untie
that man."

He gestured with the whip-butt toward Trece, still
bound and gagged.

Talatashar got over his surprise.

"You're a cube-ghost. You're not real!"

The whip hissed in the air and a long red welt ap-

peared on Talatashar's wrist. The drops of blood began
to float beside him in the air before he could speak
again.

Veesey could say nothing; her mind and body seemed
to be blanking out.

As she sank to the floor, she saw Talatashar shake
himself, walk over to Trece and begin untying the
knots.

When Talatashar got the gag out of Trece's mouth,
Trece spoke—not to him, but to the stranger:

"Who are you?"

"I do not exist," said the stranger, "but I can kill
you, any of you, if I wish. You had better do as I say.
Listen carefully. You too," he added, turning halfway
around and looking at Veesey. "You listen too, because
it's you who called me."

All three listened. The fight was gone out of them.
Trece rubbed his wrists and shook his hands to get the
circulation going in them again.

The stranger turned, in courtly and elegant fashion,
so that he spoke most directly to Talatashar.

"I derive from the young lady's cube. Did you notice
the lights dim? Tiga-belas left a false cube in her freeze-
box but he hid me in the ship. When she thought the
key notions at me, there was a fraction of a microvolt
which called for more power at my terminals. I am
made from the brain of some small animal, but I bear
the personality and the strength of Tiga-belas. I shall
last a billion years. When the current came on full
power, I became operative as a distortion in your
minds. I do not exist," said he, specifically addressing
himself to Talatashar, "but if I needed to take out my
imaginary pistol and to shoot you in the head with it,
my control is so strong that your bone would comply
with my command. The hole would appear in your head
and your blood and your brains would pour out, just as
much as blood is pouring from your hand just now. Look
at your hand and believe me, if you wish."

Talatashar refused to look.

The stranger went on in a very deliberate tone. "No

bullet would come from my pistol, no ray, no blast, nothing. Nothing at all. But your flesh would believe me, even if your thoughts did not. Your bone structure would believe me, whether you thought so or not. I am communicating to every separate single cell in your body, to everything which I feel to be alive. If I think *bullet* at you, your bone will pull aside for the imaginary wound. Your skin will part, your blood will pour out, your brains will splash. They will not do it by physical force but by communication from me. Communication direct, you fool. That may not be real violence, but it serves my purpose just as well. Now do you understand me? Look at your wrist."

Talatashar did not avert his eyes from the stranger. In an odd cold voice he said, "I believe you. I guess I am crazy. Are you going to kill me?"

"I don't know," said the stranger.

Trece said, "Please, are you a person or machine?"

"I don't know," said the stranger to him too.

"What's your name?" asked Veesey. "Did you get a name when they made you and sent you with us?"

"My name," said the stranger, with a bow to her, "is Sh'san."

"Glad to meet you, Sh'san," said Trece, holding out his own hand.

They shook hands.

"I felt your hand," said Trece. He looked at the other two in amazement. "I felt his hand, I really did. What were you doing out in space all this time?"

The stranger smiled. "I have work to do, not talk to make."

"What do you want us to do," said Talatashar, "now that you've taken over?"

"I haven't taken over," said Sh'san, "and you will do what you have to do. Isn't that the nature of people?"

"But, please—" said Veesey.

The stranger had vanished and the three of them were alone in the spaceboat cabin again. Trece's gag and bindings had finally drifted down to the carpet but Tala's blood hung gently in the air beside him.

Very heavily, Talatashar spoke. "Well, we're through that. Would you say I was crazy?"

"Crazy?" said Veesey. "I don't know the word."

"Damaged in the thinking," explained Trece to her. Turning to Talatashar he began to speak seriously. "I think that—" He was interrupted by the control board. Little bells rang and a sign lighted up. They all saw it. *Visitors expected* said the glowing sign.

The storage door opened and a beautiful woman came into the cabin with them. She looked at them as though she knew them all. Veesey and Trece were inquisitive and startled, but Talatashar turned white, dead white.

5

Veesey saw that the woman wore a dress of the style which had vanished a generation ago—a style now seen only in the story-boxes. There was no back to it. The lady had a bold cosmetic design fanning out from her spinal column. In front, the dress hung from the usual magnet tabs which had been inserted into the shallow fatty area of the chest, but in her case the tabs were above the clavicles, so that the dress rose high, with an air of old-fashioned prudishness. Magnet tabs were at the usual place just below the ribcage, holding the half-skirt, which was very full, in a wide sweep of unpressed pleats. The lady wore a necklace and matching bracelet of off-world coral. The lady did not even look at Veesey. She went straight to Talatashar and spoke to him with peremptory love.

"Tal, be a good boy. You've been bad."

"Mama," gasped Talatashar. "Mama, you're dead!"

"Don't argue with me," she snapped. "Be a good boy. Take care of the little girl. Where is the little girl?" She looked around and saw Veesey. "That little girl," she added, "be a good boy to *that* little girl. If you don't, you will break your mother's heart, you will ruin your mother's life, you will break your mother's heart, just like your father did. Don't make me tell you twice."

She leaned over and kissed him on the forehead, and it seemed to Veesey that both sides of the man's face were equally twisted, for that moment.

She stood up, looked around, nodded politely at Trece and Veesey, and walked back into the storage room, closing the door after her.

Talatashar plunged after her, opening the door with a bang and shutting it with a slam. Trece called after him:

"Don't stay in there too long. You'll freeze."

Trece added, speaking to Veesey, "This is something your cube is doing. That Sh'san, he's the most powerful warden I ever saw. Your psychological guard must have been a genius. And you know what's the matter with *him*?" He nodded at the closed door. "He told me once, just in general. His own mother raised him. He was born in the asteroid belt and she didn't turn him in."

"You mean, his very own mother?" said Veesey.

"Yes, his genealogical mother," said Trece.

"How *dirty*!" said Veesey. "I never heard of anything like it."

Talatashar came back into the room and said nothing to either of them.

The mother did not reappear.

But Sh'san, the eidetic man imprinted in the cube, continued to assert his authority over all three of them.

Three days later Marcia herself appeared, talked to Veesey for half an hour about her adventures with the Moon Men, and then disappeared again. Marcia never pretended that she was real. She was too pretty to be real. A thick cascade of yellow hair crowned a well-formed head; dark eyebrows arched over vivid brown eyes; and an enchantingly mischievous smile pleased Veesey, Trece and Talatashar. Marcia admitted that she was the imaginary heroine of a dramatic series from the story-boxes. Talatashar had calmed down completely after the apparition of Sh'san followed by that of his mother. He seemed anxious to get to the bottom of the phenomena. He tried to do it by asking Marcia.

She answered his questions willingly.

"What are you?" he demanded. The friendly smile on the good side of his face was more frightening than a scowl would have been.

"I'm a little girl, silly," said Marcia.

"But you're not real," he insisted.

"No," she admitted, "but are you?" She laughed a happy girlish laugh—the teen-ager tying up the bewildered adult in his own paradox.

"Look," he persisted, "you know what I mean. You're just something that Veesey saw in the story-boxes and you've come to give her imaginary red shoes."

"You can feel the shoes after I've left," said Marcia.

"That means the cube has made them out of something on this ship," said Talatashar, very triumphantly.

"Why not?" said Marcia. "I don't know about ships. I guess he does."

"But even if the shoes are real, you're not," said Talatashar. "Where do you go when you 'leave' us?"

"I don't know," said Marcia. "I came here to visit Veesey. When I go away I suppose that I will be where I was before I came."

"And where was that?"

"Nowhere," said Marcia, looking solid and real.

"Nowhere? So you admit you're nothing?"

"I will if you want me to," said Marcia, "but this conversation doesn't make much sense to me. Where were you before you were here?"

"Here? You mean in this boat? I was on Earth," said Talatashar.

"Before you were in this universe, where were you?"

"I wasn't born, so I didn't exist."

"Well," said Marcia, "it's the same with me, only a little bit different. Before I existed I didn't exist. When I exist, I'm here. I'm an echo out of Veesey's personality and I'm helping her to remember that she is a pretty young girl. I feel as real as you feel. So there!"

Marcia went back to talking about her adventures

with the Moon Men and Veesey was fascinated to hear all the things they had had to leave out of the story-box version. When Marcia was through, she shook hands with the two men, gave Veesey a little peck of a kiss on her left cheek and walked through the hull into the gnawing emptiness of space, marked only by the starless rhomboids of the sails which cut off part of the heavens from view.

Talatashar pounded his fist in his other, open hand. "Science has gone too far. They will kill us with their precautions."

Trece said, deadly calm, "And what might you have done?"

Talatashar fell into a gloomy silence.

And on the tenth day after the apparitions began, they ended. The power of the cube drew itself into a whole thunderbolt of decision. Apparently the cube and the ship's computers had somehow filled in each other's data.

The person who came in this time was a space captain, gray, wrinkled, erect, tanned by the radiation of a thousand worlds.

"You know who I am," he said.

"Yes, sir, a captain," said Veesey.

"I don't know you," said Talatashar, "and I'm not sure I believe in you."

"Has your hand healed?" asked the captain, grimly.

Talatashar fell silent.

The captain called them to attention. "Listen. You are not going to live long enough to get to the stars on your present course. I want Trece to set the macro-chronography for intervals of ninety-five years, and then I want to watch while he gives two of you at a time five years on watch. That will do to set the sails, check the tangling of the pod lines, and send out report beacons. This ship should have a sailor, but there is not enough equipment to turn one of you into a sailor, so we'll have to take a chance on the robot controls while all three of you sleep in your freezebeds. Your sailor died of a blood clot and the robots pushed him out of the cabin before they woke you—"

Trece winced. "I thought he had committed suicide."

"Not a bit," said the captain. "Now listen. You'll get through in about three sleeps if you obey orders. If you don't, you'll never get there."

"It doesn't matter about me," said Talatashar, "but this little girl has got to get to Wereld Schemering while she still has some life. One of your blasted apparitions told me to take care of her, but the idea is a good one, anyhow."

"Me too," said Trece. "I didn't realize that she was just a kid until I saw her talking to that other kid Marcia. Maybe I'll have a daughter like her some day."

The captain said nothing to these comments but gave them the full, happy smile of an old, wise man.

An hour later they were through with the checkup of the boat. The three were ready to go to their separate freezebeds. The captain was getting ready to make his farewell.

Talatashar spoke up. "Sir, I can't help asking it, but who are you?"

"A captain," said the captain promptly.

"You know what I mean," said Tala wearily.

The captain seemed to be looking inside himself. "I am a temporary, artificial personality created out of your minds by the personality which you call Sh'san. Sh'san is on the ship, but hidden from you, so that you will do him no harm. Sh'san was imprinted with the personality of a man, a real man, by the name of Tigabelas. Sh'san was also imprinted with the personalities of five or six good space officers, just in case those skills might be needed. A small amount of static electricity keeps Sh'san on the alert, and when he is in the right position, he has a triggering mechanism which can call for more current from the ship's supply."

"But what *is* he? What *are* you?" Talatashar kept on, almost pleading. "I was about to commit a terrible crime and you ghosts came in and saved me. Are you imaginary? Are you real?"

"That's philosophy. I'm made by science. I wouldn't know," said the captain.

"Please," said Veesey, "could you tell us what it seems like to you? Not what it is. What it seems like."

The captain sagged, as though the discipline had gone out of him—as though he suddenly felt terribly old. "When I'm talking and doing things, I suppose that I feel about like any other space captain. If I stop to think about it, I find myself pretty upsetting. I know that I'm just an echo in your minds, combined with the experience and wisdom which has gone into the cube. So I guess that I do what real people do. I just don't think about it very much. I mind my business." He stiffened and straightened and was himself again. "My own business," he repeated.

"And Sh'san," said Trece, "how do you feel about him?"

A look of awe—almost a look of terror—came upon the captain's face. "He? Oh, him." The tone of wonder enriched his voice and made it echo in the small cabin of the spaceboat. "Sh'san. He is the thinker of all thinking, the 'to be' of being, the doer of doings. He is powerful beyond your strongest imagination. He makes me come living out of your living minds. In fact," said the captain with a final snarl, "he is a dead mouse-brain laminated with plastic and I have no idea at all of who *I* am. Good night to you all!"

The captain set his cap on his head and walked straight through the hull. Veesey ran to a viewpoint but there was nothing outside the ship. Nothing. Certainly no captain.

"What can we do," said Talatashar, "but obey?"

They obeyed. They climbed into their freezebeds. Talatashar attached the correct electrodes to Veesey and to Trece before he went to his bed and attached his own. They called to each other pleasantly as the lids came down.

They slept.

6

At destination, the people of Wereld Schemering did the ingathering of pods, sails and ship themselves. They did not wake the sleepers till they had them all assured of safety on the ground.

They woke the three cabinmates together. Veesey, Trece and Talatashar were so busy answering questions about the dead sailor, about the repaired sails and about their problems on the trip that they did not have time to talk to each other. Veesey saw that Talatashar seemed to be very handsome. The port doctors had done something to restore his face, so that he seemed a strangely dignified young-old man. At last Trece had a chance to talk to her.

"Good-bye, kid," he said. "Go to school for a while here and then find yourself a good man. I'm sorry."

"Sorry for what?" she said, a terrible fear rising within her.

"For smooching around with you before that trouble came. You're just a kid. But you're a good kid." He ran his fingers through her hair, turned on his heel and was gone.

She stood, utterly forlorn, in the middle of the room. She wished that she could weep. What use had she been on the trip?

Talatashar had come up to her unnoticed.

He held out his hand. She took it.

"Give it time, child," said he.

Is it *child* again? she thought to herself. To him she said, politely, "Maybe we'll see each other again. This is a pretty small world."

His face lit up in an oddly agreeable smile. It made such a wonderful difference for the paralysis to be gone from one side. He did not look old at all, not really old.

His voice took on urgency. "Veesey, remember that I remember. I remember what almost happened. I remember what we thought we saw. Maybe we did see all those things. We won't see them on the ground. But I want you to remember this. You saved us all. Me too. And Trece, and the thirty thousand out behind."

"Me?" she said. "What did I do?"

"You tuned in help. You let Sh'san work. It all came through you. If you hadn't been honest and kind and friendly, if you hadn't been terribly intelligent, no cube could have worked. That wasn't any dead mouse working miracles on us. It was your mind and your own goodness that saved us. The cube just added the sound effects. I tell you, if you hadn't been along, two dead men would be sailing off into the Big Nothing with thirty thousand spoiling bodies trailing along behind. You saved us all. You may not know how you did it, but you did."

An official tapped him on the arm; Tala said, firmly but politely, to him, "Just a moment."

"That's it, I guess," he said to her.

A contrary spirit seized her; she had to speak, though she risked unhappiness by talking. "And what you said about girls . . . then . . . that time?"

"I remember it." His face twisted almost back to its old ugliness for a moment. "I remember it. But I was wrong. Wrong."

She looked at him and she thought in her own mind about the *blue* sky, about the *two* doors behind them, and about the *red shoes* in her luggage. Nothing miraculous happened. No Sh'san, no voices, no magic cubes.

Except that he turned around, came back to her and said, "Look. Let's make sure that we see each other next week. These people at the desk can tell us where we are going to be, so that we'll find each other. Let's pester them."

Together they went to the immigration desk.

The Colonel Came Back from the Nothing-at-All

1. The Naked and Alone

WE LOOKED THROUGH the peephole of the hospital door.

Colonel Harkening had torn off his pajamas again and lay naked face down on the floor.

His body was rigid.

His face was turned sharply to the left so that the neck muscles showed. His right arm stuck out straight from the body. The elbow formed a right angle, with the forearm and hand pointing straight upward. The left arm also pointed straight out, but in this case the hand and forearm pointed downward in line with the body.

The legs were in the grotesque parody of a running position.

Except that Colonel Harkening wasn't running.

He was lying flat on the floor.

Flat, as though he were trying to squeeze himself out of the third dimension and to lie in two planes only. Grosbeck stood back and gave Timofeyev his turn at the peephole.

"I still say he needs a naked woman," said Grosbeck. Grosbeck always went in for the elementals.

We had atropine, surgital, a whole family of the digitalinids, assorted narcotics, electrotherapy, hydrotherapy, subsonictherapy, temperature shock, audiovisual shock, mechanical hypnosis, and gas hypnosis.

None of these had had the least effect on Colonel Harkening.

When we picked the colonel up he tried to lie down.

When we put clothes on him he tore them off.

We had already brought his wife to see him. She had wept because the world had acclaimed her husband a hero, dead in the vast, frightening emptiness of space. His miraculous return had astonished seven continents on Earth and the settlements on Venus and Mars.

Harkening had been test pilot for the new device which had been developed by a team at the Research Office of the Instrumentality.

They called it a chronoplast, though a minority held out for the term planoform.

The theory of it was completely beyond me, though the purpose was simple enough. Crudely stated, the theory sought to compress living, material bodies into a two-dimensional frame while skipping the living body and its material adjuncts through two dimensions only to some inconceivably remote point in space. As our technology now stood it would have taken us a century at the least to reach Alpha Centauri, the nearest star.

Desmond, the Harkening, who held the titular rank of colonel under the Chiefs of the Instrumentality, was one of the best space navigators we had. His eyes were perfect, his mind cool, his body superb, his experience first-rate: What more could we ask?

Humanity had sent him out in a minute space ship not much larger than the elevator in an ordinary private home. Somewhere between Earth and the Moon with millions of televideo watchers following his course, he had disappeared.

Presumably he had turned on the chronoplast and had been the first man to planoform.

We never saw his craft again.

But we found the colonel, all right.

He lay naked in the middle of Central Park in New York, which lay about a hundred miles west of the Ancient Ruins.

He lay in the grotesque position in which we had just observed him in the hospital cell, forming a sort of human starfish.

Four months had passed and we had made very little progress with the colonel.

It was not much trouble keeping him alive since we fed him by massive rectal and intravenous administrations of the requisites of medical survival. He did not oppose us. He did not fight except when we put clothes on him or tried to keep him too long out of the horizontal plane.

When kept upright too long he would awaken just enough to go into a mad, silent, gloating rage, fighting the attendants, the straitjacket, and anything else that got in his way.

We had had one hellish time in which the poor man suffered for an entire week, bound firmly in canvas and struggling every minute of the week to get free and to resume his nightmarish position.

The wife's visit last week had done no more good than I expected Grosbeck's suggestion to do this week.

The colonel paid no more attention to her than he paid to us doctors.

If he had come back from stars, come back from the cold beyond the Moon, come back from all the terrors of the Up-and-Out, come back by means unknown to any man living, come back in a form not himself and nevertheless himself, how could we expect the crude stimuli of previous human knowledge to awaken him?

When Timofeyev and Grosbeck turned back to me after looking at him for the some-thousandth time, I told them I did not think we could make any progress with the case by ordinary means.

"Let's start all over again. This man is here. He can't be here because nobody can come back from the stars, mother-naked in his own skin, and land from outer space in Central Park so gently that he shows not the slightest abrasion from a fall. Therefore, he isn't in that room, you and I aren't talking about anything, and there isn't any problem. Is that right?"

"No," they chorused simultaneously.

I turned on Grosbeck as the more obdurate of the two. "Have it your way then. He is there, major premise. He can't be there, minor premise. We don't exist. Q.E.D. That suit you any better?"

"No, sir and doctor, Chief and Leader," said Grosbeck, sticking to the courtesies even though he was angry. "You are trying to destroy the entire context of this
case, and, by doing so, are trying to lead us even further
into unorthodox methods of treatment. Lord and
Heaven, sir! we can't go any further that way. This
man is crazy. It doesn't matter how he got into Central
Park. That's a problem for the engineers. It's not a
medical problem. His craziness *is* a medical problem.
We can try to cure it, or we can try not to cure it. But
we won't get anywhere if we mix the medicine with the
engineering—"

"It's not that bad," interjected Timofeyev gently.

As the older of my associates he had the right to address me by my short title. He turned to me. "I agree
with you, sir and doctor Anderson, that the engineering
is mixed up with this man's mental and physical state.
After all, he is the first person to go out in a chronoplast and neither we nor the engineers nor anybody else
has the faintest idea of what happened to him. The engineers can't find the machine, and we can't find his
consciousness. Let's leave the machine to the engineers,
but let's persevere on the medical side of the case."

I said nothing, waiting for them to let off steam until
they were prepared to reason with me and not just shout
at me in their desperation.

They looked at me, keeping their silence grudgingly,
and trying to make me take the initiative in the unpleasant case.

"Open the cell door," I said. "He's not going to run
away in that position. All he wants to do is be flat."

"Flatter than a Scotch pancake in a Chinese hell,"
said Grosbeck, "and you're not going to get anywhere
by leaving him in his flatness. He was a human being
once and the only way to make a human being be a
human being is to appeal to the human being side of
him, not to some imaginary flat side that got thrown
into him while he was out—wherever he was."

Grosbeck himself smiled a lopsided grin; he was capable of seeing the humor of his own vehemence at

times. "Shall we say he was out *underneath space,* sir and doctor, Chief and Leader?"

"That's a good way to put it," I said. "You can try your naked woman idea later on, but I frankly don't think it's going to do any good. That man isn't corticating at a level above that of the simplest invertebrates except when he's in that grotesque position. If he's not thinking, he's not seeing. If he's not seeing, he won't see a woman any more than anything else. There's nothing wrong with the body. The trouble lies in the brain. I still see it as a problem of getting into the brain."

"Or the soul," breathed Timofeyev, whose full name was Herbert Hoover Timofeyev, and who came from the most religious part of Russia. "You can't leave the soul out sometimes, doctor . . ."

We had entered the cell and stood there looking helplessly at the naked man.

The patient breathed very quietly. His eyes were open; we had not been able to make the eyes blink, even with a photoflash. The patient acquired a grotesque and elementary humanity when he was taken out of his flat position. His mind reached, intellectually speaking, a high point no higher than that of a terrorized, panicked, momentarily deranged squirrel. When clothed or out of position he fought madly, hitting indiscriminately at objects and persons.

Poor Colonel Harkening! We three were supposed to be the best doctors on Earth, and we could do nothing for him.

We had even tried to study his way of fighting to see whether the muscular and eye movements involved in the struggle revealed where he had been or what experiences he had undergone. Even that was fruitless. He fought something after the fashion of a nine-month-old infant, using his adult strength, but using it indiscriminately.

We never got a sound out of him.

He breathed hard as he fought. His sputum bubbled. Froth appeared on his lips. His hands made clumsy movements to tear away the shirts and robes and walkers which we put on him. Sometimes his fingernails or toenails tore his own skin as he got free of gloves or shoes.

He always went back to the same position:

On the floor.

Face down.

Arms and legs in swastika form.

There he was back from outer space. He was the first man to return, and yet he had not really returned.

As we stood there helpless, Timofeyev made the first serious suggestion we had gotten that day.

"Do you dare to try a secondary telepath?"

Grosbeck looked shocked.

I dared to give the subject thought. Secondary telepaths were in bad repute because they were supposed to come into the hospitals and have their telepathic capacities removed once it had been proved that they were not true telepaths with a real capacity for complete interchange.

Under the Ancient Law many of them could and did elude us.

With their dangerous part-telepathic capacities they took up charlatanism and fakery of the worst kind, pretending to talk with the dead, precipitating neurotics into psychotics, healing a few sick people and bungling ten other cases for each case that they did heal, and, in general, disturbing the good order of society.

And yet, if everything else had failed . . .

2. The Secondary Telepath

A day later we were back in Harkening's hospital cell, almost in the same position.

The three of us stood around the naked body on the floor.

There was a fourth person with us, a girl.

Timofeyev had found her. She was a member of his own religious group, the Post-Soviet Orthodox Eastern Quakers. You could tell when they spoke· Anglic because they used the word "thou" from the Ancient English Language instead of the word "thee."

Timofeyev looked at me.

I nodded at him very quietly.

He turned to the girl. "Canst thou help him, sister?"

The child was scarcely more than twelve. She was a little girl with a long, lean face, a soft, mobile mouth, quick gray-green eyes, a mop of tan hair that fell over her shoulders. She had expressive, tapering hands. She showed no shock at all at the sight of the naked man lost in the depths of his insanity.

She knelt down on the floor and spoke gently directly into the ear of Colonel Harkening.

"Canst thou hear me, brother? I have come to help thee. I am thy sister Liana. I am thy sister under the love of God. I am thy sister born of the flesh of man. I am thy sister under the sky. I am thy sister come to help thee. I am thy sister, brother. I am thy sister. Waken a little and I can help thee. Waken a little to the words of thy sister. Waken a little for the love and the hope. Waken to let the love come in. Waken to let the love awaken thee further. Waken to let mankind get thee. Waken to return again, return again to the realm of man. The realm of man is a friendly realm. The friendship of man is a friendly thing. Thy friend is thy sister, by the name of Liana. Thy friend is here. Waken a little to the words of thy friend . . ."

As she talked on I saw that she made a gentle movement with her left hand, motioning us out of the room.

I nodded to my two colleagues, jerking my head to indicate that we should step out in the corridor. We stepped just beyond the door so that we could still look in.

The child went on with her endless chant.

Grosbeck stood rigid, glaring at her as though she were an intrusion into the field of regular medicine. Timofeyev tried to look sweet, benevolent, and spiritual; he forgot and, instead, just looked excited. I got very tired and began to wonder when I could interrupt the

child. It did not seem to me that she was getting anywhere.

She herself settled the matter.

She burst into tears.

She went on talking as she wept, her voice broken
with sobs, the tears from her eyes pouring down her
cheeks and dropping on the face of the colonel just below her face.

The colonel might as well have been made of porce-
lainized concrete.

I could see his breathing, but the pupils of his eyes
did not move. He was no more alive than he had been
all these weeks. No more alive, and no less alive.

No change. At last the girl gave up her weeping and
talking and came out to the corridor to us.

She spoke to me directly. "Art thou a brave man,
Anderson, sir and doctor, Chief and Leader?"

It was a silly question. How does anybody answer a
question like that? All I could say was "I suppose so.
What do you want to do?"

"I want you three," said she as solemnly as a witch.
"I want you three to wear the helmet of the pinlighters
and ride with me into hell itself. That soul is lost. It is
frozen by a force I do not know, frozen out beyond the
stars, where the stars caught it and made it their own, so
that the poor man and brother that thou seest is truly
among us, but his soul weeps in the unholy pleasure between the stars where it is lost to the mercy of God and
to the friendship of mankind. Wilt thou, O brave man,
sir and doctor, Chief and Leader, ride with me to hell
itself?"

What could I say but yes?

3. The Return

Late that night we made the return from the Nothing-
at-All. There were five pinlighters' helmets, crude
things, mechanical correctives to natural telepathy, devices to throw the synapses of one mind into another so
that all five of us could think the same thoughts.

It was the first time that I had been in contact with the minds of Grosbeck and Timofeyev. They surprised me.

Timofeyev really was clean all the way through, as clean and simple as washed linen. He was really a very simple man. The urgencies and pressures of his everyday life did not go down to the insides.

Grosbeck was very different. He was as alive, as cackling, and as violent as a whole barnyard full of fowl: His mind was dirty in spots, clean in others. It was bright, smelly, alive, vivid, moving.

I caught an echo of my own mind from them. To Timofeyev I seemed cold, high, icy, and mysterious; to Grosbeck I looked like a solid lump of coal. He couldn't see into my mind very much and he didn't even want to.

We all sensed out toward Liana, and in reaching for the sense-of-the-mind of Liana we encountered the mind of the colonel . . .

Never have I encountered something so terrible.

It was raw pleasure.

As a doctor I have seen pleasure—the pleasure of morphine which destroys, the pleasure of fennine which kills and ruins, even the pleasure of the electrode buried in the living brain.

As a doctor I had been required to see the wickedest of men kill themselves under the law. It was a simple thing we did. We put a thin wire directly into the pleasure center of the brain. The bad man then put his head near an electric field of the right phase and voltage. It was simple enough. He died of pleasure in a few hours.

This was worse.

This pleasure was not in human form.

Liana was somewhere near and I caught her thoughts as she said, "We must go there, sirs and doctors, Chiefs and Leaders.

"We must go there together, the four of us, go to where no man was, go to the Nothing-at-All, go to the hope and the heart of the pain, go to the pain which return may this man, go to the power which is greater than space, go to the power which has sent him home,

go to the place which is not a place, find the force
which is not a force, force the force which is not a force
to give this heart and spare it back to us.

"Come with me if you come at all. Come with me to
the end of things. Come with me—"

Suddenly there was a flash as of sheet lightning in
our minds.

It was bright lightning, bright, delicate, multicolored,
gentle. Suffusing everything, it was like a cascade of
pure color, pastel in hue, but intense in its brightness.
The light came.

The light came, I say.

Strange.

And it was gone.

That was all.

The experience was so quick that it could hardly be
called instantaneous. It seemed to happen less than in-
stantaneously, if you can imagine that. We all five felt
that we had been befriended, looked at. *We felt that we
had been made the toys or the pets of some gigantic
form of life immensely beyond the limits of human imagination, and that that life in looking at the four of
us—the three doctors and Liana—had seen us and the
colonel and had realized that the colonel needed to go
back to his own kind.*

Because it was five, not four, who stood up.

The colonel was trembling, but he was sane. He was
alive. He was human again. He said very weakly:

"Where am I? Is this an Earth hospital?"

And then he fell into Timofeyev's arms.

Liana was already gliding out the door.

I followed her out.

She turned on me. "Sir and doctor, Chief and
Leader, all I ask is no thanks, and no money, no notice
and no word of what has happened. My powers come
from the goodness of the Lord's grace and from the
friendliness of mankind. I should not intrude into the
field of medicine. I should not have come if thy friend
Timofeyev had not asked me as a matter of common

mercy. Claim the credit for thy hospital, sir and doctor, Chief and Leader, but thou and thy friends should forget me."

I stammered at her, "But the reports? . . ."

"Write the reports any way thou wishes, but mention me not."

"But our patient. He is our patient, too, Liana."

She smiled a smile of great sweetness, of girlish and childish friendliness. "If he need me, I shall come to him . . ."

The world was better, but not much the wiser.

The chronoplast spaceship was never found. The colonel's return was never explained. The colonel never left Earth again. All he knew was that he had pushed a button out somewhere near the Moon and that he had then awakened in a hospital after four months had been unaccountably lost.

And all the world knew was that he and his wife had unaccountably adopted a strange but beautiful little girl, poor in family, but rich in the mild generosity of her own spirit.

From Gustible's Planet

SHORTLY AFTER THE celebration of the four thousandth anniversary of the opening of space, Angary J. Gustible discovered Gustible's planet. The discovery turned out to be a tragic mistake.

Gustible's planet was inhabited by highly intelligent life forms. They had moderate telepathic powers. They immediately mind-read Angary J. Gustible's entire mind and life history, and embarrassed him very deeply by making up an opera concerning his recent divorce.

The climax of the opera portrayed his wife throwing a teacup at him. This created an unfavorable impression concerning Earth culture, and Angary J. Gustible, who held a reserve commission as a Subchief of the Instrumentality, was profoundly embarrassed to find that it was not the higher realities of Earth which he had conveyed to these people, but the unpleasant intimate facts.

As negotiations proceeded, other embarrassments developed.

In physical appearance the inhabitants of Gustible's planet, who called themselves Apicians, resembled nothing more than oversize ducks, ducks four feet to four feet six in height. At their wing tips, they had developed juxtaposed thumbs. They were paddle-shaped and sufficed to feed the Apicians.

Gustible's planet matched Earth in several respects: in the dishonesty of the inhabitants, in their enthusiasm for good food, in their instant capacity to understand the human mind. Before Gustible began to get ready to go back to Earth, he discovered that the Apicians had copied his ship. There was no use hiding this fact. They had copied it in such detail that the discovery of Gustible's planet meant the simultaneous discovery of Earth . . .

By the Apicians.

The implications of this tragic development did not show up until the Apicians followed him home. They had a planoforming ship capable of traveling in nonspace just as readily as his.

The most important feature of Gustible's planet was its singularly close match to the biochemistry of Earth. The Apicians were the first intelligent life forms ever met by human beings who were at once capable of smelling and enjoying everything which human beings smelled and enjoyed, capable of following any human music with forthright pleasure and capable of eating and drinking everything in sight.

The very first Apicians on Earth were greeted by somewhat alarmed ambassadors who discovered that an appetite for Munich beer, Camembert cheese, tortillas and enchiladas, as well as the better grades of chow mein, far transcended any serious cultural, political or strategic interests which the new visitors might have.

Arthur Djohn, a Lord of the Instrumentality who was acting for this particular matter, delegated an Instrumentality agent named Calvin Dredd as the chief diplomatic officer of Earth to handle the matter.

Dredd approached one Schmeckst, who seemed to be the Apician leader. The interview was an unfortunate one.

Dredd began by saying, "Your Exalted Highness, we are delighted to welcome you to Earth—"

Schmeckst said, "Are those edible?" and proceeded to eat the plastic buttons from Calvin Dredd's formal coat, even before Dredd could say though not edible they were attractive.

Schmeckst said, "Don't try to eat those, they are really not very good."

Dredd, looking at his coat sagging wide open, said, "May I offer you some food?"

Schmeckst said, "Indeed, yes."

And while Schmeckst ate an Italian dinner, a Peking dinner, a red-hot peppery Szechuanese dinner, a Japanese sukiyaki dinner, two British breakfasts, a smorgasbord and four complete servings of diplomatic-level Russian zakouska, he listened to the propositions of the Instrumentality of Earth.

These did not impress him. Schmeckst was intelligent despite his gross and offensive eating habits. He pointed out: "We two worlds are equal in weapons. We can't fight. Look," said he to Calvin Dredd in a threatening tone.

Calvin Dredd braced himself, as he had learned to do. Schmeckst also braced him.

For an instant Dredd did not know what had happened. Then he realized that in putting his body into a rigid and controlled posture he had played along with the low-grade but manipulable telepathic powers of the visitors. He was frozen rigid till Schmeckst laughed and released him.

Schmeckst said, "You see, we are well matched. I can freeze you. Nothing short of utter desperation could get you out of it. If you try to fight us, we'll lick you. We are going to move in here and live with you. We have enough room on our planet. You can come and live with us too. We would like to hire a lot of those cooks of yours. You'll simply have to divide space with us, and that's all there is to it."

That really was all there was to it. Arthur Djohn reported back to the Lords of the Instrumentality that, for the time being, nothing could be done about the disgusting people from Gustible's planet.

They kept their greed within bounds—by their standards. A mere seventy-two thousand of them swept the Earth, hitting every wine shop, dining hall, snack bar, soda bar and pleasure center in the world. They ate popcorn, alfalfa, raw fruit, live fish, birds on the wing, prepared foods, cooked and canned foods, food concentrates, and assorted medicines.

Outside of an enormous capacity to hold many times what the human body could tolerate in the way of food, they showed very much the same effects as persons. Thousands of them got various local diseases, sometimes called by such undignified names as the Yangtze rapids, Delhi belly, the Roman groanin', or the like. Other thousands became ill and had to relieve themselves in the fashion of ancient emperors. Still they came.

Nobody liked them. Nobody disliked them enough to wish a disastrous war.

Actual trade was minimal. They bought large quantities of foodstuffs, paying in rare metals. But their economy on their own planet produced very little which the world itself wanted. The cities of mankind had long since developed to a point of comfort and corruption where a relatively monocultural being, such as the citizens of Gustible's planet, could not make much impression. The word "Apician" came to have unpleasant connotations of bad manners, greediness and prompt payment. Prompt payment was considered rude in a credit society, but after all it was better than not being paid at all.

The tragedy of the relationship of the two groups came from the unfortunate picnic of the lady Ch'ao, who prided herself on having ancient Chinesian blood. She decided that it would be possible to satiate Schmeckst and the other Apicians to a point at which they would be able to listen to reason. She arranged a feast which, for quality and quantity, had not been seen since previous historic times, long before the many interruptions of war, collapse, and rebuilding of culture. She searched the museums of the world for recipes.

The dinner was set forth on the telescreens of the entire world. It was held in a pavilion built in the old Chinesian style. A soaring dream of dry bamboo and paper walls, the festival building had a thatched roof in the true ancient fashion. Paper lanterns with real candles illuminated the scene. The fifty selected Apician guests gleamed like ancient idols. Their feathers shone in the light and they clicked their paddlelike thumbs readily as they spoke, telepathically and fluently, in any Earth language which they happened to pick out of the heads of their hearers.

The tragedy was fire. Fire struck the pavilion, wrecked the dinner. The lady Ch'ao was rescued by Calvin Dredd. The Apicians fled. All of them escaped, all but one. Schmeckst himself. Schmeckst suffocated.

He let out a telepathic scream which was echoed in the living voices of all the human beings, other Apicians and animals within reach, so that the television viewers of the world caught a sudden cacophony of birds shrilling, dogs barking, cats yowling, otters screeching and one lone panda letting out a singularly high grunt. Then Schmeckst perished. The pity of it . . .

The Earth leaders stood about, wondering how to solve the tragedy. On the other side of the world, the Lords of the Instrumentality watched the scene. What they saw was amazing and horrible. Calvin Dredd, cold, disciplined agent that he was, approached the ruins of the pavilion. His face was twisted in an expression which they had difficulty in understanding. It was only after he licked his lips for the fourth time and they saw a ribbon of drool running down his chin that they realized he had gone mad with appetite. The lady Ch'ao followed close behind, drawn by some remorseless force.

She was out of her mind. Her eyes gleamed. She stalked like a cat. In her left hand she held a bowl and chopsticks.

The viewers all over the world watching the screen could not understand the scene. Two alarmed and dazed Apicians followed the humans, wondering what was going to happen.

Calvin Dredd made a sudden reach. He pulled out the body of Schmeckst.

The fire had finished Schmeckst. Not a feather remained on him. And then the flash fire, because of the peculiar dryness of the bamboo and the paper and the thousands upon thousands of candles, had baked him. The television operator had an inspiration. He turned on the smell-control.

Throughout the planet Earth, where people had gathered to watch this unexpected and singularly interesting tragedy, there swept a smell which mankind had forgotten. It was an essence of roast duck.

Beyond all imagining, it was the most delicious smell that any human being had ever smelled. Millions upon millions of human mouths watered. Throughout the world people looked away from their sets to see if there were any Apicians in the neighborhood. Just as the Lords of the Instrumentality ordered the disgusting scene cut off, Calvin Dredd and the lady Ch'ao began eating the roast Apician, Schmeckst.

Within twenty-four hours most of the Apicians on Earth had been served, some with cranberry sauce, others baked, some fried Southern style. The serious

leaders of Earth dreaded the consequences of such uncivilized conduct. Even as they wiped their lips and asked
for one more duck sandwich, they felt that this behavior
was difficult beyond all imagination.

The blocks that the Apicians had been able to put on
human action did not operate when they were applied
to human beings who, looking at an Apician, went deep
into the recesses of their personality and were animated
by a mad hunger which transcended all civilization.

The Lords of the Instrumentality managed to round
up Schmeckst's deputy and a few other Apicians and to
send them back to their ship.

The soldiers watching them licked their lips. The
captain tried to see if he could contrive an accident as
he escorted his state visitors. Unfortunately, tripping
Apicians did not break their necks, and the Apicians
kept throwing violent mind-blocks at human beings in
an attempt to save themselves.

One of the Apicians was so undiplomatic as to ask
for a chicken salad sandwich and almost lost a wing,
raw and alive, to a soldier whose appetite had been re-
stimulated by reference to food.

The Apicians went back, the few survivors. They
liked Earth well enough and Earth food was delicious,
but it was a horrible place when they considered the
cannibalistic human beings who lived there—so cannibalistic that they ate ducks!

The Lords of the Instrumentality were relieved to
note that when the Apicians left they closed the space
lane behind them. No one quite knows how they closed
it, or what defenses they had. Mankind, salivating and
ashamed, did not push the pursuit hotly. Instead, people
tried to make up chicken, duck, goose, Cornish hen, pi-
geon, sea-gull, and other sandwiches to duplicate the incomparable taste of a genuine inhabitant of Gustible's
planet. None were quite authentic and people, in their
right minds, were not uncivilized enough to invade another world solely for getting the inhabitants as tidbits.

The Lords of the Instrumentality were happy to report to one another and to the rest of the world at their

next meeting that the Apicians had managed to close
Gustible's planet altogether, had had no further interest
in dealing with Earth and appeared to possess just
enough of a technological edge on human beings to stay
concealed from the eyes and the appetites of men.

Save for that, the Apicians were almost forgotten. A
confidential secretary of the Office of Interstellar Trade
was astonished when the frozen intelligences of a meth-
ane planet ordered forty thousand cases of Munich
beer. He suspected them of being jobbers, not consum-
ers. But on the instructions of his superiors he kept the
matter confidential and allowed the beer to be shipped.

It undoubtedly went to Gustible's planet, but they did
not offer any of their own citizens in exchange.

The matter was closed. The napkins were folded.
Trade and diplomacy were at an end.

Drunkboat

PERHAPS IT IS the saddest, maddest, wildest story in the
whole long history of space. It is true that no one else
had ever done anything like it before, to travel at such a
distance, and at such speeds, and by such means. The
hero looked like such an ordinary man—when people
looked at him for the first time. The second time, ah!
that was different.

And the heroine. Small she was, and ash-blonde, intelligent, perky, and hurt. Hurt—yes, that's the right
word. She looked as though she needed comforting or
helping, even when she was perfectly all right. Men felt
more like men when she was near. Her name was Elizabeth.

Who would have thought that her name would ring

loud and clear in the wild vomiting nothing which made up space[3]?

He took an old, old rocket, of an ancient design. With it he outflew, outfled, outjumped all the machines which had ever existed before. You might almost think that he went so fast that he shocked the great vaults of the sky, so that the ancient poem might have been written for him alone. "All the stars threw down their spears and watered heaven with their tears."

Go he did, so fast, so far that people simply did not believe it at first. They thought it was a joke told by men, a farce spun forth by rumor, a wild story to while away the summer afternoon.

We know his name now.

And our children and their children will know it for always.

Rambo. Artyr Rambo of Earth Four.

But he followed his Elizabeth where no space was. He went where men could not go, had not been, did not dare, would not think.

He did all this of his own free will.

Of course people thought it was a joke at first, and got to making up silly songs about the reported trip.

"Dig me a hole for that reeling feeling! . . . " sang one.

"Push me the call for the umber number! . . ." sang another.

"Where is the ship of the ochre joker? . . ." sang a third.

Then people everywhere found it was true. Some stood stock still and got gooseflesh. Others turned quickly to everyday things. Space[3] had been found, and it had been pierced. Their world would never be the same again. The solid rock had become an open door.

Space itself, so clean, so empty, so tidy, now looked like a million million light-years of tapioca pudding—gummy, mushy, sticky, not fit to breathe, not fit to swim in.

How did it happen?

Everybody took the credit, each in his own different way.

1

"He came for me," said Elizabeth. "I died and he came for me because the machines were making a mess of my life when they tried to heal my terrible, useless death."

2

"I went myself," said Rambo. "They tricked me and lied to me and fooled me, but I took the boat and I became the boat and I got there. Nobody made me do it. I was angry, but I went. And I came back, didn't I?"

He too was right, even when he twisted and whined on the green grass of earth, his ship lost in a space so terribly far and strange that it might have been beneath his living hand, or might have been half a galaxy away.

How can anybody tell, with space³?

It was Rambo who got back, looking for his Elizabeth. He loved her. So the trip was his, and the credit his.

3

But the Lord Crudelta said, many years later, when he spoke in a soft voice and talked confidentially among friends, "The experiment was mine. I designed it. I picked Rambo. I drove the selectors mad, trying to find a man who would meet those specifications. And I had that rocket built to the old, old plans. It was the sort of thing which human beings first used when they jumped out of the air a little bit, leaping like flying fish from one wave to the next and already thinking that they were eagles. If I had used one of the regular planoform ships, it would have disappeared with a sort of reverse gurgle, leaving space milky for a little bit while it faded into nastiness and obliteration. But I did not risk that. I put the rocket on a launching pad. *And the launching pad itself was an interstellar ship!* Since we were using an ancient rocket, we did it up right, with the old, old writing, mysterious letters printed all over the machine. We even had the name of our Organization—I and O and M, for 'the Instrumentality of Mankind'—written on it good and sharp.

"How would I know," went on the Lord Crudelta, "that we would succeed more than we wanted to succeed, that Rambo would tear space itself loose from its hinges and leave that ship behind, just because he loved Elizabeth so sharply much, so fiercely much?"

Crudelta sighed.

"I know it and I don't know it. I'm like that ancient man who tried to take a water boat the wrong way around the planet Earth and found a new world instead. Columbus, he was called. And the land, that was Australia or America or something like that. That's what I did. I sent Rambo out in that ancient rocket and he found a way through space-three. Now none of us will ever know who might come bulking through the floor or take shape out of the air in front of us."

Crudelta added, almost wistfully, "What's the use of telling the story? Everybody knows it, anyhow. My part in it isn't very glorious. Now the end of it, that's pretty. The bungalow by the waterfall and all the wonderful children that other people gave to them, you could write a poem about that. But the next to the end, how he showed up at the hospital helpless and insane, looking for his own Elizabeth. That was sad and eerie, that was frightening. I'm glad it all came to the happy ending with the bungalow by the waterfall, but it took a crashing long time to get there. And there are parts of it that we will never quite understand, the naked skin against naked space, the eyeballs riding something much faster than light ever was. Do you know what an *aoudad* is? It's an ancient sheep that used to live on Old Earth, and here we are, thousands of years later, with a children's nonsense rhyme about it. The animals are gone but the rhyme remains. It'll be like that with Rambo someday.

Everybody will know his name and all about his drunkboat, but they will forget the scientific milestone that he
crossed, hunting for Elizabeth in an ancient rocket that
couldn't fly from peetle to pootle. . . . Oh, the rhyme?
Don't you know that? It's a silly thing. It goes:

> Point your gun at a murky lurky.
> *(Now you're talking ham or turkey!)*
> Shoot a shot at a dying aoudad.
> *(Don't ask the lady why or how, dad!)*

Don't ask me what 'ham' and 'turkey' are. Probably
parts of ancient animals, like beefsteak or sirloin. But
the children still say the words. They'll do that with
Rambo and his drunken boat some day. They may even
tell the story of Elizabeth. But they will never tell the
part about how he got to the hospital. That part is too
terrible, too real, too sad and wonderful at the end.
They found him on the grass. Mind you, naked on the
grass, and nobody knew where he had come from!"

4

They found him naked on the grass and nobody
knew where he had come from. They did not even
know about the ancient rocket which the Lord Crudelta
had sent beyond the end of nowhere with the letters I,
O and M written on it. They did not know that this was
Rambo, who had gone through space[3]. The robots noticed him first and brought him in, photographing everything that they did. They had been programmed that
way, to make sure that anything unusual was kept in the
records.

Then the nurses found him in an outside room.

They assumed that he was alive, since he was not
dead, but they could not prove that he was alive, either.

That heightened the puzzle.

The doctors were called in. Real doctors, not machines. They were very important men. Citizen Doctor

Timofeyev, Citizen Doctor Grosbeck and the director himself, Sir and Doctor Vomact. They took the case.

(Over on the other side of the hospital Elizabeth waited, unconscious, and nobody knew it at all. Elizabeth, for whom he had jumped space, and pierced the stars, but nobody knew it yet!)

The young man could not speak. When they ran eye-prints and fingerprints through the Population Machine, they found that he had been bred on Earth itself, but had been shipped out as a frozen and unborn baby to Earth Four. At tremendous cost, they queried Earth Four with an "instant message," only to discover that the young man who lay before them in the hospital had been lost from an experimental ship on an intergalactic trip.

Lost.

No ship and no sign of ship.

And here he was.

They stood at the edge of space, and did not know what they were looking at. They were doctors and it was their business to repair or rebuild people, not to ship them around. How should such men know about space^3 when they did not even know about space^2 except for the fact that people got on the planoform ships and made trips through it? They were looking for sickness when their eyes saw engineering. They treated him when he was well.

All he needed was time, to get over the shock of the most tremendous trip ever made by a human being, but the doctors did not know that and they tried to rush his recovery.

When they put clothes on him, he moved from coma to a kind of mechanical spasm and tore the clothing off. Once again stripped, he lay himself roughly on the floor and refused food or speech.

They fed him with needles while the whole energy of space, had they only known it, was radiating out of his body in new forms.

They put him all by himself in a locked room and watched him through the peephole.

He was a nice-looking young man, even though his mind was blank and his body was rigid and unconscious. His hair was very fair and his eyes were light blue but his face showed character—a square chin; a handsome, resolute, sullen mouth; old lines in the face which looked as though, when conscious, he must have lived many days or months on the edge of rage.

When they studied him the third day in the hospital, their patient had not changed at all.

He had torn off his pajamas again and lay naked, face down, on the floor.

His body was as immobile and tense as it had been on the day before.

(One year later, this room was going to be a museum with a bronze sign reading, "Here lay Rambo after he left the Old Rocket for Space Three," but the doctors still had no idea of what they were dealing with.)

His face was turned so sharply to the left that the neck muscles showed. His right arm stuck out straight from the body. The left arm formed an exact right angle from the body, with the left forearm and hand pointing rigidly upward at 90° from the upper arm. The legs were in the grotesque parody of a running position.

Doctor Grosbeck said, "It looks to me like he's swimming. Let's drop him in a tank of water and see if he moves." Grosbeck sometimes went in for drastic solutions to problems.

Timofeyev took his place at the peephole. "Spasm, still," he murmured. "I hope the poor fellow is not feeling pain when his cortical defenses are down. How can a man fight pain if he does not even know what he is experiencing?"

"And you, Sir and Doctor," said Grosbeck to Vomact, "what do you see?"

Vomact did not need to look. He had come early and had looked long and quietly at the patient through the peephole before the other doctors arrived. Vomact was a wise man, with good insight and rich intuitions. He could guess in an hour more than a machine could diagnose in a year; he was already beginning to understand that this was a sickness which no man had ever had before. Still, there were remedies waiting.

The three doctors tried them.

They tried hypnosis, electrotherapy, massage, subsonics, atropine, surgital, a whole family of the digitalinids, and some quasi-narcotic viruses which had been grown in orbit where they mutated fast. They got the beginning of a response when they tried gas hypnosis combined with an electronically amplified telepath; this showed that something still went on inside the patient's mind. Otherwise the brain might have seemed to be mere fatty tissue, without a nerve in it. The other attempts had shown nothing. The gas showed a faint stirring away from fear and pain. The telepath reported glimpses of unknown skies. (The doctors turned the telepath over to the Space Police promptly, so they could try to code the star patterns which he had seen in the patient's mind, but the patterns did not fit. The telepath, though a keen-witted man, could not remember them in enough detail for them to be scanned against the samples of piloting sheets.)

The doctors went back to their drugs and tried ancient, simple remedies—morphine and caffeine to counteract each other, and a rough massage to make him dream again, so that the telepath could pick it up.

There was no further result that day, or the next.

Meanwhile the Earth authorities were getting restless. They thought, quite rightly, that the hospital had done a good job of proving that the patient had not been on Earth until a few moments before the robots found him on the grass. How had he gotten on the grass?

The airspace of Earth reported no intrusion at all, no vehicle marking a blazing arc of air incandescing against metal, no whisper of the great forces which drove a planoform ship through space[2].

(Crudelta, using faster-than-light ships, was creeping slow as a snail back toward Earth, racing his best to see if Rambo had gotten there first.)

On the fifth day, there was the beginning of a breakthrough.

5

Elizabeth had passed.

This was found out only much later, by a careful check of the hospital records.

The doctors only knew this much:

Patients had been moved down the corridor, sheet-covered figures immobile on wheeled beds.

Suddenly the beds stopped rolling.

A nurse screamed.

The heavy steel-and-plastic wall was bending inward. Some slow, silent force was pushing the wall into the corridor itself.

The wall ripped.

A human hand emerged.

One of the quick-witted nurses screamed, *"Push* those beds! *Push* them out of the way."

The nurses and robots obeyed.

The beds rocked like a group of boats crossing a wave when they came to the place where the floor, bonded to the wall, had bent upward to meet the wall as it tore inward. The peach-colored glow of the lights flicked. Robots appeared.

A second human hand came through the wall. Pushing in opposite directions, the hands tore the wall as though it had been wet paper.

The patient from the grass put his head through.

He looked blindly up and down the corridor, his eyes not quite focusing, his skin glowing a strange red-brown from the burns of open space.

"No," he said. Just that one word.

But that "No" was heard. Though the volume was not loud, it carried through the hospital. The internal telecommunications system relayed it. Every switch in the place went negative. Frantic nurses and robots, with even the doctors helping them, rushed to turn all the machines back on—the pumps, the ventilators, the artificial kidneys, the brain re-recorders, even the simple air engines which kept the atmosphere clean.

Far overhead an aircraft spun giddily. Its "off" switch, surrounded by triple safeguards, had suddenly been thrown into the negative position. Fortunately the robot-pilot got it going again before crashing into earth.

The patient did not seem to know that his word had this effect.

(Later the world knew that this was part of the "drunkboat effect." The man himself had developed the capacity for using his neurophysical system as a machine control.)

In the corridor, the machine-robot who served as policeman arrived. He wore sterile, padded velvet gloves with a grip of sixty metric tons inside his hands. He approached the patient. The robot had been carefully trained to recognize all kinds of danger from delirious or psychotic humans; later he reported that he had an input of "danger, extreme" on every band of sensation. He had been expecting to seize the prisoner with irreversible firmness and to return him to his bed, but with this kind of danger sizzling in the air, the robot took no chances. His wrist itself contained a hypodermic pistol which operated on compressed argon.

He reached out toward the unknown, naked man who stood in the big torn gap of the wall. The wrist-weapon hissed and a sizeable injection of condamine, the most powerful narcotic in the known universe, spat its way through the skin of Rambo's neck. The patient collapsed.

The robot picked him up gently and tenderly, lifted him through the torn wall, pushed the door open with a kick which broke the lock and put the patient back on his bed. The robot could hear doctors coming, so he used his enormous hands to pat the steel wall back into its proper shape. Work-robots or underpeople could finish the job later, but meanwhile it looked better to have that part of the building set at right angles again.

Doctor Vomact arrived, followed closely by Grosbeck.

"What happened?" he yelled, shaken out of a lifelong calm. The robot pointed at the ripped wall.

"He tore it open. I put it back," said the robot.

The doctors turned to look at the patient. He had crawled off his bed again and was on the floor, but his breathing was light and natural.

"What did you give him?" cried Vomact to the robot.

"Condamine," said the robot, "according to rule forty-seven-B. The drug is not to be mentioned outside the hospital."

"I know that," said Vomact absentmindedly and a little crossly. "You can go along now. Thank you."

"It is not usual to thank robots," said the robot, "but you can read a commendation into my record if you want to."

"Get the blazes out of here!" shouted Vomact at the officious robot.

The robot blinked. "There are no blazes but I have the impression you mean me. I shall leave, with your permission." He jumped with odd gracefulness around the two doctors, fingered the broken doorlock absentmindedly, as though he might have wished to repair it, and then, seeing Vomact glare at him, left the room completely.

A moment later soft muted thuds began. Both doctors listened a moment and then gave up. The robot was out in the corridor, gently patting the steel floor back into shape. He was a tidy robot, probably animated by an amplified chicken-brain, and when he got tidy he became obstinate.

"Two questions, Grosbeck," said the Sir and Doctor Vomact.

"Your service, sir!"

"Where was the patient standing when he pushed the wall into the corridor, and how did he get the leverage to do it?"

Grosbeck narrowed his eyes in puzzlement. "Now that you mention it, I have no idea of how he did it. In fact, he could not have done it. But he has. And the other question?"

"What do you think of condamine?"

"Dangerous, of course, as always. Addiction can—"

"Can you have addiction with no cortical activity?" interrupted Vomact.

"Of course," said Grosbeck promptly. "Tissue addiction."

"Look for it, then," said Vomact.

Grosbeck knelt beside the patient and felt with his fingertips for the muscle endings. He felt where they knotted themselves into the base of the skull, the tips of the shoulders, the striped area of the back.

When he stood up there was a look of puzzlement on his face. "I never felt a human body like this one before. I am not even sure that it *is* human any longer."

Vomact said nothing. The two doctors confronted one another. Grosbeck fidgeted under the calm stare of the senior man. Finally he blurted out:

"Sir and Doctor, I know what we *could* do."

"And that," said Vomact levelly, without the faintest hint of encouragement or of warning, "is what?"

"It wouldn't be the first time that it's been done in a hospital."

"What?" said Vomact, his eyes—those dreaded eyes!—making Grosbeck say what he did not want to say.

Grosbeck flushed. He leaned toward Vomact so as to whisper, even though there was no one standing near them. His words, when they came, had the hasty indecency of a lover's improper suggestion,

"Kill the patient, Sir and Doctor. Kill him. We have plenty of records of him. We can get a cadaver out of the basement and make it into a good simulacrum. Who knows what we will turn loose among mankind if we let him get well?"

"Who knows?" said Vomact without tone or quality to his voice. "But Citizen and Doctor, what is the twelfth duty of a physician?"

" 'Not to take the law into his own hands, keeping healing for the healers and giving to the state or the Instrumentality whatever properly belongs to the state or the Instrumentality.' " Grosbeck sighed as he retracted his own suggestion. "Sir and Doctor, I take it back. It wasn't medicine which I was talking about. It was government and politics which were really in my mind."

"And now . . . ?" asked Vomact.

"Heal him, or let him be until he heals himself."

"And which would you do?"

"I'd try to heal him."

"How?" said Vomact.

"Sir and Doctor," cried Grosbeck, "do not ride my weaknesses in this case! I know that you like me because I am a bold, confident sort of man. Do not ask me to be myself when we do not even know where this body came from. If I were bold as usual, I would give him typhoid and condamine, stationing telepaths nearby. But this is something new in the history of man. We are people and perhaps he is not a person any more. Perhaps he represents the combination of people with some kind of a new force. How did he get here from the far side of nowhere? How many million times has he been enlarged or reduced? We do not know what he is or what has happened to him. How can we treat a man when we are treating the cold of space, the heat of suns, the frigidity of distance? We know what to do with flesh, but this is not quite flesh any more. Feel him yourself, Sir and Doctor! You will touch something which nobody has ever touched before."

"I have," Vomact declared, "already felt him. You are right. We will try typhoid and condamine for half a day. Twelve hours from now let us meet each other at this place. I will tell the nurses and the robots what to do in the interim."

They both gave the red-tanned spread-eagled figure on the floor a parting glance. Grosbeck looked at the body with something like distaste mingled with fear; Vomact was expressionless, save for a wry wan smile of pity.

At the door the head nurse awaited them. Grosbeck was surprised at his chief's orders.

"Ma'am and Nurse, do you have a weaponproof vault in this hospital?"

"Yes, sir," she said. "We used to keep our records in it until we telemetered all our records into Computer Orbit. Now it is dirty and empty."

"Clean it out. Run a ventilator tube into it. Who is your military protector?"

"My what?" she cried, in surprise.

"Everyone on Earth has military protection. Where are the forces, the soldiers, who protect this hospital of yours?"

"My Sir and Doctor!" she called out. "My Sir and Doctor! I'm an old woman and I have been allowed to work here for three hundred years. But I never thought of that idea before. Why would I need soldiers?"

"Find who they are and ask them to stand by. They are specialists too, with a different kind of art from ours. Let them stand by. They may be needed before this day is out. Give my name as authority to their lieutenant or sergeant. Now here is the medication which I want you to apply to this patient."

Her eyes widened as he went on talking, but she was a disciplined woman and she nodded as she heard him out, point by point. Her eyes looked very sad and weary at the end but she was a trained expert herself and she had enormous respect for the skill and wisdom of the Sir and Doctor Vomact. She also had a warm, feminine pity for the motionless young male figure on the floor, swimming forever on the heavy floor, swimming between archipelagoes which no man living had ever dreamed before.

6

Crisis came that night.

The patient had worn handprints into the inner wall of the vault, but he had not escaped.

The soldiers, looking oddly alert with their weapons gleaming in the bright corridor of the hospital, were really very bored, as soldiers always become when they are on duty with no action.

Their lieutenant was keyed up. The wirepoint in his

hand buzzed like a dangerous insect. Sir and Doctor
Vomact, who knew more about weapons than the soldiers thought he knew, saw that the wirepoint was set to
HIGH, with a capacity of paralyzing people five stories
up, five stories down or a kilometer sideways. He said
nothing. He merely thanked the lieutenant and entered
the vault, closely followed by Grosbeck and Timofeyev.

The patient swam here too.

He had changed to an arm-over-arm motion, kicking
his legs against the floor. It was as though he had swum
on the other floor with the sole purpose of staying
afloat, and had now discovered some direction in which
to go, albeit very slowly. His motions were deliberate,
tense, rigid, and so reduced in time that it seemed as
though he hardly moved at all. The ripped pajamas lay
on the floor beside him.

Vomact glanced around, wondering what forces the
man could have used to make those handprints on the
steel wall. He remembered Grosbeck's warning that the
patient should die, rather than subject all mankind to
new and unthought risks, but though he shared the feeling, he could not condone the recommendation.

Almost irritably, the great doctor thought to himself—where could the man be going?

*(To Elizabeth, the truth was, to Elizabeth, now only
sixty meters away. Not till much later did people understand what Rambo had been trying to do—crossing
sixty mere meters to reach his Elizabeth when he had
already jumped an uncount of light-years to return to
her. To his own, his dear, his well-beloved who needed
him!)*

The condamine did not leave its characteristic mark
of deep lassitude and glowing skin: perhaps the typhoid
was successfully contradicting it. Rambo did seem more
lively than before. The name had come through on the
regular message system, but it still did not mean anything to the Sir and Doctor Vomact. It would. It would.

Meanwhile the other two doctors, briefed ahead of
time, got busy with the apparatus which the robots and
the nurses had installed.

Vomact murmured to the others, "I think he's better off. Looser all around. I'll try shouting."

So busy were they that they just nodded.

Vomact screamed at the patient, "Who are you? What are you? Where do you come from?"

The sad blue eyes of the man on the floor glanced at him with a surprisingly quick glance, but there was no other real sign of communication. The limbs kept up their swim against the rough concrete floor of the vault. Two of the bandages which the hospital staff had put on him had worn off again. The right knee, scraped and bruised, deposited a sixty-centimeter trail of blood— some old and black and coagulated, some fresh, new and liquid—on the floor as it moved back and forth.

Vomact stood up and spoke to Grosbeck and Timofeyev. "Now," he said, "let us see what happens when we apply the pain."

The two stepped back without being told to do so.

Timofeyev waved his hand at a small white-enameled orderly-robot who stood in the doorway.

The pain net, a fragile cage of wires, dropped down from the ceiling.

It was Vomact's duty, as senior doctor, to take the greatest risk. The patient was wholly encased by the net of wires, but Vomact dropped to his hands and knees, lifted the net at one corner with his right hand, thrust his own head into it next to the head of the patient. Doctor Vomact's robe trailed on the clean concrete, touching the black old stains of blood left from the patient's "swim" throughout the night.

Now Vomact's mouth was centimeters from the patient's ear.

Said Vomact, "Oh."

The net hummed.

The patient stopped his slow motion, arched his back, looked steadfastly at the doctor.

Doctors Grosbeck and Timofeyev could see Vomact's face go white with the impact of the pain machine, but Vomact kept his voice under control and said evenly and loudly to the patient:

"Who—are—you?"

The patient said flatly, "Elizabeth."

The answer was foolish but the tone was rational.

Vomact pulled his head out from under the net, shouting again at the patient, *"Who—are—you?"*

The naked man replied, speaking very clearly:

> "Chwinkle, chwinkle, little chweeble,
> I am feeling very feeble!"

Vomact frowned and murmured to the robot, "More pain. Turn it up to pain ultimate."

The body threshed under the net, trying to resume its swim on the concrete.

A loud wild braying cry came from the victim under the net. It sounded like a screamed distortion of the name Elizabeth, echoing out from endless remoteness.

It did not make sense.

Vomact screamed back, *"Who—are—you?"*

With unexpected clarity and resonance, the voice came back to the three doctors from the twisting body under the net of pain:

"I'm the shipped man, the ripped man, the gypped man, the dipped man, the hipped man, the tripped man, the tipped man, the slipped man, the flipped man, the nipped man, the ripped man, the clipped man—aah!" His voice choked off with a cry and he went back to swimming on the floor, despite the intensity of the pain net immediately above him.

The doctor lifted his hand. The pain net stopped buzzing and lifted high into the air.

He felt the patient's pulse. It was quick. He lifted an eyelid. The reactions were much closer to normal.

"Stand back," he said to the others.

"Pain on both of us," he said to the robot.

The net came down on the two of them.

"Who are you?" shrieked Vomact, right into the patient's ear, holding the man halfway off the floor and not quite knowing whether the body which tore steel

walls might not, somehow, tear both of them apart as they stood.

The man babbled back at him: "I'm the most man, the post man, the host man, the ghost man, the coast man, the boast man, the dosed man, the grossed man, the toast man, the roast man, no! no! no!"

He struggled in Vomact's arms. Grosbeck and Timofeyev stepped forward to rescue their chief when the patient added, very calmly and clearly:

"Your procedure is all right, Doctor, whoever you are. More fever, please. More pain, please. Some of that dope to fight the pain. You're pulling me back. I know I am on Earth. Elizabeth is near. For the love of God, get me Elizabeth! But don't rush me. I need days and days to get well."

The rationality was so startling that Grosbeck, without waiting for orders from Vomact, as chief doctor, ordered the pain net lifted.

The patient began babbling again: "I'm the three man, the he man, the tree man, the me man, the three man, the three man. . . ." His voice faded and he slumped unconscious.

Vomact walked out of the vault. He was a little unsteady.

His colleagues took him by the elbows.

He smiled wanly at them. "I wish it were lawful. . . . I could use some of that condamine myself. No wonder the pain nets wake the patients up and even make dead people do twitches! Get me some liquor. My heart is old."

Grosbeck sat him down while Timofeyev ran down the corridor in search of medicinal liquor.

Vomact murmured, "How are we going to find *his* Elizabeth? There must be millions of them. And he's from Earth Four too."

"Sir and Doctor, you have worked wonders," said Grosbeck. "To go under the net. To take those chances. To bring him to speech. I will never see anything like it again. It's enough for any one lifetime, to have seen this day."

"But what do we do next?" asked Vomact wearily, almost in confusion.

That particular question needed no answer.

7

The Lord Crudelta had reached Earth.

His pilot landed the craft and fainted at the controls with sheer exhaustion.

Of the escort cats, who had ridden alongside the space craft in the miniature spaceships, three were dead, one was comatose and the fifth was spitting and raving.

When the port authorities tried to slow the Lord Crudelta down to ascertain his authority, he invoked Top Emergency, took over the command of troops in the name of the Instrumentality, arrested everyone in sight but the troop commander and requisitioned the troop commander to take him to the hospital. The computers at the port had told him that one Rambo, "sans origine," had arrived mysteriously on the grass of a designated hospital.

Outside the hospital, the Lord Crudelta invoked Top Emergency again, placed all armed men under his own command, ordered a recording monitor to cover all his actions if he should later be channeled into a court-martial, and arrested everyone in sight.

The tramp of heavily armed men, marching in combat order, overtook Timofeyev as he hurried back to Vomact with a drink. The men were jogging along on the double. All of them had live helmets and their wire-points were buzzing.

Nurses ran forward to drive the intruders out, ran backward when the sting of the stun-rays brushed cruelly over them. The whole hospital was in an uproar.

The Lord Crudelta later admitted that he had made a serious mistake.

The Two Minutes' War broke out immediately.

You have to understand the pattern of the Instrumentality to see how it happened. The Instrumentality was a self-perpetuating body of men with enormous powers and a strict code. Each was a plenum of the low, the middle and the high justice. Each could do anything he found necessary or proper to maintain the Instrumentality and to keep the peace between the worlds. But if he made a mistake or committed a wrong—ah, then, it was suddenly different. Any Lord could put another Lord to death in an emergency, but he was assured of death and disgrace himself if he assumed this responsibility. The only difference between ratification and repudiation came in the fact that Lords who killed in an emergency and were proved wrong were marked down on a very shameful list, while those who killed other Lords rightly (as later examination might prove) were listed on a very honorable list, but still killed.

With three Lords, the situation was different. Three Lords made an emergency court; if they acted together, acted in good faith, and reported to the computers of the Instrumentality, they were exempt from punishment, though not from blame or even reduction to citizen status. Seven Lords, or all the Lords on a given planet at a given moment, were beyond any criticism except that of a dignified reversal of their actions should a later ruling prove them wrong.

This was all the business of the Instrumentality. The Instrumentality had the perpetual slogan: "Watch, but do not govern; stop war, but do not wage it; protect, but do not control; and first, survive!"

The Lord Crudelta had seized the troops—not his troops, but the light regular troops of Manhome Government—because he feared that the greatest danger in the history of man might come from the person whom he himself had sent through space[3].

He never expected that the troops would be plucked out from his command—an overriding power reinforced by robotic telepathy and the incomparable communications net, both open and secret, reinforced by thousands of years in trickery, defeat, secrecy, victory and sheer experience, which the Instrumentality had perfected since it emerged from the Ancient Wars.

Overriding, overridden!

These were the commands which the Instrumentality had used before recorded time began. Sometimes they suspended their antagonists on points of law, sometimes by the deft and deadly insertion of weapons, most often by cutting in on other peoples' mechanical and social controls and doing their will, only to drop the controls as suddenly as they had taken them.

But not Crudelta's hastily called troops.

8

The war broke out with a change of pace.

Two squads of men were moving into that part of the hospital where Elizabeth lay, waiting the endless returns to the jelly-baths which would rebuild her poor ruined body.

The squads changed pace.

The survivors could not account for what happened.

They all admitted to great mental confusion—afterward.

At the time it seemed that they had received a clear, logical command to turn and to defend the women's section by counterattacking their own main battalion right in their rear.

The hospital was a very strong building. Otherwise it would have melted to the ground or shot up in flame.

The leading soldiers suddenly turned around, dropped for cover and blazed their wirepoints at the comrades who followed them. The wirepoints were cued to organic material, though fairly harmless to inorganic. They were powered by the power relays which every soldier wore on his back.

In the first ten seconds of the turnaround, twenty-seven soldiers, two nurses, three patients and one orderly were killed. One hundred and nine other people were wounded in that first exchange of fire.

The troop commander had never seen battle, but he had been well trained. He immediately deployed his reserves around the external exits of the building and sent his favorite squad, commanded by a Sergeant Lansdale whom he trusted well, down into the basement, so that it could rise vertically from the basement into the women's quarters and find out who the enemy was.

As yet, he had no idea that it was his own leading troops turning and fighting their comrades.

He testified later, at the trial, that he personally had no sensations of eerie interference with his own mind. He merely knew that his men had unexpectedly come upon armed resistance from antagonists—identity unknown!—who had weapons identical with theirs. Since the Lord Crudelta had brought them along in case there might be a fight with unspecified antagonists, he felt right in assuming that a Lord of the Instrumentality knew what he was doing. This was the enemy, all right.

In less than a minute, the two sides had balanced out. The line of fire had moved right into his own force. The lead men, some of whom were wounded, simply turned around and began defending themselves against the men immediately behind them. It was as though an invisible line, moving rapidly, had parted the two sections of the military force.

The oily black smoke of dissolving bodies began to glut the ventilators.

Patients were screaming, doctors cursing, robots stamping around and nurses trying to call each other.

The war ended when the troop commander saw Sergeant Lansdale, whom he himself had sent upstairs, leading a charge out of the women's quarters—directly at his own commander!

The officer kept his head.

He dropped to the floor and rolled sidewise as the air chittered at him, the emanations of Lansdale's wirepoint killing all the tiny bacteria in the air. On his helmet phone he pushed the manual controls to TOP VOLUME and to NONCOMS ONLY and he commanded, with a sudden flash of brilliant mother-wit:

"Good job, Lansdale!"

Lansdale's voice came back as weak as if it had been

off-planet. "We'll keep them out of this section yet, sir!"

The troop commander called back very loudly but calmly, not letting on that he thought his sergeant was psychotic, "Easy now. Hold on. I'll be with you."

He changed to the other channel and said to his nearby men, "Cease fire. Take cover and wait."

A wild scream came to him from the phones.

It was Lansdale. "Sir! Sir! I'm fighting *you*, sir. I just caught on. It's getting me again. Watch out."

The buzz and burr of the weapons suddenly stopped.

The wild human uproar of the hospital continued.

A tall doctor, with the insignia of high seniority, came gently to the troop commander and said, "You can stand up and take your soldiers out now, young fellow. The fight was a mistake."

"I'm not under your orders," snapped the young officer. "I'm under the Lord Crudelta. He requisitioned this force from the Manhome Government. Who are you?"

"You may salute me, captain," said the doctor. "I am Colonel General Vomact of the Earth Medical Reserve. But you had better not wait for the Lord Crudelta."

"But *where* is he?"

"In my bed," said Vomact.

"Your *bed?*" cried the young officer in complete amazement.

"In bed. Doped to the teeth. I fixed him up. He was excited. Take your men out. We'll treat the wounded on the lawn. You can see the dead in the refrigerators downstairs in a few minutes, except for the ones that went smoky from direct hits."

"But the fight? . . ."

"A mistake, young man, or else—"

"Or else what?" shouted the young officer, horrified at the utter mess of his own combat experience.

"Or else a weapon no man has ever seen before. Your troops fought each other. Your command was intercepted."

"I could see that," snapped the officer, "as soon as I saw Lansdale coming at me."

"But do you know what took him over?" said Vomact gently, while taking the officer by the arm and beginning to lead him out of the hospital. The captain went willingly, not noticing where he was going, so eagerly did he watch for the other man's words.

"I think I know," said Vomact. "Another man's dreams. Dreams which have learned how to turn themselves into electricity or plastic or stone. Or anything else. Dreams coming to us out of space-three."

The young officer nodded dumbly. This was too much. "Space-three?" he murmured. It was like being told that the really alien invaders, whom men had been expecting for fourteen thousand years and had never met, were waiting for him on the grass. Until now space[3] had been a mathematical idea, a romancer's daydream, but not a fact.

The Sir and Doctor Vomact did not even ask the young officer. He brushed the young man gently at the nape of the neck and shot him through with tranquilizer. Vomact then led him out to the grass. The young captain stood alone and whistled happily at the stars in the sky. Behind him, his sergeants and corporals were sorting out the survivors and getting treatment for the wounded.

The Two Minutes' War was over.

Rambo had stopped dreaming that his Elizabeth was in danger. He had recognized, even in his deep sick sleep, that the tramping in the corridor was the movement of armed men. His mind had set up defenses to protect Elizabeth. He took over command of the forward troops and set them to stopping the main body. The powers which space[3] had worked into him made this easy for him to do, even though he did not know that he was doing it.

9

"How many dead?" said Vomact to Grosbeck and Timofeyev.

"About two hundred."

"And how many irrecoverable dead?"

"The ones that got turned into smoke. A dozen, maybe fourteen. The other dead can be fixed up, but most of them will have to get new personality prints."

"Do you know what happened?" asked Vomact.

"No, Sir and Doctor," they both chorused.

"I do. I think I do. No, I *know* I do. It's the wildest story in the history of man. Our patient did it—Rambo. He took over the troops and set them against each other. That Lord of the Instrumentality who came charging in—Crudelta. I've known him for a long long time. He's behind this case. He thought that troops would help, not sensing that troops would invite attack upon themselves. And there is something else."

"Yes?" they said, in unison.

"Rambo's woman—the one he's looking for. She must be here."

"Why?" said Timofeyev.

"Because *he's* here."

"You're assuming that he came here because of his own will, Sir and Doctor."

Vomact smiled the wise crafty smile of his family; it was almost a trademark of the Vomact house.

"I am assuming all the things which I cannot otherwise prove.

"First, I assume that he came here naked out of space itself, driven by some kind of force which we cannot even guess.

"Second, I assume he came *here* because he wanted something. A woman named Elizabeth, who must already be here. In a moment we can go inventory all our Elizabeths.

"Third, I assume that the Lord Crudelta knew something about it. He has led troops into the building. He began raving when he saw me. I know hysterical fatigue, as do you, my brothers, so I condamined him for a night's sleep.

"Fourth, let's leave our man alone. There'll be hearings and trials enough, Space knows, when all these events get scrambled out."

Vomact was right.
He usually was.
Trials did follow.

It was lucky that Old Earth no longer permitted newspapers or television news. The population would have been frothed up to riot and terror if they had ever found out what happened at the Old Main Hospital just to the west of Meeya Meefla.

10

Twenty-one days later, Vomact, Timofeyev and Grosbeck were summoned to the trial of the Lord Crudelta. A full panel of seven Lords of the Instrumentality was there to give Crudelta an ample hearing and, if required, a sudden death. The doctors were present both as doctors for Elizabeth and Rambo and as witnesses for the Investigating Lord.

Elizabeth, fresh up from being dead, was as beautiful as a newborn baby in exquisite, adult feminine form. Rambo could not take his eyes off her, but a look of bewilderment went over his face every time she gave him a friendly, calm, remote little smile. (She had been told that she was his girl, and she was prepared to believe it, but she had no memory of him or of anything else more than sixty hours back, when speech had been reinstalled in her mind; and he, for his part, was still thick of speech and subject to strains which the doctors could not quite figure out.)

The Investigating Lord was a man named Starmount.
He asked the panel to rise.
They did so.

He faced the Lord Crudelta with great solemnity. "You are obliged, my Lord Crudelta, to speak quickly and clearly to this court."

"Yes, my Lord," he answered.

"We have the summary power."

"You have the summary power. I recognize it."

"You will tell the truth or else you will lie."

"I shall tell the truth or I will lie."

"You may lie, if you wish, about matters of fact and opinion, but you will in no case lie about human relationships. If you do lie, nevertheless, you will ask that your name be entered in the Roster of Dishonor."

"I understand the panel and the rights of this panel. I will lie if I wish—though I don't think I will need to do so"—and here Crudelta flashed a weary intelligent smile at all of them—"but I will not lie about matters of relationship. If I do, I will ask for dishonor."

"You have yourself been well trained as a Lord of the Instrumentality?"

"I have been so trained and I love the Instrumentality well. In fact, I am myself the Instrumentality, as are you, and as are the honorable Lords beside you. I shall behave well, for as long as I live this afternoon."

"Do you credit him, my Lords?" asked Starmount.

The members of the panel nodded their mitred heads. They had dressed ceremonially for the occasion.

"Do you have a relationship to the woman Elizabeth?"

The members of the trial panel caught their breath as they saw Crudelta turn white. "My Lords!" he cried, and answered no further.

"It is the custom," said Starmount firmly, "that you answer promptly or that you die."

The Lord Crudelta got control of himself. "I am answering. I did not know who she was, except for the fact that Rambo loved her. I sent her to Earth from Earth Four, where I then was. Then I told Rambo that she had been murdered and hung desperately at the edge of death, wanting only his help to return to the green fields of life."

Said Starmount, "Was that the truth?"

"My Lord and Lords, it was a lie."

"Why did you tell it?"

"To induce rage in Rambo and to give him an over-riding reason for wanting to come to Earth faster than any man has ever come before."

"A-a-ah! A-a-ah!" Two wild cries came from Rambo, more like the call of an animal than like the sound of a man.

Vomact looked at his patient, felt himself beginning to growl with a deep internal rage. Rambo's powers, generated in the depths of space[3], had begun to operate again. Vomact made a sign. The robot behind Rambo had been coded to keep Rambo calm. Though the robot had been enameled to look like a white gleaming hospital orderly, he was actually a police-robot of high powers, built up with an electronic cortex based on the frozen midbrain of an old wolf. (A wolf was a rare animal, something like a dog.) The robot touched Rambo, who dropped off to sleep. Doctor Vomact felt the anger in his own mind fade away. He lifted his hand gently; the robot caught the signal and stopped applying the narcoleptic radiation. Rambo slept normally; Elizabeth looked worriedly at the man whom she had been told was her own.

The Lords turned back from the glances at Rambo.

Said Starmount, icily, "And why did you do that?"

"Because I wanted him to travel through space-three."

"Why?"

"To show it could be done."

"And do you, my Lord Crudelta, affirm that this man has in fact traveled through space-three?"

"I do."

"Are you lying?"

"I have the right to lie, but I have no wish to do so. In the name of the Instrumentality itself, I tell you that this is the truth."

The panel members gasped. Now there was no way out. Either the Lord Crudelta was telling the truth,

*which meant that all former times had come to an end
and that a new age had begun for all the kinds of mankind,* or else he was lying in the face of the most powerful form of affirmation which any of them knew.

Even Starmount himself took a different tone. His
teasing, restless, intelligent voice took on a new timbre
of kindness.

"You do therefore assert that this man has come
back from outside our galaxy with nothing more than
his own natural skin to cover him? No instruments? No
power?"

"I did not say that," said Crudelta. "Other people
have begun to pretend I used such words. I tell you, my
Lords, that I planoformed for twelve consecutive Earth
days and nights. Some of you may remember where
Outpost Baiter Gator is. Well, I had a good Go-captain,
and he took me four long jumps beyond there, out into
intergalactic space. I left this man there. When I
reached Earth, he had been here twelve days, more or
less. I have assumed, therefore, that his trip was more
or less instantaneous. I was on my way back to Baiter
Gator, counting by Earth time, when the doctor here
found this man on the grass outside the hospital."

Vomact raised his hand. The Lord Starmount gave
him the right to speak. "My Sirs and Lords, we did not
find this man on the grass. The robots did, and made a
record. But even the robots did not see or photograph
his arrival."

"We know that," said Starmount angrily, "and we
know that we have been told that nothing came to
Earth by any means whatever, in that particular quarter
hour. Go on, my Lord Crudelta. What relation are you
to Rambo?"

"He is my victim."

"Explain yourself!"

"I computed him out. I asked the machines where I
would be most apt to find a man with a tremendous lot
of rage in him, and was informed that on Earth Four
the rage level had been left high because that particular
planet had a considerable need for explorers and adven-

turers, in whom rage was a strong survival trait. When I got to Earth Four, I commanded the authorities to find out which border cases had exceeded the limits of allowable rage. They gave me four men. One was much too large. Two were old. This man was the only candidate for my experiment. I chose him."

"What did you tell him?"

"Tell him? I told him his sweetheart was dead or dying."

"No, no," said Starmount. "Not at the moment of crisis. What did you tell him to make him cooperate in the first place?"

"I told him," said the Lord Crudelta evenly, "that I was myself a Lord of the Instrumentality and that I would kill him myself if he did not obey, and obey promptly."

"And under what custom or law did you act?"

"Reserved material," said the Lord Crudelta promptly. "There are telepaths here who are not a part of the Instrumentality. I beg leave to defer until we have a shielded place."

Several members of the panel nodded and Starmount agreed with them. He changed the line of questioning.

"You forced this man, therefore, to do something which he did not wish to do?"

"That is right," said the Lord Crudelta.

"Why didn't you go yourself, if it is that dangerous?"

"My Lords and Honorables, it was the nature of the experiment that the experimenter himself should not be expended in the first try. Artyr Rambo has indeed traveled through space-three. I shall follow him myself, in due course." (How the Lord Crudelta did do so is another tale, told about another time.) "If I had gone and if I had been lost, that would have been the end of the space-three trials. At least for our time."

"Tell us the exact circumstances under which you last saw Artyr Rombo before you met after the battle in the Old Main Hospital."

"We had put him in a rocket of the most ancient style. We also wrote writing on the outside of it, just the way the Ancients did when they first ventured into space. Ah, that was a beautiful piece of engineering and archeology! We copied everything right down to the correct models of fifteen thousand years ago, when the Paroskii and Murkins were racing each other into space. The rocket was white, with a red and white gantry beside it. The letters IOM were on the rocket, not that the words mattered. The rocket has gone into nowhere, but the passenger sits here. It rose on a stool of fire. The stool became a column. Then the landing field disappeared."

"And the landing field," said Starmount quietly, "what was that?"

"A modified planoform ship. We have had ships go milky in space because they faded molecule by molecule. We have had others disappear utterly. The engineers had changed this around. We took out all the machinery needed for circumnavigation, for survival or for comfort. The landing field was to last three or four seconds, no more. Instead, we put in fourteen planoform devices, all operating in tandem, so that the ship would do what other ships do when they planoform—namely, drop one of our familiar dimensions and pick up a new dimension from some unknown category of space—but do it with such force as to get out of what people call space-two and move over into space-three."

"And space-three, what did you expect of that?"

"I thought that it was universal and instantaneous, in relation to our universe. That everything was equally distant from everything else. That Rambo, wanting to see his girl again, would move in a thousandth of a second from the empty space beyond Outpost Baiter Gator into the hospital where she was."

"And, my Lord Crudelta, what made you think so?"

"A hunch, my Lord, for which you are welcome to kill me."

Starmount turned to the panel. "I suspect, my Lords, that you are more likely to doom him to long life, great responsibility, immense rewards and the fatigue of being his own difficult and complicated self."

The mitres moved gently and the members of the panel rose.

"You, my Lord Crudelta, will sleep till the trial is finished."

A robot stroked him and he fell asleep.

"Next witness," said the Lord Starmount, "in five minutes."

11

Vomact tried to keep Rambo from being heard as a witness. He argued fiercely with the Lord Starmount in the intermission. "You Lords have shot up my hospital, abducted two of my patients and now you are going to torment both Rambo and Elizabeth. Can't you leave them alone? Rambo is in no condition to give coherent answers and Elizabeth may be damaged if she sees him suffer."

The Lord Starmount said to him, "You have your rules, Doctor, and we have ours. This trial is being recorded, inch by inch and moment by moment. Nothing is going to be done to Rambo unless we find that he has planet-killing powers. If that is true, of course, we will ask you to take him back to the hospital and to put him to death very pleasantly. But I don't think it will happen. We want his story so that we can judge my colleague Crudelta. Do you think that the Instrumentality would survive if it did not have fierce internal discipline?"

Vomact nodded sadly; he went back to Grosbeck and Timofeyev, murmuring sadly to them, "Rambo's in for it. There's nothing we could do."

The panel reassembled. They put on their judicial mitres. The lights of the room darkened and the weird blue light of justice was turned on.

The robot orderly helped Rambo to the witness chair.

"You are obliged," said Starmount, "to speak quickly and clearly to this court."

"You're not Elizabeth," said Rambo.

"I am the Lord Starmount," said the investigating

Lord, quickly deciding to dispense with the formalities. "Do you know me?"

"No," said Rambo.

"Do you know where you are?"

"Earth," said Rambo.

"Do you wish to lie or to tell the truth?"

"A lie," said Rambo, "is the only truth which men can share with each other, so I will tell you lies, the way we always do."

"Can you report your trip?"

"No."

"Why not, citizen Rambo?"

"Words won't describe it."

"Do you remember your trip?"

"Do you remember your pulse of two minutes ago?" countered Rambo.

"I am not playing with you," said Starmount. "We think you have been in space-three and we want you to testify about the Lord Crudelta."

"Oh!" said Rambo. "I don't like him. I never did like him."

"Will you nevertheless try to tell us what happened also to you?"

"Should I, Elizabeth?" asked Rambo of the girl, who sat in the audience.

She did not stammer. "Yes," she said, in a clear voice which rang through the big room. "Tell them, so that we can find our lives again."

"I will tell you," said Rambo.

"When did you last see the Lord Crudelta?"

"When I was stripped and fitted to the rocket, four jumps out beyond Outpost Baiter Gator. He was on the ground. He waved good-bye to me."

"And then what happened?"

"The rocket rose. It felt very strange, like no craft I had ever been in before. I weighed many, many gravities."

"And then?"

"The engines went on. I was thrown out of space itself."

"What did it seem like?"

"Behind me I left the working ships, the cloth and the food which goes through space. I went down rivers which did not exist. I felt people around me though I could not see them, red people shooting arrows at live bodies."

"*Where* were you?" asked a panel member.

"In the wintertime where there is no summer. In an emptiness like a child's mind. In peninsulas which had torn loose from the land. And I *was* the ship."

"You were what?" asked the same panel member.

"The rocket nose. The cone. The boat. I was drunk. It was drunk. I was the drunkboat myself," said Rambo.

"And where did you go?" resumed Starmount.

"Where crazy lanterns stared with idiot eyes. Where the waves washed back and forth with the dead of all the ages. Where the stars became a pool and I swam in it. Where blue turns to liquor, stronger than alcohol, wilder than music, fermented with the *red red reds* of love. I saw all the things that men have ever thought they saw, but it was me who really saw them. I've heard phosphorescence singing and tides that seemed like crazy cattle clawing their way out of the ocean, their hooves beating the reefs. You will not believe me, but I found Floridas wilder than this, where the flowers had human skins and eyes like big cats."

"What are you talking about?" asked the Lord Starmount.

"What I found in space-three," snapped Artyr Rambo. "Believe it or not. This is what I now remember. Maybe it's a dream, but it's all I have. It was years and years and it was the blink of an eye. I dreamed green nights. I felt places where the whole horizon became one big waterfall. The boat that was me met children and I showed them El Dorado, where the gold men live. The people drowned in space washed gently past me. I was a boat where all the lost spaceships lay ruined and still. Seahorses which were not real ran beside me. The summer months came and hammered

down the sun. I went past archipelagoes of stars, where
the delirious skies opened up for wanderers. I cried for
me. I wept for man. I wanted to be the drunkboat sinking. I sank. I fell. It seemed to me that the grass was a
lake, where a sad child, on hands and knees, sailed a
toy boat as fragile as a butterfly in spring. I can't forget
the pride of unremembered flags, the arrogance of pris-
ons which I suspected, the swimming of the business-
men! Then I was on the grass."

"This may have scientific value," said the Lord Starmount, "but it is not of judicial importance. Do you
have any comment on what you did during the battle in
the hospital?"

Rambo was quick and looked sane. "What I did, I
did not do. What I did not do, I cannot tell. Let me go,
because I am tired of you and space, big men and big
things. Let me sleep and let me get well."

Starmount lifted his hand for silence.

The panel members stared at him.

Only the few telepaths present knew that they had all
said, *"Aye. Let the man go. Let the girl go. Let the
doctors go.* But bring back the Lord Crudelta later on.
He has many troubles ahead of him, and we wish to add
to them."

12

Between the Instrumentality, the Manhome Government and the authorities at the Old Main Hospital,
everyone wished to give Rambo and Elizabeth happiness.

As Rambo got well, much of his Earth Four memory
returned. The trip faded from his mind.

When he came to know Elizabeth, he hated the girl.

This was not his girl—his bold, saucy Elizabeth of
the markets and the valleys, of the snowy hills and the
long boat rides. This was somebody meek, sweet, sad
and hopelessly loving.

Vomact cured that.

He sent Rambo to the Pleasure City of the Hesperides, where bold and talkative women pursued him because he was rich and famous.

In a few weeks—a very few indeed—he wanted *his* Elizabeth, this strange shy girl who had been cooked back from the dead while he rode space with his own fragile bones.

"Tell the truth, darling." He spoke to her once gravely and seriously. "The Lord Crudelta did not arrange the accident which killed you?"

"They say he wasn't there," said Elizabeth. "They say it was an actual accident. I don't know. I will never know."

"It doesn't matter now," said Rambo. "Crudelta's off among the stars, looking for trouble and finding it. We have our bungalow, and our waterfall and each other."

"Yes, my darling," she said, "each other. And no fantastic Floridas for us."

He blinked at this reference to the past, but he said nothing. A man who has been through space[3] needs very little in life, outside of *not* going back to space[3]. Sometimes he dreamed he was the rocket again, the old rocket taking off on an impossible trip. Let other men follow! he thought. Let other men go! I have Elizabeth and I am here.

Western Science Is So Wonderful

THE MARTIAN WAS sitting at the top of a granite cliff. In order to enjoy the breeze better he had taken on the shape of a small fir tree. The wind always felt very pleasant through nondeciduous needles.

At the bottom of the cliff stood an American, the first the Martian had ever seen.

The American extracted from his pocket a fantastically ingenious device. It was a small metal box with a nozzle which lifted up and produced an immediate flame. From this miraculous device the American readily lit a tube of bliss-giving herbs. The Martian understood that these were called *cigarettes* by the Americans. As the American finished lighting his cigarette, the Martian changed his shape to that of a fifteen-foot, red-faced, black-whiskered Chinese demagogue, and shouted to the American in English, "Hello, friend!"

The American looked up and almost dropped his teeth.

The Martian stepped off the cliff and floated gently down toward the American, approaching slowly so as not to affright him too much.

Nevertheless, the American did seem to be concerned, because he said, "You're not real, are you? You can't be. Or can you?"

Modestly the Martian looked into the mind of the American and realized that fifteen-foot Chinese demagogues were not reassuring visual images in an everyday American psychology. He peeked modestly into the mind of the American, seeking a reassuring image. The first image he saw was that of the American's mother, so the Martian promptly changed into the form of the American's mother and answered, "What is real, darling?"

With this the American turned slightly green and put his hand over his eyes. The Martian looked once again into the mind of the American and saw a slightly confused image.

When the American opened his eyes, the Martian had taken on the form of a Red Cross girl halfway through a strip-tease act. Although the maneuver was designed to be pleasant, the American was not reassured. His fear began to change into anger and he said, "What the hell are you?"

The Martian gave up trying to be obliging. He changed himself into a Chinese Nationalist major general with an Oxford education and said in a distinct

British accent, "I'm by way of being one of the local characters, a bit on the Supernatural side, you know. I do hope you do not mind. Western science is so wonderful that I had to examine that fantastic machine you have in your hand. Would you like to chat a bit before you go on?"

The Martian caught a confused glimpse of images in the American's mind. They seemed to be concerned with something called *prohibition,* something else called "on the wagon," and the reiterated question, "How the hell did *I* get here?"

Meanwhile the Martian examined the lighter.

He handed it back to the American, who looked stunned.

"Very fine magic," said the Martian. "We do not do anything of that sort in these hills. I am a fairly low-class Demon. I see that you are a captain in the illustrious army of the United States. Allow me to introduce myself. I am the 1,387,229th Eastern Subordinate Incarnation of a Lohan. Do you have time for a chat?"

The American looked at the Chinese Nationalist uniform. Then he looked behind him. His Chinese porters and interpreter lay like bundles of rags on the meadowy floor of the valley; they had all fainted dead away. The American held himself together long enough to say, "What is a Lohan?"

"A Lohan is an Arhat," said the Martian.

The American did not take in this information either and the Martian concluded that something must have been missing from the usual amenities of getting acquainted with American officers. Regretfully the Martian erased all memory of himself from the mind of the American and from the minds of the swooned Chinese. He planted himself back on the cliff top, resumed the shape of a fir tree, and woke the entire gathering. He saw the Chinese interpreter gesticulating at the American and he knew that the Chinese was saying, "There are Demons in these hills . . ."

The Martian rather liked the hearty laugh with which

the American greeted this piece of superstitious Chinese nonsense.

He watched the party disappear as they went around the miraculously beautiful little Lake of the Eight-Mouthed River.

That was in 1945.

The Martian spent many thoughtful hours trying to materialize a lighter, but he never managed to create one which did not dissolve back into some unpleasant primordial effluvium within hours.

Then it was 1955. The Martian heard that a Soviet officer was coming, and he looked forward with genuine pleasure to making the acquaintance of another person from the miraculously up-to-date Western world.

Peter Farrer was a Volga German.

The Volga Germans are about as much Russian as the Pennsylvania Dutch are Americans.

They have lived in Russia for more than two hundred years, but the terrible bitterness of the Second World War led to the breakup of most of their communities.

Farrer himself had fared well in this. After holding the noncommissioned rank of *yefreitor* in the Red Army for some years he had become a sublieutenant. In a technikum he had studied geology and survey.

The chief of the Soviet military mission to the province of Yunnan in the People's Republic of China had said to him, "Farrer, you are getting a real holiday. There is no danger in this trip, but we do want to get an estimate on the feasibility of building a secondary mountain highway along the rock cliffs west of Lake Pakou. I think well of you, Farrer. You have lived down your German name and you're a good Soviet citizen and officer. I know that you will not cause any trouble with our Chinese allies or with the mountain people among whom you must travel. Go easy with them, Farrer. They are very superstitious. We need their full support, but we can take our time to get it. The liberation of India is still a long way off, but when we must move to help the Indians throw off American imperialism we do not want to have any soft areas in our rear. Do not push things too hard, Farrer. Be sure that you get a good technical job done, but that you make friends with everyone other than imperialist reactionary elements."

Farrer nodded very seriously. "You mean, comrade Colonel, that I must make friends with *everything?*"

"Everything," said the colonel firmly.

Farrer was young and he liked doing a bit of crusading on his own. "I'm a militant atheist, Colonel. Do I have to be pleasant to priests?"

"Priests, too," said the colonel, "especially priests."

The colonel looked sharply at Farrer. "You make friends with everything, everything except women. You hear me, comrade? Stay out of trouble."

Farrer saluted and went back to his desk to make preparations for the trip.

Three weeks later Farrer was climbing up past the small cascades which led to the River of the Golden Sands, the Chinshachiang, as the Long River or Yangtze was known locally.

Beside him there trotted Party Secretary Kungsun. Kungsun was a Peking aristocrat who had joined the Communist Party in his youth. Sharp-faced, sharp-voiced, he made up for his aristocracy by being the most violent Communist in all of northwestern Yunnan. Though they had only a squad of troops and a lot of local bearers for their supplies, they did have an officer of the old People's Liberation Army to assure their military well-being and to keep an eye on Farrer's technical competence. Comrade Captain Li, roly-poly and jolly, sweated wearily behind them as they climbed the steep cliffs.

Li called after them, "If you want to be heroes of labor let's keep climbing, but if you are following sound military logistics let's all sit down and drink some tea. We can't possibly get to Pakouhu before nightfall anyhow."

Kungsun looked back contemptuously. The ribbon of soldiers and bearers reached back two hundred yards, making a snake of dust clutched to the rocky slope of the mountain. From this perspective he saw the caps of the soldiers and the barrels of their rifles pointing upward toward him as they climbed. He saw the towel-wrapped heads of the liberated porters and he knew without speaking to them that they were cursing him in language just as violent as the language with which they had cursed their capitalist oppressors in days gone past. Far below them all the thread of the Chinshachiang was woven like a single strand of gold into the gray-green of the twilight valley floor.

He spat at the army captain, "If you had your way about it, we'd still be sitting there in an inn drinking the hot tea while the men slept."

The captain did not take offense. He had seen many party secretaries in his day. In the New China it was much safer to be a captain. A few of the party secretaries he had known had got to be very important men. One of them had even got to Peking and had been assigned a whole Buick to himself together with three Parker 51 pens. In the minds of the Communist bureaucracy this represented a state close to absolute bliss. Captain Li wanted none of that. Two square meals a day and an endless succession of patriotic farm girls, preferably chubby ones, represented his view of a wholly liberated China.

Farrer's Chinese was poor, but he got the intent of the argument. In thick but understandable Mandarin he called, half laughing at them, "Come along, comrades. We may not make it to the lake by nightfall, but we certainly can't bivouac on this cliff either." He whistled *Ich hatt' ein Kameraden* through his teeth as he pulled ahead of Kungsun and led the climb on up the mountain.

Thus it was Farrer who first came over the lip of the cliff and met the Martian face to face.

This time the Martian was ready. He remembered his disappointing experience with the American, and he did not want to affright his guest so as to spoil the social nature of the occasion. While Farrer had been climbing the cliff, the Martian had been climbing Farrer's mind, chasing in and out of Farrer's memories as happily as a squirrel chases around inside an immense oak tree. From Farrer's own mind he had extracted a great many pleasant memories. He had then hastened back to the top of the cliff and had incorporated these in very substantial-looking phantoms.

Farrer got halfway across the lip of the cliff before he realized what he was looking at. Two Soviet military trucks were parked in a tiny glade. Each of them had tables in front of it. One of the tables was set with a very elaborate Russian *zakouska* (the Soviet equivalent of a smorgasbord). The Martian hoped he would be able to keep these objects materialized while Farrer ate them, but he was afraid they might disappear each time Farrer swallowed them because the Martian was not very well acquainted with digestive processes of human beings and did not want to give his guest a violent stomachache by allowing him to deposit through his esophagus and into his stomach objects of extremely improvised and uncertain chemical makeup.

The first truck had a big red flag on it with white Russian letters reading "WELCOME TO THE HEROES OF BRYANSK."

The second truck was even better. The Martian could see that Farrer was very fond of women, so he had materialized four very pretty Soviet girls, a blonde, a brunette, a redhead, and an albino just to make it interesting. The Martian did not trust himself to make them all speak the correctly feminine and appealing forms of the Russian language, so having materialized them he set them all in lounge chairs and put them to sleep. He had wondered what form he himself should take and decided that it would be very hospitable to assume the appearance of Mao Tze-tung.

Farrer did not come on over the cliff. He stayed where he was. He looked at the Martian and the Martian said, very oilily, "Come on up. We are waiting for you."

"Who the hell are you?" barked Farrer.

"I am a pro-Soviet Demon," said the apparent Mr. Mao Tze-tung, "and these are materialized Communist hospitality arrangements. I hope you like them."

At this point both Kungsun and Li appeared. Li climbed up the left side of Farrer, Kungsun on the right. All three stopped, gaping.

Kungsun recovered his wits first. He recognized Mao Tze-tung. He never passed up a chance to get acquainted with the higher command of the Communist Party. He said in a very weak, strained, incredulous voice, "Mr. Party Chairman Mao, I never thought that we would see you here in these hills, or are you you, and if you aren't you, who are you?"

"I am not your party chairman," said the Martian. "I am merely a local Demon who has strong pro-Communist sentiments and would like to meet companionable people like yourselves."

At this point Li fainted and would have rolled back down the cliff knocking over soldiers and porters if the Martian had not reached out his left arm, concurrently changing the left arm into the shape of a python, picking up the unconscious Li and resting his body gently against the side of the picnic truck. The Soviet sleeping beauties slept on. The python turned back into an arm.

Kungsun's face had turned completely white; since he was a pale and pleasant ivory color to start with, his whiteness had a very marked tinge.

"I think this *wang-pa* is a counterrevolutionary impostor," he said weakly, "but I don't know what to do about him. I am glad that the Chinese People's Republic has a representative from the Soviet Union to instruct us in difficult party procedure."

Farrer snapped, "If he is a goose, he is a Chinese goose. He is not a Russian goose. You'd better not call him that dirty name. He seems to have some powers that do work. Look at what he did to Li."

The Martian decided to show off his education and said very conciliatorily, "If I am a *wang-pa* you are a *wang-pen.*" He added brightly, in the Russian language,

"That's an ingrate, you know. Much worse than an illegitimate one. Do you like my shape, comrade Farrer? Do you have a cigarette lighter with you? Western science is so wonderful, I can never make very solid things, and you people make airplanes, atom bombs, and all sorts of refreshing entertainments of that kind."

Farrer reached into his pocket, groping for his lighter.

A scream sounded behind him. One of the Chinese enlisted men had left the stopped column behind and had stuck his head over the edge of the cliff to see what was happening. When he saw the trucks and the figure of Mao Tze-tung he began shrieking, "There are devils here! There are devils here!"

From centuries of experience, the Martian knew there was no use trying to get along with the local people unless they were very, very young or very, very old. He walked to the edge of the cliff so that all the men could see him. He expanded the shape of Mao Tze-tung until it was thirty-five feet high. Then he changed himself into the embodiment of an ancient Chinese god of war with whiskers, ribbons, and sword tassels blowing in the breeze. They all fainted dead away as he had intended. He packed them snugly against the rocks so that none of them would fall back down the slope. Then he took on the shape of a Soviet WAC—a rather pretty little blonde with sergeant's insignia—and rematerialized himself beside Farrer.

By this point Farrer had his lighter out.

The pretty little blonde said to Farrer, "Do you like this shape better?"

Farrer said, "I don't believe this at all. I am a militant atheist. I have fought against superstition all my life." Farrer was twenty-four.

The Martian said, "I don't think you like me being a girl. It bothers you, doesn't it?"

"Since you do not exist you cannot bother me. But if you don't mind could you please change your shape again?"

The Martian took on the appearance of a chubby little Buddha. He knew this was a little impious, but he felt Farrer give a sigh of relief. Even Li seemed cheered up, now that the Martian had taken on a proper religious form.

"Listen, you obscene demonic monstrosity," snarled Kungsun, "this is the Chinese People's Republic. You have absolutely no business taking on supernatural images or conducting unatheistic activities. Please abolish yourself and those illusions yonder. What do you want, anyhow?"

"I would like," said the Martian mildly, "to become a member of the Chinese Communist Party."

Farrer and Kungsun stared at each other. Then they both spoke at once, Farrer in Russian and Kungsun in Chinese. "But we can't let you in the Party."

Kungsun said, "If you're a demon you don't exist, and if you do exist you're illegal."

The Martian smiled. "Take some refreshments. You may change your minds. Would you like a girl?" he said, pointing at the assorted Russian beauties who still slept in their lounge chairs.

But Kungsun and Farrer shook their heads.

With a sigh the Martian dematerialized the girls and replaced them with three striped Siberian tigers. The tigers approached.

One tiger stopped cozily behind the Martian and sat down. The Martian sat on him. Said the Martian brightly, "I like tigers to sit on. They're so comfortable. Have a tiger."

Farrer and Kungsun were staring open-mouthed at their respective tigers. The tigers yawned at them and stretched out.

With a tremendous effort of will the two young men sat down on the ground in front of their tigers. Farrer sighed. "What *do* you want? I suppose you won this trick . . ."

Said the Martian, "Have a jug of wine."

He materialized a jug of wine and a porcelain cup in front of each, including himself. He poured himself a drink and looked at them through shrewd, narrowed eyes. "I would like to learn all about Western science. You see, I am a Martian student who was exiled here to become the 1,387,229th Eastern Subordinate Incarnation of a Lohan and I have been here more than two thousand years, and I can only perceive in a radius of ten leagues. Western science is very interesting. If I could, I would like to be an engineering student, but since I cannot leave this place I would like to join the Communist Party and have many visitors come to see me."

By this time Kungsun made up his mind. He was a Communist, but he was also a Chinese—an aristocratic Chinese and a man well versed in the folklore of his own country. Kungsun used a politely archaic form of the Peking court dialect when he spoke again in much milder terms. "Honored, esteemed Demon, sir, it's just no use at all your trying to get into the Communist Party. I admit it is very patriotic of you as a Chinese Demon to want to join the progressive group which leads the Chinese people in their endless struggle against the vicious American imperialists. Even if you convinced me I don't think you can convince the party authorities, esteemed sir. The only thing for you to do in our new Communist world of the New China is to become a counterrevolutionary refugee and migrate to capitalist territory."

The Martian looked hurt and sullen. He frowned at them as he sipped his wine. Behind him Li began snoring where he slept against the wheel of a truck.

Very persuasively the Martian began to speak. "I see, young man, that you're beginning to believe in me. You don't have to recognize me. Just believe in me a little bit. I am happy to see that you, Party Secretary Kungsun, are prepared to be polite. I am not a Chinese Demon, since I was originally a Martian who was elected to the Lesser Assembly of Concord, but who made an inopportune remark and who must live on as the 1,387,229th Eastern Subordinate Incarnation of a Lohan for three hundred thousand springs and autumns before I can return. I expect to be around a very long time indeed. On the other hand, I would like to study engineering and I think it would be much better for me to become a member of the Communist Party than to go to a strange place."

Farrer had an inspiration. Said he to the Martian, "I have an idea. Before I explain it, though, would you please take those damned trucks away and remove that *zakouska?* It makes my mouth water and I'm very sorry, but I just can't accept your hospitality."

The Martian complied with a wave of his hand. The trucks and the tables disappeared. Li had been leaning against a truck. His head went thump against the grass. He muttered something in his sleep and then resumed his snoring. The Martian turned back to his guests.

Farrer picked up the thread of his own thoughts. "Leaving aside the question of whether you exist or not, I can assure you that I know the Russian Communist Party and my colleague, Comrade Kungsun here, knows the Chinese Communist Party. Communist parties are very wonderful things. They lead the masses in the fight against wicked Americans. Do you realize that if we didn't fight on with the revolutionary struggle all of us would have to drink Coca-Cola every day?"

"What is Coca-Cola?" asked the Demon.

"I don't know," replied Farrer.

"Then why be afraid to drink any?"

"Don't be irrelevant. I hear that the capitalists make everybody drink it. The Communist Party cannot take time to open up supernatural secretariats. It would spoil irreligious campaigns for us to have a demonic secretary. I can tell you the Russian Communist Party won't put up with it and our friend here will tell you there is no place in the Chinese Communist Party. We want you to be happy. You seem to be a very friendly demon. Why don't you just go away? The capitalists will welcome you. They are very reactionary and very religious. You might even find people there who would believe in you."

The Martian changed his shape from that of a roly-poly Buddha and assumed the appearance and dress of a young Chinese man, a student of engineering at the

University of the Revolution in Peking. In the shape of
the student he continued, "I don't want to be believed
in. I want to study engineering, and I want to learn all
about Western science."

Kungsun came to Farrer's support. He said, "It's just
no use trying to be a Communist engineer. You look
like a very absentminded demon to me and I think that
even if you tried to pass yourself off as a human being
you would keep forgetting and changing shapes. That
would ruin the morale of any class."

The Martian thought to himself that the young man
had a point there. He hated keeping any one particular
shape for more than half an hour. Staying in one bodily
form made him itch. He also liked to change sexes every few times; it seemed sort of refreshing. He did not
admit to the young man that Kungsun had scored a
point with that remark about shape-changing, but he
nodded amiably at them and asked, "But how could I
get abroad?"

"Just go," said Kungsun, wearily. "Just go. You're a
Demon. You can do anything."

"I can't do that," snapped the student-Martian. "I
have to have something to go by."

He turned to Farrer. "It won't do any good, your giving me something. If you gave me something Russian
and I would end up in Russia, from what you say they
won't want to have a Communist Martian any more
than these Chinese people do. I won't like to leave my
beautiful lake anyhow, but I suppose I will have to if I
am to get acquainted with Western science."

Farrer said, "I have an idea." He took off his wrist-
watch and handed it to the Martian.

The Martian inspected it. Many years before, the
watch had been manufactured in the United States of
America. It had been traded by a G.I. to a fraulein, by
the fraulein's grandmother to a Red Army man for
three sacks of potatoes, and by the Red Army man for
five hundred rubles to Farrer when the two of them met
in Kuibyshev. The numbers were painted with radium,
as were the hands. The second hand was missing, so the

Martian materialized a new one. He changed the shape
of it several times before it fitted. On the watch there
was written in English "MARVIN WATCH COMPANY." At
the bottom of the face of the watch there was the name
of a town: "WATERBURY, CONN."

The Martian read it. Said he to Farrer, "Where is this
place Waterbury, *Kahn?*"

"The Conn. is the short form of the name of one of
the American states. If you are going to be a reactionary
capitalist that is a very good place to be a capitalist in."

Still white-faced, but in a sickly ingratiating way,
Kungsun added his bit. "I think *you* would like Coca-
Cola. It's very reactionary."

The student-Martian frowned. He still held the watch
in his hand. Said he, "I don't care whether it's reactionary or not. I want to be in a very scientific place."

Farrer said, "You couldn't go any place more scientific
than Waterbury, Conn., especially Conn.—that's the
most scientific place they have in America and I'm sure
they are very pro-Martian and you can join one of the
capitalist parties. They won't mind. But the Communist
parties would make a lot of trouble for you."

Farrer smiled and his eyes lit up. "Furthermore," he
added, as a winning point, "you can keep my watch for
yourself, for always."

The Martian frowned. Speaking to himself the
student-Martian said, "I can see that Chinese Communism is going to collapse in eight years, eight hundred
years, or eighty thousand years. Perhaps I'd better go to
this Waterbury, Conn."

The two young Communists nodded their heads vig-
orously and grinned. They both smiled at the Martian.

"Honored, esteemed Martian, sir, please hurry along
because I want to get my men over the edge of the cliff
before darkness falls. Go with our blessing."

The Martian changed shape. He took on the image of
an Arhat, a subordinate disciple of Buddha. Eight feet
tall, he loomed above them. His face radiated unearthly
calm. The watch, miraculously provided with a new
strap, was firmly strapped to his left wrist.

"Bless you, my boys," said he. "I go to Waterbury."
And he did.

Farrer stared at Kungsun. "What's happened to Li?"
Kungsun shook his head dazedly. "I don't know. I
feel funny."

(In departing for that marvelous strange place, Waterbury, Conn., the Martian had taken with him all their
memories of himself.)

Kungsun walked to the edge of the cliff. Looking
over, he saw the men sleeping.

"Look at that," he muttered. He stepped to the edge
of the cliff and began shouting. "Wake up, you fools,
you turtles. Haven't you any more sense than to sleep
on a cliff as nightfall approaches?"

The Martian concentrated all his powers on the loca-
tion of Waterbury, Conn.

He was the 1,387,229th Eastern Subordinate Incarnation of a Lohan (or an Arhat), and his powers were
limited, impressive though they might seem to outsiders.

With a shock, a thrill, a something of breaking, a
sense of things done and undone, he found himself in
flat country. Strange darkness surrounded him. Air,
which he had never smelled before, flowed quietly
around him. Farrer and Li, hanging on a cliff high
above the Chinshachiang, lay far behind him in the
world from which he had broken. He remembered that
he had left his shape behind.

Absentmindedly he glanced down at himself to see
what form he had taken for the trip.

He discovered that he had arrived in the form of a
small, laughing Buddha seven inches high, carved in
yellowed ivory.

"This will never do!" muttered the Martian to himself. "I must take on one of the local forms . . ."

He sensed around in his environment, groping telepathically for interesting objects near him.

"Aha, a milk truck."

Thought he, Western science is indeed very wonderful. Imagine a machine made purely for the purpose of transporting milk!

Swiftly he transferred himself into a milk truck.

In the darkness, his telepathic senses had not distinguished the metal of which the milk truck was made nor the color of the paint.

In order to remain inconspicuous, he turned himself into a milk truck made of solid gold. Then, without a driver, he started up his own engine and began driving himself down one of the main highways leading into Waterbury, Connecticut . . . So if you happen to be passing through Waterbury, Conn., and see a solid gold milk truck driving itself through the streets, you'll know it's the Martian, otherwise the 1,387,229th Eastern Subordinate Incarnation of a Lohan, and that he still thinks Western science is wonderful.

Nancy

TWO MEN FACED Gordon Greene as he came into the room. The young aide was a nonentity. The general was not. The commanding general sat where he should, at his own desk. It was placed squarely in the room, and yet the infinite courtesy of the general was shown by the fact that the blinds were so drawn that the light did not fall directly into the eyes of the person interviewed.

At that time the colonel general was Wenzel Wallenstein, the first man ever to venture into the very deep remoteness of space. He had not reached a star. Nobody had, at that time, but he had gone farther than any man had ever gone before.

Wallenstein was an old man and yet the count of his years was not high. He was less than ninety in a period

in which many men lived to one hundred and fifty. The
thing that made Wallenstein look old was the suffering
which came from mental strain, not the kind which
came from anxiety and competition, not the kind which
came from ill health.

It was a subtler kind—a sensitivity which created its
own painfulness.

Yet it was real.

Wallenstein was as stable as men came, and the
young lieutenant was astonished to find that at his first
meeting with the commander in chief his instinctive
emotional reaction should be one of quick sympathy for
the man who commanded the entire organization.

"Your name?"

The lieutenant answered, "Gordon Greene."

"Born that way?"

"No, sir."

"What was your name originally?"

"Giordano Verdi."

"Why did you change? Verdi is a great name too."

"People just found it hard to pronounce, sir. I followed along the best I could."

"I kept my name," said the old general. "I suppose it
is a matter of taste."

The young lieutenant lifted his hand, left hand, palm
outward, in the new salute which had been devised by
the psychologists. He knew that this meant military
courtesy could be passed by for the moment and that
the subordinate officer was requesting permission to
speak as man to man. He knew the salute and yet in
these surroundings he did not altogether trust it.

The general's response was quick. He countersigned,
left hand, palm outward.

The heavy, tired, wise, strained old face showed no
change of expression. The general was alert. Mechani-
cally friendly, his eyes followed the lieutenant. The lieutenant was sure that there was nothing behind those
eyes, except world upon world of inward troubles.

The lieutenant spoke again, this time on confident
ground.

"Is this a special interview, General? Do you have something in mind for me? If it is, sir, let me warn you, I have been declared to be psychologically unstable. Personnel doesn't often make a mistake but they may have sent me in here under error."

The general smiled. The smile itself was mechanical. It was a control of muscles, not a quick spring of human emotion.

"You will know well enough what I have in mind when we talk together, Lieutenant. I am going to have another man sit with me and it will give you some idea of what your life is leading you toward. You know perfectly well that you have asked for deep space and that so far as I'm concerned you've gotten it. The question is now, 'Do you really want it?' Do you want to take it? Is that all that you wanted to abridge courtesy for?"

"Yes, sir," said the lieutenant.

"You didn't have to call for the courtesy sign for that kind of a question. You could have asked me even within the limits of service. Let's not get too psychological. We don't need to, do we?"

Again the general gave the lieutenant a heavy smile.

Wallenstein gestured to the aide, who sprang to attention.

Wallenstein said, "Send him in."

The aide said, "Yes, sir."

The two men waited expectantly. With a springy, lively, quick, happy step a strange lieutenant entered the room.

Gordon Greene had never seen anybody quite like this lieutenant. The lieutenant was old, almost as old as the general. His face was cheerful and unlined. The muscles of his cheeks and forehead bespoke happiness, relaxation, an assured view of life. The lieutenant wore the three highest decorations of his service. There weren't any others higher and yet there he was, an old man and still a lieutenant.

Lieutenant Greene couldn't understand it. He didn't know who this man was. It was easy enough for a young man to be a lieutenant but not for a man in his seventies

or eighties. People that age were colonels, or retired, or
out.

Or they had gone back to civilian life.

Space was a young man's game.

The general himself arose in courtesy to his contemporary. Lieutenant Greene's eyes widened. This too was
odd. The general was not known to violate courtesy at
all irregularly.

"Sit down, sir," said the strange old lieutenant.

The general sat.

"What do you want with me now? Do you want to
talk about the Nancy routine one more time?"

"The Nancy routine?" asked the general blindly.

"Yes, sir. It's the same story I've told these young-
sters before. You've heard it and I've heard it, there's no
use of pretending."

The strange lieutenant said, "My name's Karl Vonderleyen. Have you ever heard of me?"

"No, sir," said the young lieutenant.

The old lieutenant said, "You will."

"Don't get bitter about it, Karl," said the general. "A
lot of other people have had troubles, besides you. I
went and did the same things you did, and I'm a general. You might at least pay me the courtesy of envying
me."

"I don't envy you, General. You've had your life,
and I've had mine. You know what you've missed, or
you think you do, and I know what I've had, and I'm
sure I do."

The old lieutenant paid no more attention to the commander in chief. He turned to the young man and said,

"You're going to go out into space and we are putting
on a little act, a vaudeville act. The general didn't get
any Nancy. He didn't ask for Nancy. He didn't turn for
help. He got out into the Up-and-Out, he pulled
through it. Three years of it. Three years that are closer
to three million years, I suppose. He went through hell
and he came back. Look at his face. He's a success.
He's an utter, blasted success, sitting there worn out,
tired, and, it would seem, hurt. Look at me. Look at me

carefully, Lieutenant. I'm a failure. I'm a lieutenant and
the Space Service keeps me that way."

The commander in chief said nothing, so Vonderleyen talked on.

"Oh, they will retire me as general, I suppose, when
the time comes. I'm not ready to retire. I'd just as soon
stay in the Space Service as anything else. There is not
much to do in this world. I've had it."

"Had what, sir?" Lieutenant Greene dared to ask.

"I found Nancy. He didn't," he said. "That's as simple as it is."

The general cut back into the conversation. "It's not
that bad and it's not that simple, Lieutenant Greene.
There seems to be something a little wrong with Lieutenant Vonderleyen today. The story is one we have to
tell you and it is something you have to make up your
own mind on. There is no regulation way of handling
it."

The general looked very sharply at Lieutenant
Greene.

"Do you know what we have done to your brain?"

"No, sir."

"Have you heard of the *sokta* virus?"

"The what, sir?"

"The *sokta* virus. *Sokta* is an ancient word, gets its
name from Chosen-mal, the language of Old Korea.
That was a country west of where Japan used to be. It
means 'maybe' and it is a 'maybe' that we put inside
your head. It is a tiny crystal, more than microscopic.
It's there. There is actually a machine on the ship, not a
big one because we can't waste space; it has resonance
to detonate the virus. If you detonate *sokta,* you will be
like him. If you don't, you will be like me—assuming,
in either case, that you live. You may not live and you
may not get back, in which case what we are talking
about is academic."

The young man nerved himself to ask, "What does
this do to me? Why do you make this big fuss over it?"

"We can't tell you too much. One reason is it is not
worth talking about."

"You mean you really can't, sir?"

The general shook his head sadly and wisely.

"No, I missed it, he got it, and yet it somehow gets out beyond the limits of talking."

At this point while he was telling the story, many years later, I asked my cousin, "Well, Gordon, if they said you can't talk about it, how can you?"

"Drunk, man, drunk," said the cousin. "How long do you think it took me to wind myself up to this point? I'll never tell it again—never again. Anyhow, you're my cousin, you don't count. And I promised Nancy I wouldn't tell anybody."

"Who's Nancy?" I asked him.

"Nancy's what it's all about. That is what the story is. That's what those poor old goops were trying to tell me in the office. They didn't know. One of them, he had Nancy; the other one, he hadn't."

"Is Nancy a real person?"

With that he told me the rest of the story.

The interview was harsh. It was clean, stark, simple, direct. The alternatives were flat. It was perfectly plain that Wallenstein wanted Greene to come back alive. It was actual space command policy to bring the man back as a live failure instead of letting him become a dead hero. Pilots were not that common. Furthermore, morale would be worsened if men were told to go out on suicide operations.

The whole thing was psychological and before Greene got out of the room he was more confused than when he went in.

They kept telling them, both of them in their different ways—the general happily, the old lieutenant unhappily—that this was serious. The grim old general was very cheerful about telling him. The happy lieutenant kept being very sympathetic.

Greene himself wondered why he could be so sympathetic toward the commanding general and be so perfectly carefree about a failed old lieutenant. His sympathies should have been the other way around.

Fifteen hundred million miles later, four months later in ordinary time, four lifetimes later by the time which he'd gone through, Greene found out what they were talking about. It was an old psychological teaching. The men died if they were left utterly alone. The ships were designed to be protected against that. There were two men on each ship. Each ship had a lot of tapes, even a few quite unnecessary animals; in this case a pair of hamsters had been included on the ship. They had been sterilized, of course, to avoid the problem of feeding the young, but nevertheless they made a little family of their own in a miniature of life's happiness on Earth.

Earth was very far away.

At that point, his copilot died.

Everything that had threatened Greene then came true.

Greene suddenly realized what they were talking about.

The hamsters were his one hope. He thrust his face close to their cage and talked to them. He attributed moods to them. He tried to live their lives with them, all as if they were people.

As if he, himself, were a part of people still alive and not out there with the screaming silence beyond the thin wall of metal. There was nothing to do except to roam like a caged animal in machinery which he would never understand.

Time lost its perspectives. He knew he was crazy and he knew that by training he could survive the partial craziness. He even realized that the instability in his own personality which had made him think that he wouldn't fit the Space Service probably contributed to the hope that went in with service to this point.

His mind kept coming back to Nancy and to the *sokta* virus.

What was it they had said?

They had told him that he could waken Nancy, whoever Nancy was. Nancy was no pet name of his.

And yet somehow or other the virus always worked. He only needed to move his head toward a certain point, press the resonating stud on the wall, one pressure, his mission would fail, he would be happy, he would come home alive.

He couldn't understand it. Why such a choice?

It seemed three thousand years later that he dictated his last message back to Space Service. He didn't know what would happen. Obviously, that old lieutenant, Vonderleyen, or whatever his name was, was still alive. Equally obviously the general was alive. The general had pulled through. The lieutenant hadn't.

And now, Lieutenant Greene, fifteen hundred million miles out in space, had to make his choice. He made it. He decided to fail.

But he wanted, as a matter of discipline, to speak up for the man who was failing and he dictated, for the records of the ship when it got back to Earth, a very simple message concluding with an appeal for justice.

". . . and so, gentlemen, I have decided to activate the stud. I do not know what the reference to Nancy signifies. I have no concept of what the *sokta* virus will do except that it will make me fail. For this I am heartily ashamed. I regret the human weakness that has driven me to this. The weakness is human and you, gentlemen, have allowed for it. In this respect, it is not I who is failing, but the Space Service itself in giving me an authorization to fail. Gentlemen, forgive the bitterness with which I say *good-bye* to you in these seconds, but now I do say good-bye."

He stopped dictating, blinked his eyes, took one last look at the hamsters—who might they be by the time the *sokta* virus went to work?—pressed the stud and leaned forward.

Nothing happened. He pressed the stud again.

The ship suddenly filled with a strange odor. He couldn't identify the odor. He didn't know what it was.

It suddenly came to him that this was new-mown hay with a slight tinge of geraniums, possibly of roses, too, on the far side. It was a smell that was common on the farm a few years ago where he had gone for a summer. It was the smell of his mother being on the porch and calling him back to a meal, and of himself, enough of a man to be indulgent even toward the woman in his own mother, enough of a child to turn happily back to a familiar voice.

He said to himself, "If this is all there is to that virus, I can take it and work on with continued efficiency."

He added, "At fifteen hundred million miles out, and nothing but two hamsters for years of loneliness, a few hallucinations won't hurt me any."

The door opened.

It couldn't open.

The door opened nevertheless.

At this point, Greene knew a fear more terrible than anything else he had ever encountered. He said to himself, "I'm crazy, I'm crazy," and stared at the opening door.

A girl stepped in. She said, "Hello, you there. You know me, don't you?"

Greene said, "No, no, miss, who are you?"

The girl didn't answer. She just stood there and she gave him a smile.

She wore a blue serge skirt cut so that it had broad, vertical stripes, a neat little waist, a belt of the same material, a very simple blouse. She was not a strange girl and she was by no means a creature of outer space.

She was somebody he had known and known well. Perhaps loved. He just couldn't place her—not at that moment, not in that place.

She still stood staring at him. That was all.

It all came to him. Of course, she was Nancy. She was not just that Nancy they were talking about, she was *his* Nancy, his own Nancy he had always known and never met before.

He managed to pull himself together and say it to her,

"How do I know you if I don't know you? You're Nancy and I've known you all my life and I have always wanted to marry you. You are the girl I have al-

ways been in love with and I never saw you before.
That's funny, Nancy. It's terribly funny. I don't understand it, do you?"

Nancy came over and put her hand on his forehead.
It was a real little hand and her presence was dear and
precious and very welcome to him. She said, "It's going
to take a bit of thinking. You see, I am not real, not to
anybody except you. And yet I am more real to you
than anything else will ever be. That is what the *sokta*
virus is, darling. It's me. I'm you."

He stared at her.

He could have been unhappy but he didn't feel unhappy, he was so glad to have her there. He said,

"What do you mean? The *sokta* virus has made you?
Am I crazy? Is this just a hallucination?"

Nancy shook her head and her pretty curls spun.

"It's not that. I'm simply every girl that you ever
wanted. I am the illusion that you always wanted but I
am you because I am in the depths of you. I am everything that your mind might not have encountered in life.
Everything that you might have been afraid to dig up.
Here I am and I'm going to stay. And as long as we are
here in this ship with the resonance we will get along
well."

*My cousin at this point began weeping. He picked up
a wine flask and poured down a big glass of heavy Dago
Red. For a while he cried. Putting his head on the table,
he looked up at me and said, "It's been a long, long
time. It's been a very long time and I still remember
how she talked with me. And I see now why they say
you can't talk about it. A man has got to be fearfully
drunk to tell about a real life that he had and a good
one, and a beautiful one and let it go, doesn't he?"*

"That's right," I said, to be encouraging.

Nancy changed the ship right away. She moved the
hamsters. She changed the decorations. She checked the
records. The work went on more efficiently than ever
before.

But the home they made for themselves, that was something different. It had baking smells, and it had wind smells, and sometimes he would hear the rain although the nearest rain by now was one thousand six hundred million miles away, and there was nothing but the grating of cold silence on the cold, cold metal at the outside of the ship.

They lived together. It didn't take long for them to get thoroughly used to each other.

He had been born Giordano Verdi. He had limitations.

And the time came for them to get even more close than lover and lover. He said,

"I just can't take you, darling. That is not the way we can do it, even in space and not the way, even if you are not real. You are real enough to me. Will you marry me out of the prayer book?"

Her eyes lit up and her incomparable lips gleamed in a smile that was all peculiarly her own. She said, "Of course."

She flung her arms around him. He ran his fingers over the bones of her shoulder. He felt her ribs. He felt the individual strands of her hair brushing his cheeks. This was real. This was more real than life itself, yet some fool had told him that it was a virus—that Nancy didn't exist. If this wasn't Nancy, what was it? he thought.

He put her down and, alive with love and happiness, he read the prayer book. He asked her to make the responses. He said,

"I suppose I'm captain, and I suppose I have married you and me, haven't I, Nancy?"

The marriage went well. The ship followed an immense perimeter like that of a comet. It went far out. So far that the sun became a remote dot. The interference of the solar system had virtually no effect on the instruments.

Nancy came to him one day and said, "I suppose you know why you are a failure now."

"No," he said.

She looked at him gravely. She said,

"I think with your mind. I live in your body. If you die while on this ship, I die too. Yet as long as you live, I am alive and separate. That's funny, isn't it?"

"Funny," he said, an old new pain growing in his heart.

"And yet I can tell you something which I know with that part of your mind I use. I know without you that I am. I suppose I recognize your technical training and feel it somehow even though I don't feel the lack of it. I had the education you thought I had and you wanted me to have. But do you see what's happening? We are working with our brain at almost half-power instead of one-tenth power. All your imagination is going into making me. All your extra thoughts are of me. I want them just as I want you to love me but there are none left over for emergencies and there is nothing left over for the Space Service. You are doing the minimum, that's all. Am I worth it?"

"Of course you are worth it, darling. You're worth anything that any man could ask of the sweetheart, and of love, and of a wife and a true companion."

"But don't you see? I am taking all the best of you. You are putting it into me and when the ship comes home there won't be any me."

In a strange way he realized that the drug was working. He could see what was happening to himself as he looked at his well-beloved Nancy with her shimmering hair and he realized the hair needed no prettying or hairdos. He looked at her clothes and he realized that she wore clothes for which there was no space on the ship. And yet she changed them, delightfully, winsomely, attractively, day in and day out. He ate the food that he knew couldn't be on the ship. None of this worried him. And now he couldn't even be worried at the thought of losing Nancy herself. Any other thought he could have rejected from his subconscious mind and could have surrendered to the idea that it was not a hallucination after all.

This was too much. He ran his fingers through her hair. He said,

"I know I'm crazy, darling, and I know that you don't exist—"

"But I do exist. I am you. I am a part of Gordon Greene as surely as if I'd married you. I'll never die until you do because when you get home, darling, I'll drop back, back into your deeper mind but I'll live in your mind as long as you live. You can't lose me and I can't leave you and you can't forget me. And I can't escape to anyone except through your lips. That's why they talk about it. That's why it is such a strange thing."

"And that's where I know I'm wrong," stubbornly insisted Gordon. "I love you and I know you are a phantom and I know you are going away and I know we are coming to an end and it doesn't worry me. I'll be happy just being with you. I don't need a drink. I wouldn't touch a drug. Yet the happiness is here."

They went about their little domestic chores. They checked his graph paper, they stored the records, they put a few silly things into the permanent ship's record. They then toasted marshmallows before a large fire. The fire was in a handsome fireplace which did not exist. The flames couldn't have burned but they did. There weren't any marshmallows on the ship but they toasted them and enjoyed them anyhow.

That's the way their life went—full of magic, and yet the magic had no sting or provocation to it, no anger, no hopelessness, no despair.

They were a very happy couple.

Even the hamsters felt it. They stayed clean and plump. They ate their food willingly. They got over space nausea. They peered at him.

He let one of them, the one with the brown nose, out and let it run around the room. He said, "You're a real army character. You poor thing. Born for space and serving out here in it."

Only one other time did Nancy take up the question of their future. She said,

"We can't have children, you know. The *sokta* drug

doesn't allow for that. And you may have children
yourself but it is going to be funny having them if you
marry somebody else with me always there just in the
background. And I will be there."

They made it back to Earth. They returned.

As he stepped out of the gate, a harsh, weary medical
colonel gave him one sharp glance. He said,

"Oh, we thought that had happened."

"What, sir?" said a plump and radiant Lieutenant
Greene.

"You got Nancy," said the colonel.

"Yes, sir. I'll bring her right out."

"Go get her," said the colonel.

Greene went back into the rocket and he looked.
There was no sign of Nancy. He came to the door astonished. He was still not upset. He said,

"Colonel, I don't seem to see her there but I'm sure
that she's somewhere around."

The colonel gave him a strange, sympathetic, fatigued
smile. "She always will be somewhere around, Lieutenant. You've done the minimum job. I don't know
whether we ought to discourage people like you. I suppose you realize that you are frozen in your present
grade. You'll get a decoration, Mission Accomplished.
Mission successful, farther than anybody has gone before. Incidentally, Vonderleyen says he knows you and
will be waiting over yonder. We have to take you into
the hospital to make sure that you don't go into shock."

*"At the hospital," said my cousin, "there was no
shock."*

*He didn't even miss Nancy. How could he miss her
when she hadn't left? She was always just around the
corner, just behind the door, just a few minutes away.*

At breakfast time he knew he'd see her for lunch. At
lunch, he knew she'd drop by in the afternoon. At the
end of the afternoon, he knew he'd have dinner with
her.

He knew he was crazy. Crazy as he could be.

He knew perfectly well that there was no Nancy and never had been. He supposed that he ought to hate the *sokta* drug for doing that to him, but it brought its own relief.

The effect of Nancy was an immolation in perpetual hope, the promise of something that could never be lost, and a promise of something that cannot be lost is often better than a reality which can be lost.

That's all there was to it. They asked him to testify against the use of the *sokta* drug and he said,

"Me? Give up Nancy? Don't be silly."

"You haven't got her," said somebody.

"That's what you think," said my cousin, Lieutenant Greene.

The Fife of Bodidharma

Music (said Confucius) *awakens the mind, propriety finishes it, melody completes it.*
          —The *Lun Yu,* Book VIII, Chapter 8

1

IT WAS PERHAPS in the second period of the proto-Indian Harappa culture, perhaps earlier in the very dawn of metal, that a goldsmith accidentally found a formula to make a magical fife. To him, the fife became death or bliss, an avenue to choosable salvations or dooms. Among later men, the fife might be recognized as a chancy prediscovery of psionic powers with sonic triggering.

Whatever it was, it worked! Long before the Buddha, long-haired Dravidian priests learned that it worked.

Cast mostly in gold despite the goldsmith's care with the speculum alloy, the fife emitted shrill whistlings but it also transmitted supersonic vibrations in a narrow range—narrow and intense enough a range to rearrange synapses in the brain and to modify the basic emotions of the hearer.

The goldsmith did not long survive his instrument. They found him dead.

The fife became the property of priests; after a short, terrible period of use and abuse, it was buried in the tomb of a great king.

2

Robbers found the fife, tried it and died. Some died amid bliss, some amid hate, others in a frenzy of fear and delusion. A strong survivor, trembling after the ordeal of inexpressibly awakened sensations and emotions, wrapped the fife in a page of holy writing and presented it to Bodidharma the Blessed One just before Bodidharma began his unbelievably arduous voyage from India across the ranges of the spines of the world over to far Cathay.

Bodidharma the Blessed One, the man who had seen Persia, the aged one bringing wisdom, came across the highest of all mountains in the year that the Northern Wei dynasty of China moved their capital out of divine Loyang. (Elsewhere in the world where men reckoned the years from the birth of their Lord Jesus Christ, the year was counted as Anno Domini 554, but in the high land between India and China the message of Christianity had not yet arrived and the word of the Lord Gautama Buddha was still the sweetest gospel to reach the ears of men.)

Bodidharma, clad by only a thin robe, climbed across the glaciers. For food he drank the air, spicing it with prayer. Cold winds cut his old skin, his tired bones; for a cloak he drew his sanctity about him and bore within his indomitable heart the knowledge that the pure, unspoiled message of the Lord Gautama Buddha had, by the will of time and chance themselves, to be carried from the Indian world to the Chinese.

Once beyond the peaks and passes he descended into the cold frigidity of high desert. Sand cut his feet but the skin did not bleed because he was shod in sacred spells and magical charms.

At last animals approached. They came in the ugliness of their sin, ignorance, and shame. Beasts they were, but more than beasts—they were the souls of the wicked condemned to endless rebirth, now incorporated in vile forms because of the wickedness with which they had once rejected the teachings of eternity and the wisdom which lay before them as plainly as the trees or the nighttime heavens. The more vicious the man, the more ugly the beast: this was the rule. Here in the desert the beasts were very ugly.

Bodidharma the Blessed One shrank back.

He did not desire to use the weapon. "O Forever Blessed One, seated in the Lotus Flower, Buddha, help me!"

Within his heart he felt no response. The sinfulness and wickedness of these beasts was such that even the Buddha had turned his face gently aside and would offer no protection to his messenger, the missionary Bodidharma.

Reluctantly Bodidharma took out his fife.

The fife was a dainty weapon, twice the length of a man's finger. Golden in strange, almost ugly forms, it hinted at a civilization which no one living in India now remembered. The fife had come out of the early beginnings of mankind, had ridden across a mass of ages, a legion of years, and survived as a testimony to the power of early men.

At the end of the fife was a little whistle. Four touch holes gave the fife pitches and a wide variety of combination of notes.

Blown once the fife called to holiness. This occurred if all stops were closed.

Blown twice with all stops opened the fife carried its
own power. This power was strange indeed. It magni-
fied every chance emotion of each living thing within
range of its sound.

Bodidharma the Blessed One had carried the fife because it comforted him. Closed, its notes reminded him
of the sacred message of the Three Treasures of the
Buddha which he carried from India to China. Opened,
its notes brought bliss to the innocent and their own
punishment to the wicked. Innocence and wickedness
were not determined by the fife but by the hearers
themselves, whoever they might be. The trees which
heard these notes in their own treelike way struck even
more mightily into the earth and up to the sky reaching
for nourishment with new but dim and treelike hope.
Tigers became more tigerish, frogs more froggy, men
more good or bad, as their characters might dispose
them.

"Stop!" called Bodidharma the Blessed One to the
beasts.

Tiger and wolf, fox and jackal, snake and spider,
they advanced.

"Stop!" he called again.

Hoof and claw, sting and tooth, eyes alive, they advanced.

"Stop!" he called for the third time.

Still they advanced. He blew the fife wide open,
twice, clear and loud.

Twice, clear and loud.

The animals stopped. At the second note, they began
to thresh about, imprisoned even more deeply by the
bestiality of their own natures. The tiger snarled at his
own front paws, the wolf snapped at his own tail, the
jackal ran fearfully from his own shadow, the spider hid
beneath the darkness of rocks, and the other vile beasts
who had threatened the Blessed One let him pass.

Bodidharma the Blessed One went on. In the streets
of the new capital at Anyang the gentle gospel of
Buddhism was received with curiosity, with calm and
with delight. Those voluptuous barbarians, the Toba

Tartars, who had made themselves masters of North China, now filled their hearts and souls with the hope of death instead of the fear of destruction. Mothers wept with pleasure to know that their children, dying, had been received into blessedness. The Emperor himself laid aside his sword in order to listen to the gentle message that had come so bravely over illimitable mountains.

When Bodidharma the Blessed One died he was buried in the outskirts of Anvang, his fife in a sacred onyx case beside his right hand. There he and it both slept for thirteen hundred and forty years.

3

In the year 1894 a German explorer—so he fancied himself to be—looted the tomb of the Blessed One in the name of science.

Villagers caught him in the act and drove him from the hillside.

He escaped with only one piece of loot, an onyx case with a strange copperlike fife. Copper it seemed to be, although the metal was not as corroded as actual copper should have been after so long a burial in intermittently moist country. The fife was filthy. He cleaned it enough to see that it was fragile and to reveal the un-Chinese character of the declarations along its side.

He did not clean it enough to try blowing it: *he* lived because of that.

The fife was presented to a small municipal museum named in honor of a German grand duchess. It occupied case No. 34 of the Dorotheum and lay there for another fifty-one years.

4

The B-29s had gone. They had roared off in the direction of Rastatt.

Wolfgang Huene climbed out of the ditch. He hated himself, he hated the Allies, and he almost hated Hitler.

A Hitler youth, he was handsome, blond, tall, craggy.
He was also brave, sharp, cruel and clever. He was a
Nazi. Only in a Nazi world could he hope to exist. His
parents, he knew, were soft rubbish. When his father
had been killed in a bombing, Wolfgang did not mind.
When his mother, half-starved, died of influenza, he did
not worry about her. She was old and did not matter.
Germany mattered.

Now the Germany which mattered to him was coming apart, ripped by explosions, punctured by shock
waves, and fractured by the endless assault of Allied air
power.

Wolfgang as a young Nazi did not know fear, but he
did know bewilderment.

In an animal, instinctive way, he knew—without
thinking about it—that if Hitlerism did not survive he
himself would not survive either. He even knew that he
was doing his best, what little best there was still left to
do. He was looking for spies while reporting the weak-
hearted ones who complained against the Fuehrer or the
war. He was helping to organize the Volkssturm and he
had hopes of becoming a Nazi guerrilla even if the Allies did cross the Rhine. Like an animal, but like a very
intelligent animal, he knew he had to fight, while at the
same time, he realized that the fight might go against
him.

He stood in the street watching the dust settle after
the bombing.

The moonlight was clear on the broken pavement.

This was a quiet part of the city. He could hear the
fires downtown making a crunching sound, like the familiar noise of his father eating lettuce. Near himself he
could hear nothing; he seemed to be all alone, under the
moon, in a tiny forgotten corner of the world.

He looked around.

His eyes widened in astonishment: the Dorotheum
museum had been blasted open.

Idly, he walked over to the ruin. He stood in the dark
doorway.

Looking back at the street and then up at the sky to

make sure that it was safe to show a light, he then flashed on his pocket electric light and cast the beam around the display room. Cases were broken; in most of them glass had fallen in on the exhibits. Window glass looked like puddles of ice in the cold moonlight as it lay broken on the old stone floors.

Immediately in front of him a display case sagged crazily.

He cast his flashlight beam on it. The light picked up a short tube which looked something like the barrel of an antique pistol. Wolfgang reached for the tube. He had played in a band and he knew what it was. It was a fife.

He held it in his hand a moment and then stuck it in his jacket. He cast the beam of his light once more around the museum and then went out in the street. It was no use letting the police argue.

He could now hear the laboring engines of trucks as they coughed, sputtering with their poor fuel, climbing up the hill toward him.

He took his light in his pocket. Feeling the fife, he took it out.

Instinctively, the way that any human being would, he put his fingers over all four of the touch holes before he began to blow. The fife was stopped up.

He applied force.

He blew hard.

The fife sounded.

A sweet note, golden beyond imagination, softer and wilder than the most thrilling notes of the finest symphony in the world, sounded in his ears.

He felt different, relieved, happy.

His soul, which he did not know he had, achieved a condition of peace which he had never before experienced. In that moment a small religion was born. It was a small religion because it was confined to the mind of a single brutal adolescent, but it was a true religion, nevertheless, because it had the complete message of hope, comfort and fulfillment of an order beyond the limits of this life. Love, and the tremendous meaning of love, poured through his mind. Love relaxed the muscles of his back and even let his aching eyelids drop over his eyes in the first honest fatigue he had admitted for many weeks.

The Nazi in him had been drained off. The call to holiness, trapped in the forgotten magic of Bodidharma's fife, had sounded even to him. Then he made his mistake, a mortal one.

The fife had no more malice than a gun before it is fired, no more hate than a river before it swallows a human body, no more anger than a height from which a man may slip; the fife had its own power, partly in sound itself, but mostly in the mechanopsionic linkage which the unusual alloy and shape had given the Harappa goldsmith forgotten centuries before.

Wolfgang Huene blew again, holding the fife between two fingers, with none of the stops closed. This time the note was wild. In a terrible and wholly convincing moment of vision he reincarnated in himself all the false resolutions, the venomous patriotism, the poisonous bravery of Hitler's Reich. He was once again a Hitler youth, consummately a Nordic man. His eyes gleamed with a message he felt pouring out of himself.

He blew again.

This third note was the perfecting note—the note which had protected Bodidharma the Blessed One fifteen hundred and fifty years before in the frozen desert north of Tibet.

Huene became even more Nazi. No longer the boy, no longer the human being. He was the magnification of himself. He became all fighter, but he had forgotten who he was or what it was that he was fighting for.

The blacked-out trucks came up the hill. His blind eyes looked at them. Fife in hand, he snarled at them.

A crazy thought went through his mind. "Allied tanks . . ."

He ran wildly toward the leading truck. The driver did not see more than a shadow and jammed on the brakes too late. The front bumper burst a soft obstruction.

The front wheel covered the body of the boy. When the truck stopped the boy was dead and the fife, half crushed, was pressed against the rock of a German road.

5

Hagen von Grün was one of the German rocket scientists who worked at Huntsville, Alabama. He had gone on down to Cape Canaveral to take part in the fifth series of American launchings. This included in the third shot of the series a radio transmitter designed to hit standard wave radios immediately beneath the satellite. The purpose was to allow ordinary listeners throughout the world to take part in the tracking of the satellite. This particular satellite was designed to have a relatively short life. With good luck it would last as long as five weeks, not longer.

The miniaturized transmitter was designed to pick up the sounds, minute though they might be, produced by the heating and cooling of the shell and to transmit a sound pattern reflecting the heat of cosmic rays and also to a certain degree to relay the visual images in terms of a sound pattern.

Hagen von Grün was present at the final assembly. A small part of the assembly consisted of inserting a tube which would serve the double function of a resonating chamber between the outer skin of the satellite and a tiny microphone half the size of a sweet pea which would then translate the sound made by the outer shell into radio signals which amateurs on the earth surface fifteen hundred miles below could follow.

Von Grün no longer smoked. He had stopped smoking that fearful night in which Allied planes bombed the truck convoy carrying his colleagues and himself to safety. Though he had managed to scrounge cigarettes throughout the war he had even given up carrying his cigarette holder. He carried instead an odd old copper ~ife he had found in the highway and had put back into

Superstitious at his luck in living, and grateful

that the fife reminded him not to smoke, he never bothered to clean it out and blow it. He had weighed it, found its specific gravity, measured it, like the good German that he was, down to the last millimeter and milligram but he kept it in his pocket though it was a little clumsy to carry.

Just as they put the last part of the nose cone together, the strut broke.

It could not break, but it did.

It would have taken five minutes and a ride down the elevator to find a new tube to serve as a strut.

Acting on an odd impulse, Hagen von Grün remembered that his lucky fife was within a millimeter of the length required, and was of precisely the right diameter. The holes did not matter. He picked up a file, filed the old fife and inserted it.

They closed the skin of the satellite. They sealed the cone.

Seven hours later the message rocket took off, the first one capable of reaching every standard wave radio on earth. As Hagen von Grün watched the great rocket climb he wondered to himself, Does it make any difference whether those stops were opened or closed?

Angerhelm

*Funny funny funny. It's sort of funny funny funny
to think without a brain—it is really something
like a trick but not a trick to think without a brain.
Talking is even harder but it can be done.*

I STILL REMEMBER the way that phrase came ringing
through when we finally got hold of old Nelson Angerhelm and sat him down with the buzzing tape.

The story began a long time before that. I never
knew the beginnings.

My job is an assistant to Mr. Spatz, and Spatz has
been shooting holes in budgets now for eighteen years.
He is the man who approves, on behalf of the Director
of the Budget, all requests for special liaison between
the Department of the Army and the intelligence community.

He is very good at his job. More people have shown
up asking for money and have ended up with about
one-tenth of what they asked than you could line up in
any one corridor of the Pentagon. That is saying a lot.

The case began to break some months ago after the
Russians started to get back those odd little recording
capsules. The capsules came out of their Sputniks. We
didn't know what was in the capsules as they returned
from upper space. All we knew was that there was
something in them.

The capsules descended in such a way that we could
track them by radar. Unfortunately they all fell into
Russian territory except for a single capsule which

landed in the Atlantic. At the seven-million-dollar point we gave up trying to find it.

The Commander of the Atlantic fleet had been told by his intelligence officer that they might have a chance of finding it if they kept on looking. The Commander referred the matter to Washington, and the budget people saw the request. That stopped it, for a while.

The case began to break from about four separate directions at once. Khrushchev himself said something very funny to the Secretary of State. They had met in London after all.

Khrushchev said at the end of a meeting, "You play jokes sometimes, Mr. Secretary?"

The Secretary looked very surprised when he heard the translation.

"Jokes, Mr. Prime Minister?"

"Yes."

"What kind of jokes?"

"Jokes about apparatus."

"Jokes about machinery don't sit very well," said the American.

They went on talking back and forth as to whether it was a good idea to play practical jokes when each one had a serious job of espionage to do.

The Russian leader insisted that he had no espionage, never heard of espionage and that his espionage worked well enough so that he knew damn well that he didn't have any espionage.

To this display of heat, the Secretary replied that he didn't have any espionage either and that we knew nothing whatever that occurred in Russia. Furthermore not only did we not know anything about Russia but we knew we didn't know it and we made sure of that. After this exchange both leaders parted, each one wondering what the other had been talking about.

The whole matter was referred back to Washington. I was somewhere down on the list to see it.

At that time I had "Galactic" clearance. Galactic clearance came a little bit after universal clearance. It wasn't very strong but it amounted to something. I was supposed to see those special papers in connection with my job of assisting Mr. Spatz in liaison. Actually it didn't do any good except fill in the time when I wasn't working out budgets for him.

The second lead came from some of the boys over in the Valley. We never called the place by any other name and we don't even like to see it in the federal budget. We know as much as we need to about it and then we stop thinking.

It is much safer to stop thinking. It is not our business to think about what other people are doing, particularly if they are spending several million dollars of Uncle Sam's money every day, trying to find out what they think and most of the time ending up with nothing conclusive.

Later we were to find out that the boys in the Valley had practically every security agent in the country rushing off to Minneapolis to look for a man named Angerhelm. Nelson Angerhelm.

The name didn't mean anything then but before we got through it ended up as the largest story of the twentieth century. If they ever turn it loose it is going to be the biggest story in two thousand years.

The third part of the story came along a little later. Colonel Plugg was over in G-2. He called up Mr. Spatz and he couldn't get Mr. Spatz so he called me.

He said, "What's the matter with your boss? Isn't he ever in his room?"

"Not if I can help it. I don't run him, he runs me. What do you want, Colonel?" I said.

The colonel snarled.

"Look, I am supposed to get money out of you for liaison purposes. I don't know how far I am going to have to go to liaise or if it is any of my business. I asked my old man what I ought to do about it and he doesn't know. Perhaps we ought to get out and just let the Intelligence boys handle it. Or we ought to send it to State. You spend half your life telling me whether I can have liaison or not and then giving me the money for it.

Why don't you come on over and take a little responsibility for a change?"

I rushed over to Plugg's office. It was an Army problem.

These are the facts.

The Soviet Assistant Military Attaché, a certain Lieutenant Colonel Potariskov, asked for an interview. When he came over he brought nothing with him. This time he didn't even bring a translator. He spoke very funny English but it worked.

The essence of Potariskov's story was that he didn't think it was very sporting of the American military to interfere in solemn weather reporting by introducing practical jokes in Soviet radar. If the American army didn't have anything else better to do would they please play jokes on each other but not on the Soviet forces?

This didn't make much sense.

Colonel Plugg tried to find out what the man was talking about. The Russian sounded crazy and kept talking about jokes.

It finally turned out that Potariskov had a piece of paper in his pocket. He took it out and Plugg looked at it.

On it there was an address. Nelson Angerhelm, 2322 Ridge Drive, Hopkins, Minnesota.

It turned out that Hopkins, Minnesota, was a suburb of Minneapolis. That didn't take long to find out.

This meant nothing to Colonel Plugg and he asked if there was anything that Potariskov really wanted.

Potariskov asked if the Colonel would confess to the Angerhelm joke.

Potariskov said that in Intelligence they never tell you about the jokes they play with the Signal Corps. Plugg still insisted that he didn't know. He said he would try to find out and let Potariskov know later on. Potariskov went away.

Plugg called up the Signal Corps, and by the time he got through calling he had a lead back into the Valley. The Valley people heard about it and they immediately sent a man over.

It was about this time that I came in. He couldn't get hold of Mr. Spatz and there was real trouble.

The point is that all three of them led together. The Valley people had picked up the name (and it is not up to me to tell you how they got hold of it). The name Angerhelm had been running all over the Soviet communications system. Practically every Russian official in the world had been asked if he knew anything about Nelson Angerhelm and almost every official, at least as far as the boys in the Valley could tell, had replied that he didn't know what it was all about.

Some reference back to Mr. Khrushchev's conversation with the Secretary of State suggested that the Angerhelm inquiry might have tied in with this. We pursued it a little further. Angerhelm was apparently the right reference. The Valley people already had something about him. They had checked with the F.B.I.

The F.B.I. had said that Nelson Angerhelm was a 62-year-old retired poultry farmer. He had served in World War I.

His service had been rather brief. He had gotten as far as Plattsburg, New York, broken an ankle, stayed four months in a hospital, and the injury had developed complications. He had been drawing a Veterans Administration allowance ever since. He had never visited outside the United States, never joined a subversive organization, had never married, and never spent a nickel. So far as the F.B.I. could discover, his life was not worth living.

This left the matter up in the air. There was nothing whatever to connect him with the Soviet Union.

It turned out that I wasn't needed after all. Spatz came into the office and said that a conference had been called for the whole Intelligence community, people from State were sitting in, and there was a special representative from OCBM from the White House to watch what they were doing.

The question arose, "Who was Nelson Angerhelm? And what were we to do about him?"

An additional report had been made out by an agent

who specialized in pretending to be an Internal Revenue man.

The "Internal Revenue agent" was one of the best people in the F.B.I. for checking on subversive activities. He was a real expert on espionage and he knew all about bad connections. He could smell a conspirator two miles off on a clear day. And by sitting in a room for a little while he could tell whether anybody had an illegal meeting there for the previous three years. Maybe I am exaggerating a little bit but I am not exaggerating much.

This fellow, who was a real artist at smelling out Commies and anything that even faintly resembles a Commie, came back with a completely blank ticket on Angerhelm.

There was only one connection that Angerhelm had with the larger world. He had a younger brother, whose name was Tice. Funny name and I don't know why he got it. Somebody told us later on that the full name tied in with Theiss Ankerhjelm, which was the name of a Swedish admiral a couple hundred years ago. Perhaps the family was proud of it.

The younger brother was a West Pointer. He had had a regular career; that came easily enough out of the Adjutant General's Office.

What did develop, though, was that the younger brother had died only two months previously. He too was a bachelor. One of the psychiatrists who got into the case said, "What a mother!"

Tice Angerhelm had traveled a great deal. He had something to do, as a matter of fact, with two or three of the projects that I was liaising on. There were all sorts of issues arising from this.

However, he was dead. He had never worked directly on Soviet matters. He had no Soviet friends, had never been in the Soviet Union, and had never met Soviet forces. He had never even gone to the Soviet Embassy to an official reception.

The man was no specialist, outside of Ordnance, a little tiny bit of French and the missile program. He was a card player, an awfully good man with trout and something of a Saturday evening Don Juan.

It was then time for the fourth stage.

Colonel Plugg was told to get hold of Lieutenant Colonel Potariskov and find out what Potariskov had to give him. This time Potariskov called back and said that he would rather have his boss, the Soviet Ambassador himself, call on the Secretary or the Undersecretary of State.

There was some shilly-shallying back and forth. The Secretary was out of town, the Undersecretary said he would be very glad to see the Soviet Ambassador if there were anything to ask about. He said that we had found Angerhelm, and if the Soviet authorities wanted to interview Mr. Angerhelm themselves they jolly well could go to Hopkins, Minnesota, and interview him.

This led to a real flash of embarrassment when it was discovered that the area of Hopkins, Minnesota, was in the "no travel" zone prescribed to Soviet diplomats in retaliation against their "no travel" zones imposed on American diplomats in the Soviet Union.

This was ironed out. The Soviet Ambassador was asked, would he like to go see a chicken farmer in Minnesota?

When the Soviet Ambassador stated that he was not particularly interested in chicken farmers, but that he would be willing to see Mr. Angerhelm at a later date if the American government didn't mind, the whole thing was let go.

Nothing happened at all. Presumably the Russians were relaying things back to Moscow by courier, letter or whatever mysterious ways the Russians use when they are acting very deliberate and very solemnly.

I heard nothing and certainly the people around the Soviet Embassy saw no unusual contacts at that time.

Nelson Angerhelm hadn't come into the story yet. All he knew was that several odd characters had asked him about veterans that he scarcely knew, saying that they were looking for security clearances.

And an Internal Revenue man had a long and very

exhausting talk with him about his brother's estate. That didn't seem to leave much.

Angerhelm went on feeding his chickens. He had television and Minneapolis has a pretty good range of stations. Now and then he showed up at the church; more frequently he showed up at the general store.

He almost always went away from town to avoid the new shopping centers. He didn't like the way Hopkins had developed and preferred to go to the little country centers where they still have general stores. In its own funny way this seemed to be the only pleasure the old man had.

After nineteen days, and I can now count almost every hour of them, the answer must have gotten back from Moscow. It was probably carried in by the stocky brown-haired courier who made the trip about every fortnight. One of the fellows from the Valley told me about that. I wasn't supposed to know and it didn't matter then.

Apparently the Soviet Ambassador had been told to play the matter lightly. He called on the Undersecretary of State and ended up discussing world butter prices and the effect of American exports of ghee to Pakistan on the attempts of the Soviet Union to trade ghee for hemp.

Apparently this was an extraordinary and confidential thing for the Soviet Ambassador to discuss. The Undersecretary would have been more impressed if he had been able to find out why the Soviet Ambassador just out of the top of his head announced that the Soviet Union had given about a hundred and twenty million dollars' credit to Pakistan for some unnecessary highways and was able to reply, therefore, somewhat tartly to the general effect that if the Soviet Union ever decided to stabilize world markets with the cooperation of the United States we would be very happy to cooperate. But this was no time to discuss money or fair business deals when they were dumping every piece of export rubbish they could in our general direction.

It was characteristic of this Soviet Ambassador that he took the rebuff calmly. Apparently his mission was to have no mission. He left and that was all there was from him.

Potariskov came back to the Pentagon, this time accompanied by a Russian civilian. The new man's English was a little more than perfect. The English was so good that it was desperately irritating.

Potariskov himself looked like a rather horsey, brown-faced schoolboy, with chestnut hair and brown eyes. I got to see him because they had me sitting in the back of Plugg's office pretending just to wait for somebody else.

The conversation was very simple. Potariskov brought out a recording tape. It was standard American tape.

Plugg looked at it and said, "Do you want to play it right now?"

Potariskov agreed.

The stenographer got a tape recorder in. By that time three or four other officers wandered in and none of them happened to leave. As a matter of fact one of them wasn't even an officer but he happened to have a uniform on that very day.

They played the tape and I listened to it. It was *buzz, buzz, buzz*. And there was some hissing, then it went *clickety, clickety, clickety*. Then it was *buzz, buzz, buzz* again. It was the kind of sound in which you turn on a radio and you don't even get static. You just get funny buzzing sounds which indicate that somebody has some sort of radio transmission somewhere but it is not consistent enough to be the loud *whee, wheeeee* kind of static which one often hears.

All of us stood there rather solemnly. Plugg thoroughly a soldier, listened at rigid attention, moving his eyes back and forth from the tape recorder to Potariskov's face. Potariskov looked at Plugg and then ran his eyes around the group.

The little Russian civilian, who was as poisonous as a snake, glanced at every single one of us. He was obviously taking our measure and he was anxious to find out if any of us could hear anything he couldn't hear. None of us heard anything.

At the end of the tape Plugg reached out to turn off the machine.

"Don't stop it," Potariskov said.

The other Russian interjected, "Didn't you hear it?" All of us shook our heads. We had heard nothing.

With that, Potariskov said with singular politeness, "Please play it again."

We played it again. Nothing happened, except for the buzzing and clicking.

After the fifteen-minute point it was beginning to get pretty stale for some of us. One or two of the men actually wandered out. They happened to be the bona fide visitors. The non-bona fide visitors slouched down in the room.

Colonel Plugg offered Potariskov a cigarette which Potariskov took. They both smoked and we played it a third time. Then the third time Potariskov said, "Turn it off."

"Didn't you hear it?" said Potariskov.

"Hear what?" said Plugg.

"Hear the name and the address."

At that the funniest feeling came over me. I knew that I had heard something and I turned to the Colonel and said, "Funny, I don't know where I heard it or how I heard it but I do know something that I didn't know."

"What is that?" said the little Russian civilian, his face lighting up.

"Nelson," said I, intending to say, "Nelson Angerhelm, 2322 Ridge Drive, Hopkins, Minnesota." Just as I had seen it in the "galactic" secret documents. Of course I didn't go any further. That was in the document and was very secret indeed. How should I know it?

The Russian civilian looked at me. There was a funny, wicked, friendly, crooked sort of smile on his face. He said, "Didn't you hear 'Nelson Angerhelm, 2322 Ridge Drive, Hopkins, Minnesota,' just now, and yet did you not know *where* you heard it?"

The question then arose, "What had happened?"

Potariskov spoke with singular candor. Even the Russian with him concurred.

"We believe that this is a case of marginal perception. We have played this. This is obviously a copy. We have many such copies. We have played it to all our people. Nobody can even specify at what point he has heard it. We have had our best experts on it. Some put it at minute three. Others put it at minute twelve. Some put it at minute thirteen and a half and at different places. But different people under different controls all come out with the idea that they have heard 'Nelson Angerhelm, 2322 Ridge Drive, Hopkins, Minnesota.' We have tried it on Chinese people."

At that the Russian civilian interrupted. "Yes, indeed, they tried it on Chinese persons and even they heard the same thing, Nelson Angerhelm. Even when they do not know the language they hear 'Nelson Angerhelm.' Even when they know nothing else they hear that and they hear the street numbers. The numbers are always in English. They cannot make a recording. The recording is only of this noise and yet it comes out. What do you make of that?"

What they said turned out to be true. We tried it also, after they went away.

We tried it on college students, foreigners, psychiatrists, White House staff members, and passers-by. We even thought of running it on a municipal radio somewhere as a quiz show and offering prizes for anyone that got it. That was a little too heavy, so we accepted a much safer suggestion that we try it out on the public address system of the SAC base. The SAC was guarded night and day.

No one happened to be getting much leave anyhow and it was easy enough to cut off the leave for an extra week. We played that damn thing six times over and almost everybody on that base wanted to write a letter to Nelson Angerhelm, 2322 Ridge Drive, Hopkins, Minnesota. They were even calling each other Angerhelm and wondering what the hell it meant.

Naturally there were a great many puns on the name and even some jokes of a rather smutty order. That didn't help.

The troublesome thing was that on all these different tests we too were unable to find out at what point the subliminal transmission of the name and address came.

It was subliminal, all right. There's not much trick to that. Any good psychologist can pass along either a noise message or a sight message without the recipient knowing exactly when he got it. It is simply a matter of getting down near the threshold, running a little tiny bit under the threshold and then making the message sharp and clear enough, just under the level of conscious notice, so that it slips on through.

We therefore knew what we were dealing with. What we didn't know was what the Russians were doing with it, how they had gotten it and why they were so upset about it.

Finally it all went to the White House for a conference. The conference, to which my boss Mr. Spatz went along as a sort of rapporteur and monitor to safeguard the interests of the Director of the Budget and of the American taxpayer, was a rather brief affair.

All roads led to Nelson Angerhelm. Nelson Angerhelm was already guarded by about half of the F.B.I. and a large part of the local military district forces. Every room in his house had been wired. The microphones were sensitive enough to hear his heart beat. The safety precautions we were taking on that man would have justified the program we have for taking care of Fort Knox.

Angerhelm knew that some awful funny things had been happening but he didn't know what and he didn't know who was concerned with it.

Months later he was able to tell somebody that he thought his brother had probably done some forgery or counterfeiting and that the neighborhood was being thoroughly combed. He didn't realize his safeguarding was the biggest American national treasure since the discovery of the atomic bomb.

The President himself gave the word. He reviewed the evidence. The Secretary of State said that he didn't think that Khrushchev would have brought up the question of a joke if Khrushchev himself had not missed out on the facts.

We had even tried Russians on it, of course—Russians on our side. And they didn't get any more off the record than the rest of the people. Everybody heard the same blessed thing, "Nelson Angerhelm, 2322 Ridge Drive, Hopkins, Minnesota."

But that didn't get anybody anywhere.

The only thing left was to try it on the man himself.

When it came to picking inconspicuous people to go along, the Intelligence committee were pretty thin-skinned about letting outsiders into their show. On the other hand they did not have domestic jurisdiction, particularly not when the President had turned it over to J. Edgar Hoover and said, "Ed, you handle this. I don't like the looks of it."

Somebody over in the Pentagon, presumably deviled on by Air Intelligence, got the bright idea that if the Army and the rest of the Intelligence committee couldn't fit into the show the best they could do would be to get their revenge on liaison by letting liaison itself go. This meant Mr. Spatz.

Mr. Spatz has been on the job for many, many years by always avoiding anything interesting or dramatic, always watching for everything that mattered—which was the budget and the authorization for next year—and by ditching controversial personalities long before anyone else had any idea that they were controversial.

Therefore, he didn't go. If this Angerhelm fiasco was going to turn out to be a mess he wanted to be out of it.

It was me who got the assignment.

I was made a sort of honorary member of the F.B.I. and they even let me carry the tape in the end. They must have had about six other copies of the tape so the honor wasn't as marked as it looked. We were simply supposed to go along as people who knew something about the brother.

It was a dry, reddish Sunday afternoon, looking a little bit as though the sunset were coming.

We drove up to this very nice frame house. It had double windows all the way around and looked as tight as the proverbial rug for a bug to be snug in in cold winter. This wasn't winter and the old gentleman obviously couldn't pay for air conditioning. But the house still looked snug.

There was no waste, no show. It just looked like a thoroughly livable house.

The F.B.I. man was big-hearted and let me ring the doorbell. There was no answer so I rang the doorbell some more. Again, nobody answered the bell.

We decided to wait outside and wandered around the yard. We looked at the car in the yard; it seemed in running order.

We rang the doorbell again, then walked around the house and looked into the kitchen window. We checked his car to see if the radiator felt warm. We looked at our watches. We wondered if he were hiding and peeking out at us. Once more we rang the doorbell.

Just then, the old boy came down the front walk.

We introduced ourselves and the preliminaries were the usual sort of thing. I found my heart beating violently. If something had stumped both the Soviet Union and the rest of the world, something salvaged possibly out of space itself, something which thousands of men had heard and none could identify, something so mysterious that the name of Nelson Angerhelm rang over and over again like a pitiable cry beyond all limits of understanding, what could this be?

We didn't know.

The old man stood there. He was erect, sunburned, red-cheeked, red-nosed, red-eared. Healthy as he could be, Swedish to the bone.

All we had to do was to tell him that we were concerned with his brother, Tice Angerhelm, and he listened to us. We had no trouble, no trouble at all.

As he listened his eyes got wide and he said, "I know there has been a lot of snooping around here and you people had a lot of trouble and I thought somebody was going to come and talk to me about it but I didn't think it would be this soon."

The F.B.I. man muttered something polite and vague, so Angerhelm went on. "I suppose you gentlemen are from the F.B.I. I don't think my brother was cheating. He wasn't that dishonest."

Another pause, and he continued. "But there is always a kind of a funny sleek mind—he looked like the kind of man who would play a joke."

Angerhelm's eyes lit up. "If he played a joke, gentlemen, he might even have committed a crime, I don't know. All I do is raise chickens and try to have my life."

Perhaps it was the wrong kind of Intelligence procedure but I broke in ahead of the F.B.I. and said, "Are you a happy man, Mr. Angerhelm? Do you live a life that you think is really satisfying?"

The old boy gave me a keen look. It was obvious that he thought there was something wrong and he didn't have very much confidence in my judgment.

And yet underneath the sharpness of his look he shot me a glance of sympathy and I am sure that he suspected I had been under a strain. His eyes widened a little. His shoulders went back, and he looked a little prouder.

He looked like the kind of man who might remember that he had Swedish admirals for ancestors, and that long before the Angerhelm name ran out and ran dry there in this flat country west of Minneapolis there had been something great in it and that perhaps sparks of the great name still flew somewhere in the universe.

I don't know. He got the importance of it, I suppose, because he looked me very sharply and very clearly in the eye.

"No, young man, my life hasn't been much of a life and I haven't liked it. And I hope nobody has to live a life like mine. But that is enough of that. I don't suppose you're guessing and I suppose you've got something pretty bad to show me."

The other fellow then took over.

"Yes, but it doesn't involve any embarrassment for you, Mr. Angerhelm. And even Colonel Angerhelm, your brother, wouldn't mind if he were living."

"Don't be so sure of that," said the old man. "My brother minded almost everything. As a matter of fact, my brother once said to me, 'Listen, Nels, I'd come back from Hell itself rather than let somebody put something over on me.' That's what he said. I think he meant it. There was a funny pride to him and if you've got anything here on my brother, you'd better just show it to me."

With that, we got over the small talk and we did what we were told to do. We got out the tape and put it on the portable machine, the hi-fi one which we brought along with us.

We played it for the old man.

I had heard it so often that I think I could almost have reproduced it with my vocal cords. The *clickety-click* and the *buzz, buzz*. There wasn't any *whee, whee,* but there was some more *clickety-click* and there was some *buzz, buzz,* and long periods of dull silence, the kind of contrived silence which a recording machine makes when it is playing but nothing is coming through on it.

The old gentleman listened to it and it seemed to have no effect on him, no effect at all.

No effect at all? That wasn't true.

There was an effect. When we got through the first time, he said very simply, very directly, almost coldly, "Play it again. Play it again for me. There may be something there."

We played it again.

After that second playing he started to talk.

"It is the funniest thing, I hear my own name and address there and I don't know where I hear it, but I swear to God, gentlemen, that's my brother's voice. It is my brother's voice I hear there somewhere in those clicks and noises. And yet all I can hear is Nelson Angerhelm, 2322 Ridge Drive, Hopkins, Minnesota. But I hear that, gentlemen, and it is not only plain, it is my brother's voice and I don't know where I heard it. I don't know how it came through."

We played it for him a third time.

When the tape was halfway through, he threw up his hands and said, "Turn it off. Turn it off. I can't stand it. Turn it off."

We turned it off.

He sat there in the chair breathing hard. After a while in a very funny cracked tone of voice he said, "I've got some whisky. It's back there on the shelf by the sink. Get me a shot of it, will you, gentlemen?"

The F.B.I. man and I looked at each other. He didn't want to get mixed up in accidental poisoning so he sent me. I went back. It was good enough whisky, one of the regular brands. I poured the old boy a two-ounce slug and took the glass back. I sipped a tiny bit of it myself. It seemed like a silly thing to do on duty but I couldn't risk any poison getting to him. After all my years in Army counterintelligence I wanted to stay in the Civil Service and I didn't want to take any chances on losing my good job with Mr. Spatz.

He drank the whisky and he said, "Can you record on this thing at the same time that you play?"

We said we couldn't. We hadn't thought of that.

"I think I may be able to tell you what it is saying. But I don't know how many times I can tell you, gentlemen. I am a sick man. I'm not feeling good. I never have felt very good. My brother had the life. I didn't have the life. I never had much of a life and never did anything and never went anywhere. My brother had everything. My brother got the women, he got the girl—he got the only girl I ever wanted, and then he didn't marry her. He got the life and he went away and then he died. He played jokes and he never let anybody get ahead of him. And, gentlemen, my brother's dead. Can you understand that? My brother's dead."

We said we knew his brother was dead. We didn't tell him that he had been exhumed and that the coffin had been opened and that the bones had been X-rayed. We didn't tell him that the bones had been weighed, fresh identification had been remade from what was left of the fingers, and they were in pretty good shape.

We didn't tell him that the serial number had been checked and that all the circumstances leading to the death had been checked and that everybody connected with it had been interviewed.

We didn't tell him that. We just told him we knew that his brother was dead. He knew that too.

"You know my brother is dead and then this funny thing has his voice in it. All it's got is his voice . . ."

We agreed. We said that we didn't know how his voice got in there and we didn't even know that there was a voice.

We didn't tell him that we had heard that voice ourselves a thousand times and yet never knew where we heard it.

We didn't tell him that we'd played it at the SAC base and that every man there had heard the name, Nelson Angerhelm, had heard something saying that and yet couldn't tell where.

We didn't tell him that the entire apparatus of Soviet Intelligence had been swearing over this for an unstated period of time and that our people had the unpleasant feeling that this came out of a Sputnik somewhere out in the sky.

We didn't tell him all that but we knew it. We knew that if he heard his brother's voice and if he wanted to record, it was something very serious.

"Can you get me something to dictate on?" the old man said.

"I can take notes," the F.B.I. man replied.

The old man shook his head. "That isn't enough," he said. "I think you probably want to get the whole thing if you ever get it and I begin to get pieces of it."

"Pieces of what?" said the F.B.I. man.

"Pieces of the stuff behind all that noise. It's my brother's voice talking. He's saying things—I don't like what he is saying. It frightens me and it just makes everything bad and dirty. I'm not sure I can take it and I am not going to take it twice. I think I'll go to church instead."

We looked at each other. "Can you wait ten minutes? I think I can get a recording machine by then."

The old man nodded his head. The F.B.I. man went out to the car and cranked up the radio. A great big aerial shot up out of the car, which otherwise was a very inconspicuous Chevrolet sedan. He got his office. A recording machine with a police escort was sent out from downtown Minneapolis toward Hopkins. I don't know what time it took ambulances to make it but the fellow at the other end said, "You better allow me twenty to twenty-two minutes."

We waited. The old man wouldn't talk to us and he didn't want us to play the tape. He sat there sipping the whisky.

"This might kill me and I want to have my friends around. My pastor's name is Jensen and if anything happens to me you get a hold of him there but I don't think anything will happen to me. Just get a hold of him. I may die, gentlemen, I can't take too much of this. It is the most shocking thing that ever happened to any man and I'm not going to see you or anybody else get in on it. You understand that it could kill me, gentlemen."

We pretended that we knew what he was talking about, although neither one of us had the faintest idea, beyond the suspicion that the old man might have a heart condition and might actually collapse.

The office had estimated twenty-two minutes. It took eighteen minutes for the F.B.I. assistant to come in. He brought in one of these new, tight, clean little jobs, the kind of thing that I'd love to take home. You can pack it almost anywhere. And it comes out with concert quality.

The old man brightened when he saw that we meant business.

"Give me a set of headphones and just let me talk and pick it up. I'll try to reproduce it. It won't be my brother's voice. It will be my voice you're hearing. Do you follow me?"

We turned on the tape.

He dictated, with the headset on his head.

That's when the message started. And that's the thing I started with in the very beginning.

Funny funny funny. It's sort of funny funny funny to think without a brain—it is really something like a trick but not a trick to think without a brain. Talking is even harder but it can be done.

Nels, this is Tice. I'm dead.

Nels, I don't know whether I'm in Heaven or Hell, but I think it's Hell, Nels. And I am going to play the biggest joke that anybody's ever played. And it's funny, I am an American Army officer and I am a dead one, and it doesn't matter. Nels, don't you see what it is? It doesn't matter if you're dead whether you're American or Russian or an officer or not. And even laughter doesn't matter.

But there's enough left of me, Nels, enough of the old me so that perhaps for one last time I'll have a laugh with you and the others.

I haven't got a body to laugh with, Nels, and I haven't got a mouth to laugh with and I haven't got cheeks to smile with and there really isn't any me. Tice Angerhelm is something different now, Nels. I'm dead.

I knew I was dead when I felt so different. It was more comfortable being dead, more relaxed. There wasn't anything tight.

That's the trouble, Nels, there isn't anything tight. There isn't anything around you. You can't feel the world, you can't see the world and yet you know all about it. You know all about everything.

It's awfully lonely, Nels. There are some corners that aren't lonely, some funny little corners in which you feel friendship and feel things creeping up.

Nels, it's like kittens or the faces of children or the smell of the wind on a nice day. It's any time that you turn away from yourself and you don't think about yourself.

It's the times when you don't want something and you do want something.

It's what you're not resenting, what you're not hating, what you're not fearing and what you're not jeering. That's it, Nels, that's the good part inside of death. And I suppose some people could call it Heaven. And I guess you get Heaven if you just get into the habit of having Heaven every day in your ordinary life. That's what it is. Heaven is right there, Nels, in your ordinary life, every day, day by day, right around you.

But that's not what I got. Oh, Nels, I am Tice Angerhelm all right, I am your brother and I'm dead. You can call where I am Hell since it's everything I hated.

Nels, it smells of everything that I ever wanted. It smells the way the hay smelled when I had my old Willys roadster and I made the first girl I ever made that August evening. You can go ask her. She's a Mrs. Prai Jesselton now. She lives over on the east side of St. Paul. You never knew I made her and if you don't think this is so, you can listen for yourself.

And you see, I am somewhere and I don't know what kind of a where it is.

Nels, this is me, Tice Angerhelm, and I'm going to scream this out loud with what I've got instead of a mouth. I am going to scream it loud so that any human ear that hears it can put it on this silly, silly Soviet gadget and take it back. TAKE THIS MESSAGE TO NELSON ANGERHELM, 2322 RIDGE DRIVE, HOPKINS, MINNESOTA. And I'm going to repeat that a couple more times so that you'll know that it's your brother talking and I'm somewhere and it isn't Heaven and it isn't Hell and it isn't even really out in space. I am in something different from space, Nels. It is just a somewhere with me in it and there isn't anything but me. In with me there's everything.

In with me there is everything I ever thought and everything I ever did and everything I ever wanted.

All the opposites are the same. Everything I hated and everything I loved, it's all the same. Everything I feared and everything I yearned for—that's the same. I tell you it's all the same now and the punishment is just as bad if you want something and get it as if you want something and don't get it.

The only thing that matters is those calm, nice moments in life when you don't want anything, Nels. You aren't anything. When you aren't trying for anything and the world is just around you, and you get simple things like water on the skin, when you yourself feel innocent and you are not thinking about anything else.

That's all there is to life, Nels. And I'm Tice and I'm telling you. And you know I'm dead, so I wouldn't be telling you a lie.

And I especially wouldn't be telling you on this Soviet cylinder, this Soviet gismo which will go back to them and bother them.

Nels, I hope it won't bother you too much, if everybody knows about that girl. I hope the girl forgives me but the message has got to go back.

And yet that's the message—everything I ever feared—I feared something in the war and you know what the war smells like. It smells sort of like a cheap slaughterhouse in July. It smells bad all around. There's bits of things burning, the smell of rubber burning and the funny smell of gunpowder. I was never in a big war with atomic stuff. Just the old sort of explosions. I've told you about it before and I was scared of that. And right in with that I can smell the perfume that girl had in the hotel there in Melbourne, the girl that I thought I might have wanted until she said something and then I said something and that was all there was between us. And I'm dead now.

And listen, Nels—

Listen, Nels, I am talking as though it were a trick. I don't know how I know about the rest of us—the other ones that are dead like me. I never met one and I may never talk to one. I just have the feeling that they are here too. They can't talk.

It's not that they can't talk, really.

They don't even want to talk.

They don't feel like talking. Talking is just a trick. It

is a trick that somebody can pick up and I guess it takes
a cheap, meaningless man, a man who lived his life in
spite of Hell and is now in that Hell. That's the kind of
silly man it takes to remember the trick of talking. Like
a trick with coins or a trick with cigarettes when nothing else matters.

So I am talking to you, Nels. And Nels, I suppose
you'll die the way I do. It doesn't matter, Nels. It's too
late to change—that's all.

Good-bye, Nels, you're in pretty good shape. You've
lived your life. You've had the wind in your hair.
You've seen the good sunlight and you haven't hated
and feared and loved too much.

When the old man got through dictating it, the F.B.I.
man and I asked him to do it again.

He refused.

We all stood up. We brought in the assistant.

The old man still refused to make a second dictation
from the sounds out of which only he could hear a
voice.

We could have taken him into custody and forced
him but there didn't seem to be much sense to it until
we took the recording back to Washington and had this
text appraised.

He said good-bye to us as we left his house.

"Perhaps I can do it once again maybe a year from
now. But the trouble with me, gentlemen, is that I believe it. That was the voice of my brother, Tice Angerhelm, and he is dead. And you brought me something
strange. I don't know where you got a medium or spirit
reader to record this on a tape and especially in such a
way that you can't hear it and I could. But I did hear it,
gentlemen, and I think I told you pretty good what it
was. And those words I used, they are not mine, they
are my brother's. So you go along, gentlemen, and do
what you can with it and if you don't want me to tell
anybody that the U.S. government is working on medi-
ums, I won't."

That was the farewell he gave us.

We closed the local office and hurried to the airport.

We took the tape back with us but a duplicate was already being teletyped to Washington.

That's the end of the story and that is the end of the joke. Potariskov got a copy and the Soviet Ambassador got a copy.

And Khrushchev probably wondered what sort of insane joke the Americans were playing on him. To use a medium or something weird along with subliminal perception in order to attack the U.S.S.R. for not believing in God and not believing in death. Did he figure it that way?

Here's a case where I hope that Soviet espionage is very good. I hope that their spies are so fine that they know we're baffled. I hope that they realize that we have come to a dead end, and whatever Tice Angerhelm did or somebody did in his name way out there in space recording into a Soviet Sputnik, we Americans had no hand in it.

If the Russians didn't do it and we didn't do it, who did do it?

I hope their spies find out.

The Good Friends

FEVER HAD GIVEN him a boyish look. The nurse, standing behind the doctor, watched him attentively. Her half-smile blended tenderness with an appreciation of his manly attraction.

"When can I go, doc?"

"In a few weeks, perhaps. You have to get well first."

"I don't mean home, doc. When can I go back into space? I'm captain, doc. I'm a good one. You know that, don't you?"

The doctor nodded gravely.

"I want to go back, doc. I want to go back right away. I want to be well, doc. I want to be well *now*. I want to get back in my ship and take off again. I don't even know why I'm here. What are you doing with me, doc?"

"We're trying to make you well," said the doctor, friendly, serious, authoritative.

"I'm not sick, doc. You've got the wrong man. We brought the ship in, didn't we? Everything was all right, wasn't it? Then we started to get out and everything went black. Now I'm here in a hospital. Something's pretty fishy, doc. Did I get hurt in the port?"

"No," said the doctor, "you weren't hurt at the port."

"Then why'd I faint? Why am I sick in a bed? Something must have happened to me, doc. It stands to reason. Otherwise I wouldn't be here. Some stupid awful thing must have happened, doc. After such a nice trip. Where did it happen?" A wild light came into the patient's eyes. "Did somebody do something to me, doc? I'm not hurt, am I? I'm not ruined, am I? I'll be able to go back into space, won't I?"

"Perhaps," said the doctor.

The nurse drew in her breath as though she were going to say something. The doctor looked around at her and gave her an authoritative frown, meaning *keep quiet*.

The patient saw it.

Desperation came into his voice, almost a whine. "What's the matter, doc? Why won't you talk to me? What's wrong? Something has happened to me. Where's Ralph? Where's Pete? Where's Jock? The last time I saw him he was having a beer. Where's Larry? Where's Went? Where's Betty? Where's my gang, doc? They're not killed, are they? I'm not the only one, am I? Talk to me, doc. Tell me the truth. I'm a space captain, doc. I've faced queer hells in my time, doc. You can tell me anything, doc. I'm not *that* sick. I can take it. Where's my gang, doc—my pals from the ship? What a cruise that was! Won't you talk, doc?"

"I'll talk," said the doctor, gravely.

"Okay," said the patient. "Tell me."

"What in particular?"

"Don't be a fool, doc! Tell me the straight stuff. Tell me about my friends first, and then tell me what has happened to me."

"Concerning your friends," said the doctor, measuring his words carefully, "I am in a position to tell you there has been no adverse change in the status of any of the persons you mentioned."

"All right, then, doc, if it wasn't them, it's me. Tell me. What's *happened* to me, doc? Something stinking awful must have happened or you wouldn't be standing there with a face like a constipated horse!"

The doctor smiled wryly, bleakly, briefly at the weird compliment. "I won't try to explain my own face, young fellow. I was born with it. But you are in a serious condition and we are trying to get you well. I will tell you the whole truth."

"Then do it, doc! Right away. Did somebody jump me at the port? Was I hurt badly? Was it an accident? Start talking, man!"

The nurse stirred behind the doctor. He looked around at her. She looked in the direction of the hypodermic on the tray. The doctor gave her a brief negative shake of his head. The patient saw the whole interplay and understood it correctly.

"That's right, doc. Don't let her dope me. I don't need sleep. I need the truth. If my gang's all right, why aren't they here? Is Milly out in the corridor? Milly, that was her name, the little curlyhead. Where's Jock? Why isn't Ralph here?"

"I'm going to tell you everything, young man. It may be tough but I'm counting on you to take it like a man. But it would help if you told me first."

"Told you what? Don't you know who I am? Didn't you read about my gang and me? Didn't you hear about Larry? What a navigator! We wouldn't be here except for Larry."

The late-morning light poured in through the open

window; a soft spring breeze touched the young ravaged face of the patient. There was mercy and more in the doctor's voice.

"I'm just a medical doctor. I don't keep up with the news. I know your name, age and medical history. But I don't know the details of your cruise. Tell me about it."

"Doc, you're kidding. It'd take a book. We're famous. I bet Went's out there right now, making a fortune out of the pictures he took."

"Don't tell me the whole thing, young man. Suppose you just tell me about the last couple of days before you landed, and how you got into port."

The young man smiled guiltily; there was pleasure and fond memory in his face. "I guess I can tell you, because you're a doctor and keep things confidential."

The doctor nodded, very earnest and still kind. "Do you want," said he softly, "the nurse to leave?"

"Oh, no," cried the patient. "She's a good scout. It's not as though you were going to turn it loose on the tapes."

The doctor nodded. The nurse nodded and smiled, too. She was afraid that there were tears forming at the corners of her eyes, but she dared not wipe them away. This was an extraordinarily observant patient. He might notice it. It would ruin his story.

The patient almost babbled in his eagerness to tell the story. "You know the ship, doc. It's a big one: twelve cabins, a common room, simulated gravity, lockers, plenty of room."

The doctor's eyes flickered at this but he did nothing, except to watch the patient in an attentive sympathetic way.

"When we knew we just had two days to Earth, doc, and we knew everything was all right, we had a ball. Jock found the beer in one of the lockers. Ralph helped him get it out. Betty was an old pal of mine, but I started trying to make time with Milly. Boy, did I make it! Yum." He looked at the nurse and blushed all the way down to his neck. "I'll skip the details. We had a party, doc. We were high. Drunk. Happy. Boy, did we have fun! I don't think anybody ever had more fun than we did, me and that old gang of mine. We docked all right. That Larry, he's a navigator. He was drunk as an owl and he had Betty on his lap but he put that ship in like the old lady putting a coin in the collection plate. Everything came out exactly right. I guess I should have been ashamed of landing a ship with the whole crew drunk and happy, but it was the best trip and the best gang and the best fun that anybody ever had. And we had succeeded in our mission, doc. We wouldn't have cut loose at the end of the mission if we hadn't known everything was hunky-dory. So we came in and landed, doc. And then everything went black, and here I am. Now you tell me your side of it, but be sure to tell me when Larry and Jock and Went are going to come in and see me. They're characters, doc. That little nurse of yours, she's going to have to watch them. They might bring me a bottle that I shouldn't have. Okay, doc. Shoot."

"Do you trust me?" said the doctor.

"Sure. I guess so. Why not?"

"Do you think I would tell you the truth?"

"It's something mean, doc. Real mean. Okay, shoot anyhow."

"I want you to have the shot first," said the doctor, straining to keep kindness and authority in his voice.

The patient looked bewildered. He glanced at the nurse, the tray, the hypodermic. Then he smiled at the doctor, but it was a smile in which fright lurked.

"All right, doctor. You're the boss."

The nurse helped him roll back his sleeves. She started to reach for the needle.

The doctor stopped her. He looked her straight in the face, his eyes focused right on hers. "No, intravenous. I'll do it. Do you understand?

She was a quick girl.

From the tray she took a short length of rubber tubing, twisted it quickly around the upper arm, just below the elbow.

The doctor watched, very quiet.

He took the arm, ran his thumb up and down the skin as he felt the vein.

"Now," said he.

She handed him the needle.

Patient, nurse and doctor all watched as the hypodermic emptied itself directly into the little ridge of the vein on the inside of the elbow.

The doctor took out the needle. He himself seemed relieved. Said he: "Feel anything?"

"Not yet, doc. Can you tell me now, doc? I can't make trouble with this stuff in me. Where's Larry? Where's Jock?"

"You weren't on a ship, young man. You were alone in a one-man craft. You didn't have a party for two days. You had it for twenty years. Larry didn't bring your ship in. The Earth authorities brought it in with telemetry. You were starved, dehydrated and nine-tenths dead. The boat had a freeze unit and you were fed by the emergency kit. You had the narrowest escape in the whole history of space travel. The boat had one of the new hypo kits. You must have had a second or two to slap it to your face before the boat took over. You didn't have any friends with you. They came out of your own mind."

"That's all right, doc. I'll be all right. Don't worry about me."

"There wasn't any Jock or Larry or Ralph or Milly. That was just the hypo kit."

"I get you, doc. It's all right. This dope you gave me, it's good stuff. I feel happy and dreamy. You can go away now and let me sleep. You can explain it all to me in the morning. But be sure to let Ralph and Jock in, when visiting hours open up." He turned on his side away from them.

The nurse pulled the cover up over his shoulders.

Then she and the doctor started to leave the room. At the last moment, she ran past the doctor and out of the room ahead of him. She did not want him to see her cry.